Laurence Fearnley is an award-winning novelist. Her novel *The Hut Builder* won the fiction category of the 2011 NZ Post Book Awards and was shortlisted for the international 2010 Boardman Tasker Prize for mountain writing. Her 2014 novel, *Reach*, was longlisted for the Ockham New Zealand Book Awards, *Edwin and Matilda* was runner-up in the 2008 Montana New Zealand Book Awards and her second novel, *Room*, was shortlisted for the 2001 Montana New Zealand Book Awards. In 2017 she was the joint winner of the *Landfall* essay competition and in 2016 she won the NZSA/Janet Frame Memorial Award. In 2004 Fearnley was awarded the Artists to Antarctica Fellowship and in 2007 the Robert Burns Fellowship at the University of Otago. Laurence lives in Dunedin with her husband and son.

For helping you to get through
the pandemic XX Allison

SCENTED

A NOVEL

LAURENCE
FEARNLEY

PENGUIN BOOKS

PENGUIN

UK | USA | Canada | Ireland | Australia
India | New Zealand | South Africa | China

Penguin is an imprint of the Penguin Random House group of companies,
whose addresses can be found at global.penguinrandomhouse.com.

Penguin Random House New Zealand

First published by Penguin Random House New Zealand, 2019

1 3 5 7 9 10 8 6 4 2

Cover design and photography by Keely O'Shannessy
© Penguin Random House New Zealand
Text design by Katrina Duncan © Penguin Random House New Zealand
Author photograph by Dave Fearnley
Prepress by Image Centre Group
Printed and bound in Australia by Griffin Press, an Accredited
ISO AS/NZS 14001 Environmental Management Systems Printer

A catalogue record for this book is available from
the National Library of New Zealand.

ISBN 978-0-14-377328-3
eISBN 978-0-14-377329-0

penguin.co.nz

FSC www.fsc.org MIX Paper from responsible sources FSC™ C009448

For my former lecturers in the American studies, art history, English and history departments at Canterbury University, thank you.

And for Frances, my perfume mentor and friend.

CONTENTS

BASE NOTES 13

HEART NOTES 51

TOP NOTES 229

The first perfume I ever made was for my granny Seren. It was called Gumnuts and I created it by placing a handful of gumnuts collected from the eucalyptus tree at the edge of her section into a jam jar half filled with water. The fragrance smelt of water but over time the liquid darkened and took on a dank note, slightly bitter, medicinal. I would smell it whenever I visited my grandmother and together we would dab the juice onto our pulse points – our wrists, necks, behind our ears – and inhale.

Granny Seren told me I had a natural talent for perfume making, and I believed her because she seemed to know what she was talking about and she never lied. It was Seren who introduced me to the idea of a signature scent. Some ladies, she said, only ever wear one perfume.

'One perfume at a time, you mean?'

'No, they always wear it, it's part of them. It's called a signature scent. When they walk into a room you know they're there because you can recognise them by their scent. You smell them first and that makes you turn around, and then you see them standing on the other side of the room and you think, "Oh yes, it is you. I thought so." The perfume makes them visible, you see.'

I wasn't sure I understood. 'So, without that one perfume they wouldn't know who they were?'

'That's right. They'd be incomplete.'

'So if we both wore Gumnuts every day, for the rest of our lives, we would be whole, with no missing pieces?'

'Yes, but it wouldn't be your signature. It would be our signature. So, you'd have to think up a new perfume, just for you and no one else.'

'And then I'd be whole and know who I was?'

Seren nodded. 'Yes, my love. That's right.'

Fascinated by what my grandmother said, I became more

and more curious about perfume. I consulted encyclopaedias and borrowed library books and read everything I could get my hands on about perfume history, the growers in Grasse and the great perfume houses. I was captivated by the stories surrounding roses, jasmine and lavender, and the exotic names: Galimard, Houbigant, Coty, Guerlain and Chanel. Later, as a teenager I taught myself the basics of blending oils by studying fragrance pyramids, becoming familiar with base notes, heart notes and top notes. I sniffed, inhaled deeply and quizzed myself on scents, and after many years I was able to identify and recall many individual notes and oils, filing them in my memory like words from a new, exciting dictionary.

My perfume-making experiments consumed my weekends. I gathered up empty pill bottles and filled them with my fragrant experiments. I understood that when I sniffed a perfume the first thing that grabbed my attention and drew me in was the volatile and vibrant top notes, but that when I blended a perfume, creating it from scratch, it made more sense to start at the bottom with the slow-evaporating, deeper-scented base notes. By working that way I was able to gain a greater understanding and appreciation of the overall structure of the perfume. I could also experience the various temporal shifts leading towards the drydown, the lingering twilight moment before the perfume disappeared.

As an adult I developed my own approach to perfume construction, one that made sense to me and helped to provide a framework for my creations. Base notes anchored my scent and therefore represented my past – my family background, my history and all my memories. These soul notes might not seek attention but they were always there, occasionally flaring up or entering my thoughts when I least expected. The heart notes symbolised all the things that added meaning and purpose to my life on a daily basis: my home, my work, colleagues, my interests such as perfume making and reading. The heart notes represented my centre, and carried my story, linking my past to my future. The top notes were the spark and dazzle, the flourish. They could be sharp and challenging, but they provided energy and they offered hope.

Recently I lost my job. After fourteen years as a university lecturer in the American studies department I was made redundant. The humanities were restructured and not only was I shoved aside but the department itself disappeared. Apparently, under the management for change model, it was no longer relevant or economically viable. It had no future.

When I was employed, I didn't need a signature scent to know who I was. I was a smart, professional, financially independent middle-aged woman. But lately, I've felt disembodied and confused, a collection of broken parts, and Granny Seren's description of the incomplete woman keeps coming back to me.

So, I will create a signature scent. I plan to build it, this perfume of my self, from the base notes up. The method will be simple. Identifying one note at a time, adding and subtracting notes as I go along, I will sniff and test my way to completion. The perfume will gather together all the strands of my life and tell me who I am. And when I have finished I will recognise myself once more. I will be Siân, scented.

BASE NOTES

As a child, I spent many afternoons playing alone in my grandparents' Waltham garden, a small strip of damp turf overshadowed by the Christchurch gasworks. Granny Seren was short and fat, compact, with bright white hair. She was deaf – a result of being sent to work as a weaver in the Lancashire mills when she was fourteen. The bulky battery of her hearing aid was pinned and tucked into her bra and because of that her blouse had a strange angular outline. I was fascinated by the mystery of my grandmother's mechanical inner workings, a feature emphasised by the beige-coloured, twisted wire that connected the old-fashioned aid to her ear-piece.

When Granny Seren had time she would join me outside and we would stare in silence at the gasometers with the same kind of bewildered wonderment that movie actors adopt when looking at alien spaceships.

'It's so stinky,' I'd complain.

'The gas?'

'Yes.'

'Ah. It reminds me of when we moved to Manchester to live with my aunt after my dad died. The air was so dirty compared to Wales.'

'I don't understand how the towers can go up and down. They were tall last week, and now they only reach halfway up.'

'That's true, cariad,' said my granny.

Every single time I visited I asked my grandmother to explain how the gas-holders were able to change height, but she didn't know and she wasn't bothered. 'It's science,' she'd say, before leading me inside to the kitchen where a saucepan of black tea sat simmering on the stove.

At the edge of the section was a large eucalyptus that shed long strips of red and silver bark which I sometimes persuaded my grandparents to twirl like a skipping rope while I dashed from one side to the other. When we all ran out of puff we would go and rest beneath the tree, and while my granny caught her breath and my granddad Bert finished a cigarette, I would crush the crisp leaves in my fingers and inhale, filling my lungs with the scent. 'Inhale' is really too slight a word for what I did. I'd snort the air the way addicts hoover up cocaine through a straw, and I'd encourage my grandparents to do the same. From starting with bark and leaves, it was only a matter of time before I fixated on the gumnuts, prising them open with Granny Seren's nail file in the hope that fragrant oils would infuse the water in which they soaked.

In my mind, the smell of eucalyptus will always be associated with heat and summer, clean laundry – and my grandmother. A blue shimmering haze, parched, dusty ground, long strips of silver and salmon-toned bark, gumnuts and brittle leaves. This memory of dazzling summer light and heat is false. For most of the day the garden was cast in deep shade and the air was gritty and damp. But the actual gum tree and the laundered sheets were real.

On washing day Granny would poke the hose from her broken-down washer-wringer through the laundry window, directing the soapy water towards the grid below the downspout. The water gushed in spurts, splashing onto the earth, turning the rock-hard dirt into a rivulet of foam and as she worked, Seren would murmur, 'That's nice. That's right.'

My grandmother prided herself on being the seventh child of the seventh child, and many of the stories she told me centred on her firm belief in her own psychic and magical powers, passed down to her from her mother, and her mother's Irish mother, who was, in Granny Seren's words, 'a proper gypsy queen'. One day, after listening to one of Granny's more outlandish tales, I must have expressed a hint of scepticism that took her by surprise. In the story a young Seren rode a horse to a glade carpeted in hyacinth and bluebells, which she gathered up into large bundles and placed in a silk bag. She then delivered it to a wise witch who wanted the flowers for a magic potion that would transform the colour of cows' eyes from brown to blue. The only part of the story I found unbelievable was that my granny could ride a horse. Given that she was more or less the spitting image of the grandmother in the *Giles* cartoons that Bert laughed over, it was unimaginable to me that she could get up on a horse, let alone ride one.

Rather than being offended by my response, Granny Seren took me by the hand and whispered, 'Come with me. I've something to show you.' She led me into her bedroom, a dark place with black mould on the ceiling, and made me sit on the bed while she went to her tall cupboard, lifting down a shoe-box from its shallow top shelf. Inside the box, carefully nestled in thick tissue, was a small glass bottle with a silver top. The colour of the glass was remarkable: it resembled a fluorescent yellow-green highlighter pen, though I could not have made that comparison in the 1960s. Through the glass I could see a small amount of liquid, which shifted slowly like thick syrup from one side to the other when the bottle moved.

'You may hold it but be careful,' said Granny, in a theatrical tone of voice that gave me shivers. 'This perfume bottle was given to me by the witch and it has magical powers.'

I believed it. It looked magical.

'The bottle you are holding is made from uranium glass,' she continued. 'It glows in the dark.'

'How does it glow in the dark?' I asked.

What happened next was even harder for me to believe than the horse story, the witch or the magical bottle. Seren simply shrugged and said, in her ordinary voice, 'I don't know.'

'But how can you not know?'

'Well, I never asked,' she said.

And that was that. Granny placed the bottle on top of her

dressing table, gathered up the box with its tissue and left the room.

I must have sat on the bed for an hour, waiting for the glow. Nothing happened. From that day on, I'd ask Granny if she had seen the glass glow and she'd reply, 'No. The time has not yet come . . .' or words to that effect. I spent hours sitting in the dark, watching, but never once did anything happen.

My sister Carrie was born when I was seven years old. Because she was a restless, colicky baby, I spent even more time at my grandparents' place in order to give my mother a break. Perhaps because of our age difference, and the fact I was away from home so often, I found it difficult to bond with Carrie. When we were together I noticed her smell, a mixture of baby powder and acrid, milky vomit. It was a smell I associated with sickness, hers. I'd talk or sing to her but she would cry and I never knew how to make her stop. I think I was scared of the force of her emotions compared with my own. She was loud and demanding whereas I was quiet. She drew people into her orbit and was often the centre of attention while I preferred quiet spaces and solitude. Later, she was outgoing and extroverted, surrounded by noisy groups of friends and drawn to team sports. As an older sister I loved her and admired her confidence but we were never close.

Seren died from lung cancer when I was nine, and shortly afterwards my granddad got a job making ovens at the Atlas factory off Manchester Street. At the start of the seventies, when he worked at the factory, an advertisement appeared on television for 'new look' Atlas cookers. The ovens were modern, but from the advertising you'd almost think they were futuristic. They featured a lift-up door, tilting hob, porcelain finish, electric sockets and easy to clean features. By contrast, Seren and Bert's stove was ancient. It had three hobs, rusting around the edges, and a small oven with a temperature gauge on its door. When the oven was turned on at the wall it hummed and vibrated and, for that reason, I was never allowed to touch it.

After Seren died my granddad had to learn to cook. I stayed with him often enough to know that once a week he'd make a big pan of porridge that he poured into a roasting dish and placed in the oven to keep. Every morning he would take out the roasting pan, slice off a wedge of porridge and fry it in mutton fat on top of the stove. He'd serve the porridge on a plate, eating it with a knife and fork between negotiating his pieces on the chessboard permanently set up on the table beside him. He ate slowly, and by the end of his breakfast he had usually managed to enter his next move onto one of the cards of his postal chess games.

The porridge was incredibly greasy from the fat he used and so salty that it made me gag. As a treat, therefore, he added a dollop of jam to my serving but it really didn't improve the taste. I have no idea how he managed to eat it day after day; maybe being a smoker helped. Perhaps cigarettes cut the saltiness, or maybe he'd damaged his tastebuds as a result of his pack-a-day habit? Without fail there would be a strand of grey hair in the porridge. The tip would surface as I ate and when I pulled on it the hair would detach itself slowly in a thread of greyish gloop. If I couldn't eat what was in front of me, Bert would take my plate and scrape the leftovers out for the canaries he kept in an aviary attached to the back of the garage.

After feeding the canaries we would often make a circuit of the flower beds: two strips of rose bushes either side of the front path and a small circular bed cut into the lawn at the back. Since Seren's death Bert had become more interested in roses, especially those that offered a connection to 'home' such as the fragrant red rose of Lancaster. For a short time his rose hobby happened to coincide with my own interest in the blooms. At school we were being read *Helen Keller's Teacher,* a paperback with an image of Helen Keller and her teacher, Annie Sullivan, on the cover. In the illustration, Annie held the child's hand under a stream of water pumped from a well while tapping the letters W.A.T.E.R. into her palm. It was a pivotal scene in the story but not one that made the greatest impression on me. I was far more interested in trying to negotiate my way around the rose beds by scent, with my eyes tightly shut. I was certain Helen Keller could have done it so I saw no reason why I shouldn't give it a go.

I walked slowly, one foot shuffling forward, my arms extended in front of me like a character from a classic horror movie. As my foot perceived the edge of the path I would lean forward and sniff, often losing my balance in the process.

From nearby I'd hear Bert exclaim, 'Steady on. Watch the garden', and I'd have to remind him to not talk because I was trying to be deaf as well as blind. He would grumble quietly for a bit but then my stumbling around would get the better of him.

'Careful now, don't go putting your great big foot on the "Slater's Crimson China".'

'Shush. I need quiet. I can't smell my way around if you keep talking. I have to concentrate.'

'That's a special rose,' he'd say. 'Probably the first to reach New Zealand.'

'With the Chinese?'

'No, with the missionaries.'

As I became more familiar with the paths and better at peeking through almost-closed lids without being detected by my eagle-eyed granddad, I would call out scents. 'This one smells like jam. This one is sweet. And this one is . . .'

'Just right,' joked Bert, who never took my experiments as seriously as I did.

At Christmas one year, Bert passed me a lumpy parcel wrapped in newspaper and when I opened it I discovered, to my delight, that it contained an old World War Two gas mask. 'There you are, kid,' he said. 'You can wear it when you help me with the blood and bone.' While I stood by in my gas mask, Bert made fertiliser, mixing potash with dried blood, iron sulphate and sulphate of ammonia. His 'secret ingredient' was Epsom salts, taken from the bathroom cabinet, but I was always far more interested in the large sack of dried blood kept inside the door to his garage. He liked to tease me that he had brought it out from Manchester with him and that it contained the blood and bones of an Englishman. I believed he would bring dried blood all the way from England, via Panama, but I doubted the blood itself was from an Englishman. From my limited knowledge of world history and events I assumed it had to be from a foreigner.

I never got the opportunity to get to the bottom of the blood and bone story because one day, when I called in on the way home from a friend's, I discovered Bert dead, lying on the floor by the oven. A knife covered in porridge was next to him, and a frying pan of porridge still on the hob. He'd been electrocuted.

Notes from my grandparents: gas, eucalyptus, soap, oats, rose and blood. It's a start, I suppose, though not the notes I would normally consider for a perfume base. They lack the weight and depth I desire for my foundation. But, I won't dismiss them out of hand.

My mother, Nita, had energy and vision and my father, Pete, had a sense of humour. Nita encouraged my father, who was a doctor, to carry out major renovations on our bathroom and Pete, who played along with all my mother's suggestions, went to work, roping me in as his assistant. The revamp coincided with the period in the seventies when the carpets throughout my childhood home were orange or brown shagpile, and the curtains and chairs were either purple or acid-yellow upholstery velvet.

The enormous free-standing cast-iron bath was dragged out and in its place we installed a built-in rectangular plastic bath, a shallow, three-quarter-length model fitted to its edge with dark-brown shagpile that slowly rotted and moulted over the years until it finally went bald. I helped to paper the walls and ceiling, brushing paste over lengths of the brown, orange and white wallpaper my mother had chosen while Pete swore under his breath as he tried to make it stick to the ceiling.

I can remember my father's face becoming tighter and more rigid as we went along so I tried to distract him with questions or statements intended to impress. 'Did you know that the air is full of smell molecules?'

'Hmm.'

'Well, they go up your nose and then these things called olfactory receptor . . . things, can't remember now . . . they recognise thousands and thousands of smells . . .'

'That sounds a lot.'

'Thousands, then. The olfactory reception neurons – see I remembered – send the information to these bulbs at the back of your nose and then they send that information to your brain and your brain goes, "I know what that is. That's bacon." Do you know what "olfactory" means?'

'Yes.'

'It means something to do with the sense of smell.'

'Does it?'

'You should try using it at work. If someone came in with a nose bleed you could really frighten them by saying they might have olfactory troubles.'

'Hmm.'

The final hurdle with the wallpapering was trying to cut and fit the paper around the taps, which my father had not bothered to remove before papering. He was past the stage of being open to interesting scientific facts so I tried encouragement.

'It looks really good, Dad, like in the magazines.'

He replied with a grunt.

'I could put on more glue, eh.'

'No.'

'We could use PVA instead of paste. I've got some in my pencil case.'

'No.'

'It's good where you put the paper round the taps. I like how it looks like starfish spikes where you cut it. You can hardly notice the gaps. We can patch them?'

Silence.

'I love it. You're so good at fixing stuff. It's great, heaps better than it used to . . .'

'Shush. It's best you don't talk any more.'

Nita placed stacks of *House and Garden* and bunches of dried flowers on the carpeted space at the head of the bath and, as time went on, the magazine pages wrinkled and stuck together and the flowers sprouted cobwebs and every time we shifted either the magazines or the flowers swarms of silverfish appeared, scuttling for safety, or slipping down the steep sides of the bath into the bottom, where they always died.

There were no shelves in the new bathroom cabinet we built under the sink. The pine louvre doors with white porcelain knobs – part Cornwall cottage, part Scandinavian chic – opened up to expose the plumbing and a large battered jute basket that contained everything from Vim and toilet rolls to lemon-shaped Bronnley soaps, bath salts, supplies of the medicinal shampoo my father made on prescription, hot-water bottles, dried natural sponges, crepe bandages, Dettol, potpourri and mouse poison.

The smell I most remember is that of my mother's hair removal cream, Veet. Only back then I think it may have gone by the far jauntier name, Veet-O. On first sniff, the thick, pale pink cream was similar to baby lotion: a powdery, lightly scented floral-musk that could be described as 'non-offensive'. But whereas baby lotion maintained its sweetness or innocence, Veet turned nasty. Its smell gained momentum and expanded, filling not only the bathroom but the entire floor of the house. The sweet opening appeared to rot and turn sour, like vomit, and before long the notes used to disguise the hair-removing chemicals took on an unsanitary aspect reminiscent of the smell surrounding the old metal incinerator units that were placed in the school toilets for the disposal of tampons and pads. The scent of Veet brought to mind bodily functions. It was unclean, like the scum and hairs floating on the lukewarm surface every time it was finally my turn for the bath water.

At Christmas a few patients, their families, or the pharmacist near his Brighton practice used to present my father with gifts to pass on to my mother, usually things like soap, bath salts or talc sets. As far as I could tell, he was never given anything to keep for himself – perhaps that would have seemed too familiar, lacking in respect. Apart from the soap, these presents were rarely used but the sight of them in the basket under the sink convinced me that they were the perfect solution to my own problems of finding birthday and Christmas presents for my mother. I shopped for her at the local chemist. It was a short bike ride from home, part of the Shirley shops that then included a dairy, a newsagent, a bicycle repair shop and a drapery *cum* school-uniform supplier. The shelves at the chemist had everything I could want: Potter and Moore talcum powder, Morny French Fern soap, Meadowsong deodorant, Holly Hobbie soap dishes and boxed sets of Lenthéric Tweed, Just Musk and Tramp perfumes.

The item that caught my eye, however, was packaged in the most exquisite shade of light turquoise, a colour that resembled blackbirds' eggs. This pale blue-green immediately struck me as modern and fresh and despite having no idea what the product inside smelt like, I was sure I could imagine its scent based only on the colour of the outside. Experience had taught me that yellow smelt like lemons and honeysuckle, purple like musty violets or lavender, pink like roses and baby lotion, green like ferns and lily of the valley, and brown like coal tar or beer. It made sense, then, that this product, with its unique colour and unfamiliar name, had to smell exotic, tropical, like nothing I had encountered before. Fenjal. The soap came in a hard plastic shell that gave it an air of luxury. The bath crème was packaged in a turquoise bottle with square shoulders and a nipped in waist. The scent, as I recall, was a clean jasmine. The smell didn't make me gag. It was pretty.

At that stage in my childhood, fragranced products either smelt bad (Veet) or nice (Fenjal), and I didn't understand the difference between being pleasant and being interesting. Fenjal was strangely characterless, as if the jasmine had been scrubbed, dressed up, and told to behave – like the kittens in Beatrix Potter's *The Tale of Tom Kitten*. Like polite kittens, Fenjal lacked spirit; from beginning to end the scent didn't transform, it merely faded.

Sometime around the late seventies my parents' close friend became manager of the Christchurch duty free shop, the closest thing to overseas travel that I knew. As a result my mother became the recipient of unwanted perfume samples, including a number of Guerlain mini perfume bottles. Inside geometric patterned black and white boxes, each small bottle was crowned with a rounded, cabochon-style cap of deepest sapphire blue. Within each bottle was a millilitre of golden-amber juice. The perfumes were called Mitsouko, Nahema and Shalimar. My mother shoved them, like everything else, into the basket beneath the sink.

With its absence of floral or feminine imagery, the plain zig-zag design on the packaging gave no indication of what to expect from each perfume. The names themselves meant nothing to me and so, with nothing to guide me, I carefully uncapped and sniffed each bottle. The first, Nahema, seemed rose-like. But, more than that, it conjured up a colour and texture, a very deep crimson velvet. I carefully placed the bottle on the edge of the bath and reached for Shalimar. This time, no colour came to mind. Now my thoughts went to food. I could almost taste this scent: it was like burnt custard poured over tinned apricots. Custard and apricots, that was Shalimar.

Mitsouko was next. Once again I went through the ritual of carefully unscrewing the cap and bringing it up to my nose to inhale. This time I sneezed, almost spilling the contents over my hand. I sniffed again and nothing came to mind: no colour, no food, no texture, no shape, nothing I could locate within my experience or put a word to. It was as if someone had created a smell that hadn't existed before. It was abstract, but structured. I placed my middle finger over the opening and tipped the bottle, capturing a small drop on my skin. I sniffed again. The perfume changed with each sniff and this time I thought I could detect dead flowers, stale orange juice that had been left out on a kitchen bench, and something dark and fusty. Its overall ugliness repelled me, reminding me of the rotting brown shagpile at the foot of the bath. Although it didn't strike me as something I would want to wear, I dabbed a bit on my wrist and neck.

I remember I pocketed the Nahema and Shalimar but threw the Mitsouko back into the basket under the sink.

Several hours later I was standing over the boiling kettle, making a cup of tea for my parents, when I got a hit of the most incredible smell. I think now that the steam from the kettle must have realised the scent in all its complexity, and it suddenly brought to mind the smell of the cupboard beneath the stairs, a dark cellar where we stored a range of things including tramping packs, boots and parkas, through to old *National Geographic* magazines as well as the fermenting equipment for my father's home brew and the strange concoctions of stout that exploded from time to time, leaving everything reeking of dark, malty beer. It was this combination of earthiness, cool stone and plaster, old carpet, hessian sacks, beer, wine, paper and the scent of campfires and bush held in our outdoor clothing that was now playing against my senses.

I poured the tea for my parents, then ran upstairs to the bathroom, retrieved the perfume from the basket and took it to my room, where I hid it inside the stuffing of a small grey rabbit that was coming unstitched at the seams. I had made a real perfume discovery, oakmoss, and it was love.

Notes from a seventies bathroom: Veet, jasmine, rose, citrus, vanilla, oakmoss.

Of these notes oakmoss is the one I return to time and time again. Perfumes created from the citrus-orange bergamot, the resin gathered from the sticky flowering plant Cistus ladanifer, *and oakmoss – a lichen that grows on oak trees – are referred to as chypres, and they are characterised by their complexity, their earthiness, their unwillingness to conform to stereotypes of femininity. They don't bring flowers to mind; rather, they are skanky. Historically chypres tended to appear and gain popularity during periods following war or social or economic unrest. Mitsouko was developed in 1919, and although not the first chypre in production, it created a benchmark in perfume for modern, strong, independent women. A chypre built around oakmoss is probably what I need.*

At the start of the seventies I began getting teased at school for being a Pom and talking funny. Despite being born in

New Zealand, I had my father's Mancunian accent, so words like 'grass' rhymed with 'ass' rather than 'arse.' In the playground classmates would circle me and call out words they wanted me to pronounce.

'Say "pass".'

To annoy them I'd reply, 'Parse.'

'Say "castle".'

'Carr-sel.'

'Say "plant".'

'No, you say it!'

'Say it or you'll be sorry.'

'Plarnt.'

'How do you say "grass"?' They would taunt me until I got so angry I'd yell, 'Grass like you, ass' and take a swing at them, at which point they'd yell, 'Pommy, go home' and run off.

'I am home!' I'd yell after them.

'You're a Pommy bastard!'

'No I'm not!'

'Yes you are! Pommy bastard!'

Their words always surprised me. First, because I had never felt 'Pommy', and I had no concept of home beyond the old house where I lived, which was less than five minutes' walk from school. And second, because this rudimentary introduction to nationalism happened to coincide with a very important moment in my life, my reinvention as a French orphan. Having spent many Tuesday evenings in the old brick library in the middle of town researching perfume in encyclopedias and advertisements in glossy fashion magazines, I decided that I no longer wished to be anything but French. I adopted a new name, Madeline, based on the books of that title, and in the privacy of my room began speaking fluent French, an entire language built upon the ten or twenty words I remembered from a phrase book on my mother's bookshelf. In order to be French I had to sound French, and I based my accent on two characters from television shows I regularly watched: Corporal LeBeau from *Hogan's Heroes* and Lisa Douglas, the character played by Eva Gabor on *Green Acres*.

Being French suited me. At school it became a shield that protected me from all the attacks I had become accustomed to. Now, when classmates demanded, 'Say "fast"' I no longer had to attempt the awkward sounding 'farst' but could respond with a shrug of my Gallic shoulders and the elegantly superior '*Je ne comprends pas*'. This infuriated the bullies but at least it meant they now thought I was simply stupid and weird. This was easier for me to deal with than having to negotiate questions of identity related to being a contemptible 'Pom'. In effect I had traversed the black and white territory of 'us' and 'them' and found myself in the no man's land of crazy and unknowable, a grey area outside easy classification.

At home, being French allowed me time alone to experiment with perfume. As long as I continued to do my chores and homework, my new identity was initially accepted with little comment. In fact, my mother went so far as to weave phrases into our conversation, greeting me with '*Bonjour! Comment allez-vous?*' when I returned from school or asking '*Quelle heure est-il*?' when she began thinking about dinner.

With my pocket money I bought a jar of coconut oil from the local chemist and began a series of experimentations making '*le parfum*'. The first of these, named Le Bouquet, I made by adding carnation petals and lavender heads to coconut oil and heating it gently before straining it into an almost empty bottle of almond essence. The resulting blend smelt of almonds so I wrapped it up for my mother because I knew I wouldn't wear it. I was a little more careful with my second scent. For this one I made a paste of nutmeg, cloves and cinnamon taken from the food cupboard and mixed it with orange juice before adding it to the melted coconut oil. I called it L'Hiver and gave it to my mother as a way of easing my conscience over the almond perfume. One day, not long afterwards, I discovered the small perfume jar was empty and when I pressed my mother she admitted to having added it to a fruit cake she had baked for a morning tea.

Of all the 'parfums' I made, the one I was most proud of was called Joan of Arc. It was the first time I had based a perfume on a story and it marked the beginning of a lifelong fascination with translating narrative into scent. I worked from an old book of children's stories and made notes of the aspects of Joan's life that sparked a smell response. For her childhood I wrote 'barnyard hay'. Her religious beliefs and visions of saints suggested incense. The Siege of Orléans made me think of dirt, mud and blood. But, of course, it was the fire that really captured my attention, that and the little detail of her ashes being scattered in the Seine. To represent the heat of the fire I raided the pantry once more, collecting packets of black pepper, cayenne, paprika and chilli powder. Next I scraped charcoal dust and ash from the barbecue, adding it to my spice mix. After that I took a scoop of water from the creek that ran past our house and added several drops to my dry mixture. Finally I added it to softened coconut oil and gave the finished result to my father. He applied the perfume when he came home from work and I recall my intense disappointment as the black greasy smear formed a streak across his wrist. He held his arm up to his nose and sniffed and then, to my surprise, he applied a second streak, rubbed his wrists together and asked, 'Am I doing it right? I've never had a proper perfume before.' I was so grateful for his kindness and the way he told me it was too precious for everyday use, that he would save it for special occasions to make it last longer. He was true to his word.

My year of being French ended when the flotilla of protest yachts led by the *Fri* set sail for Mururoa Atoll in 1973. In a moment of sudden irritation, my mother turned on me and asked why I was masquerading as French. Had I never heard of atom bombs or the Cold War? Why did I think she had moved to New Zealand in the first place? Had I no respect for the people of the Pacific? Was I really that stupid? It was a tirade that left me dumbfounded. Nothing in the world was worse than my mother's disapproval and so, overnight, I went back to being myself. Neither British nor a proper Kiwi like my classmates, but definitely not French.

Notes from a place called 'home': lavender, carnation, mixed spices, charcoal and ash.

In fact, my parents never called themselves Poms or used the word 'home' to describe England. They never went back to visit or for a holiday; the country very rarely featured in our conversations. Pete, in particular, seldom expressed any interest in the place where he grew up. He didn't talk about his childhood, and rarely, if ever, mentioned his family, who still lived in Manchester and were strangers to me.

My father intended to retire on his sixty-second birthday and my mother made loose plans to mark that date with a trip to Britain, before they grew too old to enjoy travelling to the places they had known and loved as a young couple. The special birthday was in September 1996 but on the fourth of July he returned home from work in agony and went into hospital. He was told he had stomach cancer and died twenty days later.

Pete was very neat in his ways, without being fanatical. When he came home from the surgery, he always tucked his bag into a dark corner beside the foot of the stairs. He placed it carefully, so that it stood upright and was always parallel with the bottom bannister. I doubt he ever took much notice of the way he lined up his bag; it was something he did automatically. On the day he came home sick, he dropped his bag in the hall and staggered up to his bed. The bag was on the rug, at an angle to the stairs, in a place it had never been before. It stayed there until after Carrie, by then a medical student, arrived to take him and my mother to hospital and then I carried it across to the foot of the stairs and placed it very carefully in its rightful place. It remained there for the next five years.

Eventually, the house I grew up in, and returned to frequently during my student years and months of unemployment, was sold to a wealthy neighbour. No one lived in it, and it fell into a state of disrepair. It was damaged in the earthquakes, and demolished. Nothing remained. The land reverted to wilderness, the growth so dense that the garden was not only unrecognisable but impassable. Even the row of lime trees gracing the driveway fell down and landed in a heap.

My father's bag sat on a shelf in my mother's new garage. As a kid I used to play with the bag as if it were a kind of doll's house. It was made to stand upright, and its main compartment was divided into drawers of various shapes and sizes, each with a small leather pull tab. I would ease open all the drawers, removing the stethoscope, the reflex hammer, the blood pressure gauge and the otoscope, examining them carefully. My father taught me how to take blood pressure, how to watch the gauge and mark the slight hiccups as the gauge dropped, and to listen to the change in volume of the heartbeat. One small drawer in the case contained disposable syringes; another flat drawer was lined with thick sponge, glass vials arranged neatly in the perforated spaces. There was a drawer full of pills, numerous small golden cylinders labelled with patients' names. Another drawer was filled with bandages, gauze and rolls of beige cotton tape. For a reason I never worked out, this drawer had a very particular smell, warm like amber or leather but somehow sweeter, as if caramelised. It was a smell I could never quite identify, though I often tried.

The last time I visited my mother, not long before she died, I brought the bag home with me. Inside were all the bandages, pills and instruments that I remembered, all there exactly as Pete had left them the day he went from doctor to patient. I opened the drawers, inspected everything as I once had, then inhaled, and in that moment my father returned to me. Not as the handyman who had renovated the bathroom, nor as the wax-pale invalid curled up in pain on a hospital bed. He returned to me as the father who had smeared sooty grease over his wrists just to make me happy.

A doctor's note: amber.

I enrolled in American studies at Canterbury University in the early 1980s, a period that's imprinted on my mind for its protests, collective energy and momentum towards creating a better world.

When I think back to that time, one of the first things I remember is the smell of sewage. I was living with my boyfriend in his rented flat on Breezes Road in Bromley, a kilometre or two from the sewage treatment station and settlement ponds. Whenever the wind blew from the east we would be enveloped in the smell of shit. The scent was not entirely unpleasant. Sometimes it was like manure or silage, at other times like bananas rotting in a fruit bowl, and every so often like jasmine.

Our flat was tiny, comprising three rooms: a kitchen that had been knocked through to the dining and living room, a bedroom and a bathroom. The laundry and toilet were in a lean-to accessed through an outside door next to the garage. Through necessity we learnt to store our toilet roll in an old bread bin for protection from the rain that entered the room through a small, paneless window above the cistern. If we forgot we would have to drape lengths of sodden two-ply over the clothes-horse in an attempt to render them useful once more.

Because my boyfriend was a window cleaner, our evening ritual was taken up with doing laundry. His pile of damp, meths-scented cloth nappies had to be washed and dried, ready for work, and for that reason we had an almost new automatic washing machine, the only truly functioning appliance in the house. In winter we arranged drying racks around the potbelly stove in the living room. Some nights the stove would begin to glow red-hot and smell of molten iron, and the room would fill with cold mist as the moisture from the rags evaporated. On still winter evenings smoke would seep through the joints on the stove and spread through the house in a dense grey haze. Then we'd have to open the windows and swing the doors on their hinges to fan the air and clear the rooms. The fact that we lived in a house with damp, wrinkled toilet paper, freezing fog or gritty smog never struck us as odd.

With the memory of my mother's stern reprimand lingering in the back of my mind, my desire to make amends steered me towards the anti-nuclear movement. Christchurch had been declared the first nuclear-free city in the world in 1982, and my real introduction to anti-nuclear protests came not long afterwards when the USS *Whipple* visited Lyttelton Harbour two years later.

My thesis supervisor, a somewhat laconic professor named Bob Strauss, was instrumental in my involvement. Originally from Nashville, he had played a significant role in the Freedom Rides and voter registration campaigns of the 1960s, and despite his reserved demeanour was a powerful presence in the local peace movement. One afternoon as I was passing his office, he caught me in the corridor and asked if I was looking forward to 'the big day'. I knew he meant the protest because we had discussed the *Whipple*'s visit during our last meeting, and I had mentioned my intention to kayak out on the harbour with my boyfriend and some other friends.

'Could you give me a lift?'

'You're not driving?' I asked.

'No. I anticipate being arrested so I'd rather leave my car near the police station so I can get home after.'

We gave him a lift out to Lyttelton but didn't see him afterwards because he was taken away and charged with trespass and disorderly behaviour. Meanwhile our small group had paddled out on the choppy harbour and braced ourselves against the wind for a day at sea. I'd been in a kayak before but had no experience of dealing with the constant harassment of the police and pro-American supporters who swept in with a roar of engines, circled our group and then accelerated away at speed. The wash from the powerful launches hit us from all directions and time and time again I thought I was going to be swamped or capsize. As the protest wore on I became not only increasingly tired from the emotional and physical effort of anticipating the next attack but also seasick. So while my male friends grew more and more emboldened, attempting to place themselves between the warship and the inner harbour, I slipped beneath a wharf and waited for the afternoon to end.

I was cold and my hands were frozen, wet and sticky from the sea. Every now and again while lurking beneath the wharf I bumped up against the piles and scraped my hands on the razor-sharp barnacles, causing my knuckles to bleed. The blood trickled in fast rivulets down the backs of my hands and I felt more and more miserable. It was gloomy beneath the wharf but every now and again, at odd angles, a strange light filtered through from above, casting streaks across the greasy, diesel-stinking water that slurped against the piers. Flotsam – bits of wood, polystyrene and cardboard – floated around me, adding to the ugliness.

The smell of diesel, combined with the constant rocking of the sea, made me horribly nauseous. But worse was the overpowering sense of shame. It was hard to accept that I wasn't as brave as I had anticipated. I had imagined being on the frontline with the other protesters, an anti-nukes Joan of Arc, but I had turned out to be frightened, unable to fight for a cause I believed in. What kind of protester did that make me?

I kayaked back to where we'd left our car. As I shivered, pulling on dry clothes over my still damp body, I could see my friends way off in the distance, their canoes so small against the bulk of the *Whipple*. Beyond them, free from all police intervention, a jet boat trailing a long 'welcome' sign zoomed back and forth, clearing a path for the visiting warship.

Not long after the protest, complaints started coming in to the university about the American studies department. Most of the criticism came from Americans and typically went, 'American studies? More like anti-American studies!' Bob, as head of department and resident expert on American foreign policy, was completely unfazed by the controversy and, to a certain extent, relished it. He gave interviews to the press and even wrote some articles for the student paper. When I asked if he was worried about possible backlash or losing his job, he shrugged.

'They're not going to touch me,' he said. 'There'd be such an uproar that half the university would walk out in support.'

In 1985, David Lange took part in the famous Oxford Union debate with the joke about smelling the uranium on his opponent's breath. As the news clip was played over and over again, a memory was triggered for me and I fetched Granny Seren's strange green bottle from my jewellery box, where it had been kept since I had inherited it following her death. I gave the bottle a rub and waited, as I had throughout my childhood, to see it glow. Though it was as vivid green as ever, it didn't shine any more brightly than usual. I tipped the bottle and then uncapped it, peering inside at the tiniest hint of a brown viscous perfume within. I took a long sniff and there, still identifiable after more than ninety years, was the distinctive bitter, forest-floor, fungal smell of oakmoss, no longer permitted in perfume in its natural state because its toxicity caused skin allergies.

Notes from a student flat: sewage, rubbish, methylated spirits, coal, diesel and oakmoss. Oakmoss again.

My career path following my masters in American studies was haphazard, to say the least. Immediately after graduating I was persuaded by my boyfriend to leave Christchurch and join an alternative community of mainly anti-logging activists on the West Coast, not far from Greymouth. He quickly adapted to a life of cold, uncomfortable self-sufficiency and possum trapping, but I didn't, and before long we parted company. I returned to the city, and all the comforts of home. Over the next several months I took on a number of part-time jobs before landing my first 'real' job, in an art museum, curating exhibitions.

I was lucky. The job was in Wellington and my boss, Charles, the museum director, was something of a maverick, a man who preferred the company of outsiders and artists to that of art-world insiders. It didn't worry him that I had no previous museum experience. In fact he preferred someone he could mould in his own image. Where his own staff was concerned, he rarely gave credit where it was due, but somehow it didn't *quite* matter because working with him was exciting, full of drama, and I respected him.

Apart from art, the thing Charles relished more than anything else was an audience. He rarely indulged in conversation, preferring to stand over people while proclaiming his latest discovery, obsession or pet peeve. He always enunciated slowly in an attempt to disguise his stutter and hesitation over long words. Like many people, Charles had favourite words, words that were touchstones, larger than life and non-negotiable. His most liked were 'absolutely', 'wonderful', 'life force' and 'aroha'. I got to know these words well because part of my job involved ghost-writing his letters, and I learnt early on that it didn't matter what I wrote as long as all these words appeared at least once on the page. As I wrote letters to artists, art collectors, museum directors and curators, the sound of his voice would be a constant racket in my ears. He was easy to mimic, and part of the fun was succeeding in making him think that he really had written each letter. His nose, usually pink, would have a way of turning blueberry-purple when he realised he had been tricked.

During my first month on the job, Charles decided to take me on a trip around the North Island to visit the artists he admired. He was a terrible driver. He always started well, moving from first to second gear like anyone else, but once he reached third gear he became deaf to the sound of the engine and would forget to change up. I remember driving along the Desert Road, doing 100k in third gear when, over the sound of the straining engine, he suddenly announced, 'When I die I want to be reincarnated as a bicycle seat in the Tour de France!' I had no idea what prompted this but I began to wonder what he had been daydreaming about as we were driving along, and the image of his face looking up from the saddle at the crotch of a Lycra-clad cyclist standing up on his pedals suddenly hit me with such force that I actually shuddered.

That introductory trip was one of the most important events in my life. It made me aware of what it meant to be a creator of objects, of artistic process on an everyday, practical level. The imagination, skill and dedication of the artists earnt my deepest respect, but it was the sensory side of the studio visits, the smell of art, that touched me personally.

One of the first studios we visited was that of a jeweller who worked with pāua. In one corner was a bench heaped with shells, all in various stages of being shaped and sanded into pieces of body adornment. As Charles held court, I went over and leant against the bench, waiting for him to finish. As I stood in my corner I began to wonder why I could smell sushi. The seaweed nuttiness of nori kept reaching me in waves and it took me a long time to realise that it was the dust from the pāua.

The next studio belonged to a ceramicist, and this time the smell of clay was undisguised and permeated the whole space. This went on throughout the week as we visited flax weavers, printmakers, textile artists, woodworkers and painters. Every studio had its own distinct smell, something that added to the vitality and life force of the art works themselves, yet neither the artists nor Charles ever remarked upon it. This lack of scent acknowledgement was even more odd given that many of the artists ended each visit by offering us coffee or showing us around their garden, two things that did attract the attention of the nose.

I spent years trying to persuade Charles to let me do a *Stop and Smell the Art* show. Most works were displayed in such a manner that they were almost impossible to appreciate except through sight. Touching was largely discouraged, sound was absent from all but kinetic objects, taste was irrelevant, but it seemed to me that we could communicate art through smell. I imagined walking visitors through darkened spaces that captured the odours of shell, clay or wood before they entered the gallery itself.

'We could prime the senses and make visitors more receptive to the exhibition.'

'Absolutely not,' said Charles.

'Why?'

He couldn't answer.

Stop and Smell the Art never happened and so, perhaps in compensation, I began to experiment with my own series of art scents. It was the first time I'd given thought to creating a range of perfumes based on medium and texture, and the five scents I chose were wood, clay, shell, paint and flax. I made them by infusing raw materials in various oils, and although I tested them on my skin I knew they weren't meant to be worn. The paint scent, for example, simply mimicked a studio with its mix of oil paint, linseed oil and a hint of turpentine. But each perfume fascinated me and I spent hours in my bedroom, testing formulas, making notes of various quantities and dilutions, until I was satisfied.

It was the thought and craft that went into making each blend that appealed to me. How a very slight variation in the dilution of one material could throw the balance of the entire perfume, turning a pale scent into a muddy one or, alternatively, a dull scent into a bright one. I learnt how to rescue a failure by going back to the place where it had begun to fall apart and starting again.

In a final attempt to convince Charles, I took my samples to work for him to sniff. He hated them all but kept them nevertheless.

Years later, after he died, I happened to mention this episode to a curator friend who was employed in an Australian museum. 'Oh, didn't you know?' he said.

'Know what?'

'Charles phoned me out of the blue one day asking if I knew any *olfactory wizards* because he'd had an idea for a show matching weaving with smell. He even had a title: *Whāriki: The Scented Mat.*'

'No!'

'I couldn't help him, of course. Korean ceramics were more my thing back then.'

Curated notes: wood shavings, cedar, pine resin, shell, seaweed, flax, oil paint, clay and a dose of bitterness.

Random smells often enter my mind and stay with me. I daydream in scents and perfumes. Recently these scents have reached me with a clarity and sharpness I haven't experienced before. Phantosmia is the word that describes olfactory hallucinations, and I have only to detect a whiff of L'Eau d'Issey, imagined or real, to immediately think of Thora.

Thora must have bought L'Eau d'Issey as soon as it was released in the early nineties. She was certainly the first among my acquaintances to wear it. I suspect that the association with the Japanese designer and the simple profile of the bottle might account for her initial attraction to the perfume, but I don't doubt that the clean and minimalist nature of the scent itself appealed to her sense of aesthetics.

Thora had started a chemistry degree and was the coolest woman I had ever met. Like me, she flatted in a large house in the Aro Valley and was part of central Wellington's arty, politically engaged social scene. She was thin, with dark hair that was cut short at the back but had a long fringe that fell over her eyes. She bleached a section of hair by her side parting, and it was a kind of dirty, greenish blonde against the blackness of the rest. She had a long nose, slightly beaky at the tip, and a downwards-curling smile. She wore black, mostly, the only hint of colour coming from her bright red lipstick. She rarely talked and struck me as shy and intelligent. I don't think we ever had a long conversation but I liked her enough to be gently teased by my two lesbian flatmates whenever her name came up in conversation.

In fact, Thora, like Charles, belonged to the period of my life when, despite one or two short-lived relationships with both men and women, I first fully embraced the freedom and independence that came with being single. I had never been greatly interested in sex – though I had never completely shut myself off from it, especially during the years spent with my former boyfriend – but while living in Wellington I realised that sex, for me, was largely irrelevant. I'd given it a go but then moved on in the same way that I might test, and ultimately reject, a new hyped-up perfume. I didn't long for intimacy and was quite satisfied with the broader social contact I enjoyed through colleagues at work, flatmates and friends. I didn't want a partner and had never felt any maternal urge, and my dream, if I had one at all, was to save enough to buy a small home of my own, a place where I could live exactly as I wished. I suppose if I had to attach a label to myself it would be 'spinster', a word that is seldom owned or used with enthusiasm or pride. I became a single woman by choice rather than as a response or reaction to hurt and disappointment, failed relationships or lack of options.

Though my sexual relationships steadily dropped by the wayside, those Aro Valley years were memorable for the number of perfumes I accrued: Shalimar by Guerlain, Christian Dior's Dune, Calyx from Prescriptives, Lancôme's Magie Noire and Calvin Klein's Obsession. Later, during long periods of unemployment, I had no spare income and was reduced to wearing my own concoctions or a syrupy fragrant oil sourced from an ethnic market stall that I think may have been a blend of patchouli oil and ylang ylang. It was sweet, a little grassy, with a smell that brought to mind overripe bananas. It was called something like Rainsong and left brown stains on my skin, collars and cuffs.

In the early nineties I was lucky enough to be offered a ticket to a Nina Simone concert, which was part of the arts festival taking place in the city. I spent hours preparing for the event by playing my flatmate's copy of 'My Baby Just Cares for Me'. I didn't particularly like the song, but it had suddenly become a hit in the late eighties and had made its way into all my friends' music collections. It wasn't until later that I discovered the reason for its sudden revival. It had been featured in a commercial for Chanel No. 5 and, as a result, had climbed to the top of the charts in Britain and Europe. Anyway, the song was upbeat and helped get me in the mood for going out. To my disappointment, the concert was anything but upbeat. The atmosphere on stage struck me as tense, and it seemed to me that Simone would have preferred to be anywhere in the world but Wellington.

As the lights came up at the end of the concert the audience stood to applaud and cheer and right up at the front, standing tall, was Alice Walker, also in town as part of the festival. As the clapping continued, Walker raised her fist in a black power salute and Simone signalled that she had seen the salute – a private show of strength between two formidable women. Next to Walker, her head lowered as if in prayer, was Thora.

When I saw Thora later I asked her what it had been like sitting next to Alice Walker all evening. I didn't imagine that she would have asked for Walker's autograph, but I thought she might have acknowledged the writer during the moments before the house lights dimmed. After all, Thora was a huge fan.

'I said "Hello",' said Thora, 'but I don't think she heard me.'

Not long afterwards I blended a perfume for Thora. In my head and on paper I had it all figured out. I would take the concept of thunder and lightning from Thora's name and link it to Alice Walker's *In Search of Our Mothers' Gardens*, one of her favourite books. In short, it would be the scent of a night garden following a storm. I decided to build the perfume around boronia. I'd only recently discovered the plant, having spotted the reddish-brown flowering bush in the botanic gardens one Sunday afternoon. The smell was sticky sweet like aged raspberry jam but with a tart, dusty base. It was the latter that gave the scent its edge. It seemed a perfect fit for Thora with her white-streaked black hair and slash of red lipstick.

Because I wanted to keep the perfume simple I added carrot seed oil for its smell of damp dug-over earth, ambrette for a hint of spicy sweetness and frankincense because I had a large unopened bottle handy and I thought it would add a nice incense-like smokiness to the drydown. The component that eluded me was petrichor, the mineral, flinty smell associated with rain falling on warm, bone-dry earth.

The perfume oil I made wasn't a bad scent – in fact it was nice – but I was disappointed that it had failed to capture my intention. It would never cause the wearer to breathe deeply and smile with pleasure or wonder. I needed something to lift it out of the ordinary, but nothing I tried worked. For some reason it remained a tad murky, like a pot of soup reheated once too often.

It was then that I thought of my grandmother's uranium bottle. I found it in my jewellery box and placed it on the table next to the boronia blend. I hadn't looked closely at the bottle since Lange's speech and I'd forgotten how lovely it was. The strange yellow-green glass was faceted, designed to resemble the surface of a scallop, though its overall shape was more like a flattened pine cone. It was more beautiful than I remembered and I spent a few minutes holding it up to the sun, tilting it this way and that to capture the light. Where the sun hit the bottle the glass was pale yellow, but where it was thickest it was the colour of unripe lemons. It was the only thing I owned from my grandmother and I'd kept it with me whenever I'd moved flats or cities. The brown gunk was still in the bottom of the bowl and I enjoyed it for one last time before carefully transferring the juice of Thora's perfume blend from its plain, dark-brown, screw-capped bottle to the rare green bottle in my hand.

I carefully carried Thora's perfume around in my pocket for two weeks before I saw her again. I grew used to the feel of its cool ribbed glass against my fingers every time I reached for my hanky or change. The perfume had started to develop in the short time since I'd created it. The individual oils were becoming less harsh and more rounded as they settled into one another. The ambrette, which had threatened to overpower the boronia, had slipped into the background, and the boronia itself was becoming more jam-like, its berry richness edging towards damask rose.

I can't recollect what I said to Thora when I handed her the perfume. I know she was very reluctant to accept my gift because she felt it was too valuable, too precious, and I had to work hard to convince her to take the bottle. I remember that I could feel my heart beating hard in my chest and that I could smell her L'Eau d'Issey, and that I took an unexpected, sudden dislike to the perfume that has stayed with me ever since. I recall the hollow, sickening sense of loss that gripped me as I comprehended the irrevocability of what I had done. More than anything, I remember how empty my pocket felt on the slow walk home.

Notes of introversion, lost friendship and regret: petrichor, boronia, ambrette, frankincense and gunk.

I stayed on at the art museum until Charles retired and then, feeling restless one day, I gave in my notice and bought a ticket to Australia. When I eventually returned, I discovered the art world had moved on without me. I took whatever part-time and contract work I could find, but my professional profile never really recovered and with every passing month I became more and more tainted by failure. With little money to my name, I had to move back home to Christchurch and, until my father's death, I was largely dependent on my parents for support. I suppose that returning to university to begin a PhD in American literature, focusing on Louisiana women writers, was part of a last-ditch attempt to save face and restore my self-esteem.

Not long after finishing my doctorate I moved to Auckland to take up employment in the American studies department at one of the most prestigious universities in the country. For more than thirteen years life was good, but then one day a cold dread began to seep through my world, sapping all the light from my day.

It started when rumours of humanities department closures took on a more threatening aspect, with talks of reviews and restructuring. The vice-chancellor, known by many as the Ice Chancellor, issued press releases hinting that sluggish university departments would be revitalised and strategies would be implemented to grow the campus. 'We see this as a positive step for the future of the university,' she said on radio and television. 'We have the chance to embrace an exciting new business model. Staff have already been asked for input and we are here to listen . . .' Photographs of the VC in front of the new 'gateway' to the campus, a large stone monument, made the local front page.

Carpetlayers moved through our department, replacing the threadbare dirty green covering with a strange purple-brown flecked carpet. The whole floor had a chemical smell, and staff who had been skulking in their offices for years were forced to open their doors to air out their rooms. Everyone felt exposed. Discussion in the staffroom began to ask whether the laying of new carpet boded well for the department. Some saw it as a vote of confidence; others of a more cynical nature regarded it as a sign that we were all to be replaced. I wasn't sure what to think.

I wanted to believe we were going to be all right, but the smell and colour of the new carpet struck me as toxic.

At night I lay awake trying to work out where I sat on the scale from 'indispensable' to 'dispensable'. I'd been at the university for longer than many people in the department and was employed full time as a senior lecturer. But I wasn't an associate professor or a professor, and had never been head of department. I had a great teaching record but my rise through the ranks hadn't been as quick as that of some of my male colleagues. My publishing record was good but not as prolific or successful as that of two of my closest colleagues: Professor Archer Hall and Associate Professor Jerome Roy.

Archer was older than me, and a real scholar. He was an expert in Early American first-person encounter narratives, those of explorers, missionaries or traders, but he also had an encyclopaedic knowledge and could have lectured on any subject from history through to religion and literature. Archer represented the institutional memory of the department, and his presence was a constant reminder of how much more valuable and flexible a well-read human brain was than a computer search engine. Jerome was younger, a career academic. He'd had great success in getting funding, and as a result had been able to buy out his teaching to further his research and publication record. As Archer once joked, Jerome was the type of guy who picked out all the dried fruit from the muesli packet. I could see Archer's point but, apart from the odd thoughtless remark, Jerome had been respectful and discreet in his dealings with me. On the other hand, I'd never posed much of a threat to him. Anyway, he was the go-to guy for twentieth-century American literature and could talk for hours about his favourite authors, James Salter and Truman Capote, a strange mixture that somehow worked. Whereas Archer served the old-fashioned concept of academic scholarship and Jerome served twenty-first century academic careerism, I fitted somewhere in the middle, serving students.

In the very early days I'd sometimes helped Archer with background research, such as when he co-authored a book about early Mormon missionaries to New Zealand or wrote a paper about nineteenth-century Māori and Pākehā pilgrims to the Salt Lake Temple in Utah for the *Journal of the American Academy of Religion*. More recently I'd also taken up the slack whenever Jerome had a break from teaching. I filled in for him and also covered course advising and marking, the least glamorous part of his job. I liked teaching, but being a good teacher didn't cut it in terms of professional development.

On the day I progressed to senior lecturer I thought my days of filling in for others had finally come to an end. From now on I would focus on big projects, research and writing for the top journals on Southern women's literature. I celebrated my new role by purchasing a bottle of Chanel No. 5, attracted to the story behind the fragrance. Ernest Beaux, its Russian-born French creator, based the famous aldehyde-centric perfume on memories of the time he spent stationed above the Arctic Circle during World War One. He wrote about the smells of the thawing rivers and lakes, notes released by the heat of the midnight sun. The aldehydes in Chanel No. 5 give it an abstract note, and the word that cropped up time and again in responses to the perfume was 'radiant'. Radiant. That was to be my future. I bought the perfume, and then a place of my own, a sanctuary, my home. I was so happy I felt as though I'd stepped into the light.

Six weeks before I lost my job I was sitting at my desk when I saw Jerome walk past my open door. He hesitated as if he might come in but then continued on without a word. Moments later he reappeared, raised his fist to tap on the doorframe but then thought better of it and suddenly looked back over his shoulder before returning the way he'd come.

Later that morning he finally knocked. Jerome was young, good looking and smart. He favoured navy and grey, checked shirts buttoned to the neck, dark wool waistcoats and chinos. He was more preppy than hipster. Around his wrist was a thin silver bangle that drew attention to the thick, dark hairs sprouting on his arm. He was Canadian, from Toronto, and had a nice accent. I imagine he was loved and supported as a child as he had an air of confidence. He wanted and expected to be the next head of department.

Always polite, Jerome asked how my day was going. I pointed to the stack of papers on my desk, marking from the Introduction to American Literature course that we shared, and answered, fine.

'You going to the restructuring meeting on Friday?'

I nodded.

He started fiddling with the silver band around his wrist. 'You've been here a long time. What do you think will happen?'

'I'm not sure, but I'm guessing it won't be good.'

'Scottie's recently started kindergarten. She's really settled in,' he said.

I nodded, glad that his daughter's name was so distinctive that I easily identified who he was talking about.

'Desna's completed her Stepping Up course and is about to become a partner at Warden, Black and Maybank. She loves the lifestyle here.'

'Yep, it's a good place for a family,' I agreed.

'How long have you been here, in the department?'

'Getting on for fourteen years,' I said.

'That's a long time.'

He hesitated, glanced past me towards the six-monthly planner on my wall. 'You'll find work at another university. If it comes to that.'

'I don't want to go to another university,' I said. 'I have an apartment here. A home I love.'

He looked startled. 'Yes, of course, but it's not like you're tied down like the rest of us . . .' He stopped short of finishing the sentence and looked at the floor, embarrassed. 'Sorry, I didn't mean it to come out like that. I know you have ties to this place. Sorry.'

'I'm sure you'll be all right,' I said. 'They won't get rid of you.'

Notes of restructuring and redundancy: carpet glue and boxes filled with books and old paper.

A list of potential base notes: gas, eucalyptus, soap, uranium, oakmoss, oats, rose, blood, jasmine, sewage, diesel, amber, oil paint, clay, wood shavings, boronia, ambrette, frankincense, industrial glue, dusty papers, old books.

Base notes provide the foundation and soul of the perfume, but that doesn't mean they are predictable and like to stay put. Like memories, they have a tendency to flare up at any time; they do more than linger in the background. They also have a way of altering and fixing the more volatile heart and top notes. There is a sense of interplay and exchange.

You need patience to appreciate base notes. Whereas top notes burst from the bottle and heart notes develop after only twenty or thirty minutes, sometimes sooner, base notes bide their time.

But for now, the heart notes need my attention.

HEART NOTES

BEFORE I HUNG MY JACKET ON THE HOOK BY THE DOOR OR placed my keys in the bowl on the side table, I always slipped off my shoes and stood with my back pressed against the exposed brick wall and inhaled. Released by the heat, the smell of wool and lanolin drew close, enfolding me in its welcome.

Home was an open-plan loft designed around a single kitchen-living space. The original steel staircase led to the mezzanine floor where I slept; a small second bedroom and bathroom were tucked off the entrance. Before the developers took over, the building was derelict. Graffiti and tagging disfigured the brickwork, the steel-framed windows were broken and the wide floorboards were damaged and encrusted with pigeon shit. My apartment was little more than disused roof space, the topmost corner of the former city wool store.

I took another deep breath. The air had substance, a pulse. It was rich and deep and made up of many notes beside the wool and lanolin. There were hints of fresh green grass, sun-bleached paddocks, the sweet coumarin warmth of hay, dust and shit . . . even human sweat, tobacco and tar. My home was a repository of past weather, seasons and years.

I walked towards the long table in the centre of the room and placed my bag gently beside an open notebook. A shaft of light filtered through the window, creating a broad track across neat rows of carefully labelled amber bottles. From my bag I took out my latest purchases and placed them in the gaps, speaking their names as I arranged them: clary sage, myrrh, birch tar, geranium, nutmeg, labdanum, vanilla and ambrette.

It was quiet in the loft. The last of the afternoon sun had slipped below the partially closed blind and the room was bathed in golden tones. The ceiling fan traced a slow circle overhead and every now and then a sound like a gentle whop, whop, whop lapped the air.

Kate Chopin's *The Awakening* lay open next to my notebook.

It was one of the department's standard texts, on the first-year reading list for as long as I could remember. For a time, it was the only novel by a woman that was required reading. When I lost my job I brought my books home. I stacked my poetry collection and novels in neat piles against the walls and placed the academic texts in numbered boxes in the spare room. I should probably have tried to sell the textbooks but I thought they might be out of date and worthless.

It had been a long time since I'd read for pleasure. At first I wasn't sure if I'd remember *how* to read without a specific purpose in mind. I guess old habits take a while to die because as I reread the story of Edna Pontellier, I copied passages and attached sticky notes whenever I came across a reference to scent. By the time I was halfway through there were fifteen blue tabs poking out from the pages.

The scents in *The Awakening* belonged to a specific time and place: summer vacations on Grand Isle, Louisana, during the 1890s. The characters seemed to float and drift through their surroundings, much like the fragrance of flowers carried on the night air. Few of the scents suggested fresh, open spaces; even the smell of the sea was dense and seductive. Rose-filled vases shared space with garlands woven from red and yellow flowers. Branches from orange and lemon trees decorated a hall, their deeply polished leaves contrasting with the gauzy muslin curtains that billowed in the warm breeze. Perfumed talcum powder – poudre de riz – was lifted from the dressing table and dabbed onto sun-flushed skin. And finally, as Edna, exhausted, slipped beneath the ocean waves, she remembered her childhood home and 'the musky odour of pinks filled the air'.

In an attempt to recreate the final, scented scenes of the book, I made a perfume with notes of carnation, clove and rose. I added bergamot and lavender. The bergamot gave the blend a hint of brightness, the lavender a contrasting cooler, herbaceous quality. The final note I selected was oak, from an expensive oakwood absolute, a highly concentrated natural extraction I kept for special occasions. It was Chopin's reference to the gnarled and stunted trees, scattered remnants of a once-vast chenier forest, that aroused my curiosity. More than the warm, salty air of the Mexican Gulf, the heady, night-time blooms, or the lush green of undergrowth, it was the hurricane-battered but tenacious water-oaks that, for me, struck at the heart of Chopin's 'rare odour'.

Jerome called in on his way home from work. He was one of the lucky ones; he still had a job.

I decided to test him on *The Awakening* perfume I had made. I wanted to see if he could identify the book from sniffing my blend, and so I devised a multi-choice question based around smells linked to the novels he taught in his Introduction to American Literature course. I amused myself all afternoon trying to decide on the other books and finally settled on Upton Sinclair's *The Jungle* for the stench of cattle and blood, Bernard Malamud's *The Natural* for the smell of grass, leather baseballs and sweat, and Marilynne Robinson's *Housekeeping* for the scent of dampened fire and burnt wood. None of these novels shared a scent profile with *The Awakening* and so I expected Jerome to have little trouble picking Chopin's novel from the choices offered.

Jerome arrived early, as he always did. I was sitting at my table when I heard the sound of the lift doors open on the floor below, followed by the hollow-sounding clunk, clunk, clunk of the steel stairs as he ran up the short flight to my landing. I'm not a hugger so we shook hands before I invited him in. I was so hooked on the lingering smell of greasy wool that permeated my loft that I tended to be surprised and disappointed when visitors didn't pause and inhale the air before taking off their shoes. When Jerome gave no indication of having noticed the warm, animal scent – at least, he didn't mention it – I felt vaguely let down and held it against him.

He had brought me a packet of oolong and as I made the tea he leant against the counter, toying with a bowl of walnuts, taking them out one by one and arranging them in a long row, like ants seeking sugar.

'How's life?' he asked.

He was too well mannered to come straight out and ask if I was having money troubles or, alternatively, had found a job, but that was what he meant.

'Still getting to grips with the changes,' I replied.

It was still early days but I'd emailed a couple of departments, putting it out that I was available for work. Apart from making good use of my academic qualifications, I was also happy to do the work that most academics found confusing: dealing with university administration, collating material for courses, updating student information, contributing to policy, committees, data entry, spreadsheets – anything that required a password and greater computer knowhow than everyday word processing skills. I slowly realised, however, that the more I emphasised how practical I was, the more my academic credentials appeared to suffer. The fact that I knew more about Southern women novelists, or, for that matter, women's personal narratives and life-writing than most other lecturers at the university, counted for little. It was as if I were no longer regarded as a scholar and teacher with an established publishing history but as a middle-aged secretary, someone capable of emptying the dishwasher and keeping track of Tupperware lids.

'It's so hard,' said Jerome.

I nodded.

'And I feel bad about what happened. I wish I could do more.'

'Well, let me know if anything comes up. I'm okay for the moment. I have holiday pay and my redundancy cheque.'

I could see that Jerome wanted to ask how much I'd been paid out but I didn't feel like talking about it so I steered him towards the table where my vial of The Awakening stood. 'I want you to smell this and then look at the four options and their perfume notes on the sheet of paper and tell me which novel it's based on.'

'What is it?'

'A blend of essential oils. I made it myself.'

'You make perfume? I didn't know that.'

'It's a secret talent,' I joked. 'Smell it and then match it to the book.'

I handed him the bottle and as he sniffed I slid the piece of paper with the four titles on it in front of him.

'It's based on one of these,' I said. 'Which one do you think?'

Barely glancing at the list, and without a second's hesitation, he responded, '*The Awakening*.'

'What? That's incredible.' I felt a sudden rush of pleasure, delight that my simple experiment had captured the fragrant essence of the novel and communicated it to someone else. I could feel myself blush with pride at my accomplishment. And then I saw my copy of Chopin's book on the table near the samples.

'You cheated!'

'No.'

'You did. You saw the book!'

He gave a 'what can I say' shrug and sniffed the bottle again.

'Can I try a bit on my skin?' he asked.

'Better not. It needs to be diluted in a carrier oil before it's safe to wear. But you could put a bit on your hanky and sniff that.'

I knew he'd have a hanky. And I was right. A freshly laundered, folded square that looked as if it had never been used.

'I like it. It smells kind of like cake, doesn't it? Like Christmas cake fresh out of the oven.'

'That's the carnation and cloves, they add spice. I was thinking of the reference to pinks at the end of the novel, when Edna's drowning and her thoughts wander back to her childhood home.'

'Pink. The colour?'

'No, the flowers. Pinks.'

Jerome shrugged and shook his head as if it were all news to him.

'There's something a bit harsh in there. What's that?'

I took the bottle and sniffed, then dabbed a drop on my wrist.

'Probably the lavender. People often describe it as screechy but I find it very relaxing.'

Jerome dipped a blotter, a narrow strip of heavy absorbent paper, into the bottle, then fanned it in front of his nose. He closed his eyes as he sniffed. 'My English grandmother used to make lavender bags for the church fair when I was a kid. I can still picture them, small drawstring bags made from scraps of floral material with purple ribbon ties. She made hundreds of them and they were in all the cupboards and drawers. They smelt scratchy and purple. Very purple.'

I passed the juice under my nose once more. 'Did you get anything bright from the perfume? I used bergamot to lift it.'

He shook his head. 'I don't know what bergamot is.'

'It's citrus. It's in Earl Grey tea, an orangey-lemon scent.'

He closed his eyes and sniffed again, the corners of his mouth tipping down in concentration. 'No, it mainly smells purple with fruit cake.'

'My favourite part will take a bit of time to develop,' I said. 'Oakwood.'

'Oak?'

'Think of the wood, the bark, or maybe imagine wine barrels if that's easier.'

Jerome took a deep breath and smiled at me, 'It's good. It's really good. You could sell it. Make your fortune.'

I enjoyed Jerome's visit. To my surprise I found that, far from resenting the fact that he had a job while I was sent home with a redundancy cheque, I was genuinely pleased that he was still valued and needed, the lone representative of *us*, the old American studies team. I'd barely been out of my office a month and I was already thinking of myself as part of a lost tribe, a passing generation, a member of the once great humanities family.

Notes for solitude, and a life short of meaning: oak. I wonder why first oakmoss and now oak has captured my attention. I'm not familiar with Chopin's water-oaks, or the live oaks of Louisiana's cheniers, but the English oak presents so much in terms of scent.

From acorns to autumn leaves, it's a broad range that includes sweet, nutty impressions through to earthy mulch. I could even add the scent of a woodpile, timber stacked and drying in a woodshed. To me, the smell of oak is rounder, less dry than the pencil-shaving smell of cedar, less resin-like than pine or birch.

If heart notes carry the main theme of a scent then oak has definite appeal. How wonderful to have a signature scent that brings to mind a species of tree that can adapt to a multitude of environments, withstand storms and live for hundreds, if not thousands, of years. Oak offers the promise of stability, of continuity, and maybe for that reason it has crept back into perfumery over the past decade – it captures the present-day nostalgia for a simpler, more authentic past. The more I think about it, the more I am attracted to oak as a key ingredient in my signature scent.

I got a job interview. Not for a university position, or for anything even remotely academic, but for the perfume counter at a newly opened department store called The Corner Dairy. I'd noticed an article about the store in the lifestyle section of the newspaper some time ago. It was portrayed as the brainchild of a New Zealand-born, Sydney-based lifestyle blogger who had wanted to gather together all the things she adored – such as vintage and upcycled products ethically sourced from around the world – into one convenient, carbon-neutral location.

I applied because I thought it would be a start, something to tide me over until a better offer came along. Even though I knew a lot about perfume, I was pleasantly surprised when I secured an interview. I had wavered over whether to include my academic qualifications in my application but I couldn't highlight my employment record, my skills or strengths, without referring to them. To make myself appear less bookish, I also drew attention to all the hours I spent working after school in a real corner dairy during the late seventies.

I arrived early for my interview and was shown into a pleasant wood-panelled room with a large vertical garden along the entire length of one wall. I was offered a cup of tea and invited to sit on a stunning-looking stool that rocked and tilted whenever I shifted my weight. The sensation of almost falling was very unsettling and to my embarrassment I capsized, spilling tea down the front of my skirt, and had to ask to use the bathroom to clean myself up. When I returned, a well-dressed young man with blotchy red skin was in my place. He didn't notice me but continued explaining something about the health benefits of core-strength balance stools to an older woman who stood listening while scrolling through a tablet in her hands. Eventually the older woman looked up, saw me and asked if I was Siân. 'Great,' she said. 'Anna. This way', and disappeared through a door in the vertical garden.

I liked Anna, who was the recruitment manager, from the start. She was warm and professional and she struck me as smart. Her description of herself as 'old-fashioned' simply meant that she preferred to interview applicants rather than rely on psychometric tests.

'I've been in business for thirty years now,' she said, 'and I still don't trust those tests. As far as I'm concerned nothing beats face-to-face communication. It keeps you honest.'

I agreed, noting that the lack of human interaction had been one of the worst aspects of my redundancy. Anna expressed sympathy and then we talked in general terms for a short while before I began to sell my ideas for the perfume counter.

'I've given it a lot of thought because I like perfume.'

'Good,' said Anna. 'That's good to know. Go on.'

'Well, I'd like to go beyond mainstream perfume retail and create a scent library. For example, we could arrange perfumes by note rather than house, with displays for chypres, orientals, florals, gourmands, aldehydes and so on.'

'Nice. Sounds good.'

'We could also spotlight individual perfumes or notes each week. You could take a classic like Chanel No. 19, for example, and tell the story of its creation and impact on iris perfumes. We could run perfume tutorials, lunchtime lectures, inviting customers to come in and sample, say, all the fruity-gourmand scents. Or,' I said, warming to the subject, 'we could focus on a single perfumer and introduce their work. For example, we could do a week of Christine Nagel perfumes. An education programme like that has a lot of potential, don't you think? We could even have a bespoke perfume experience, where we match customers to fragrances based on their favourite smells. There are so many options.'

As I outlined more and more ideas I noticed that Anna's attention was beginning to wane. She had smiled and nodded when I began but now she seemed distracted, and kept sneaking glances at her tablet. Perhaps I was out of time or maybe she'd decided that I wasn't right for the job. Instead of slowing down and regaining her attention, I did what I often do in awkward situations: I prattled on.

'Did you know,' I said, 'that there are more than two thousand perfume releases a year? That's a lot of product. We need to focus on either mainstream or niche. Who is your customer base?' I paused, took a breath, and continued without waiting for an answer. 'Probably niche, right? Hard to access, expensive perfumes, sourced from independent makers around the world. We should definitely include the Australians, they're doing some interesting work, especially the Melbourne perfumers.' By this stage I was practically talking to myself, thinking aloud. 'Then again,' I said, 'how does niche fit in with the corner dairy concept? I mean, some of those independent perfumes are $500 a bottle. Many attars are even more. Then again, customers might spend that much going to a test match or concert. How much do women pay at the hairdressers these days? Some people spend $40 to $50 on shampoo alone. We could include a few cheaper perfume brands, but the important thing is that we do something special with the perfume counter. I like the idea of a scent library, or a museum, rather than selling . . .'

Anna cleared her throat. 'Actually, what are you like at *selling* things?'

From the moment I left The Corner Dairy I knew I'd blown the interview. I had only myself to blame. I'd been too eager to prove I was serious about perfume rather than serious about retail and I'd made such a fool of myself. No one was ever going to hire me if I came across as desperate. But I could have done that job, and done it well. More than that, I needed that job. What an idiot.

On my way home, to take my thoughts off my failure, I began recalling and listing the smells associated with the neighbourhood dairy where I had worked after school and on Saturdays. An elderly couple named Mr and Mrs Bumstead owned the shop. They were my father's patients, and when Mrs Bumstead hurt her back falling off a stepladder, Dad offered my services until she recovered. It was my first paid job and I loved it so much that I stayed on long after Mrs Bumstead was back on her feet, running the show.

The dairy was typical of its day. The strongest scent memory related to the pie warmer and the smell of fruits, greasy meat, flaky pastry and fat from the apple turnovers, Cornish pasties and Stevenson's square mince pies. Next on my list was ice cream: the milky sweetness of vanilla, the buttery toffee of hokey pokey, chocolate, artificial strawberry and, during the summer months only, passion fruit. For an extra fifteen cents we'd dip the ice creams in melted chocolate to make brown derbys. It was one of my jobs to clean out the small chocolate vat at the end of each day, and for some reason the aroma of sweet cocoa tended to make me gag. I never figured out why, as I had no problem eating chocolate, but of all my tasks this was the one I dreaded most.

On a counter opposite the ice cream freezer was a shelf containing the milkshake makers and powdered mixes. Chocolate, caramel, strawberry and creaming soda were equally popular, but banana was the one most firmly fixed in my memory because it was so synthetic: it had an unexpected metallic note that wafted into the air whenever I spooned it out. Pink Smokers, small hard lollies that rattled around in the mouth like loose teeth, had a distinct smell too, similar to the sweet-musk present in the base of many of today's detergents and personal care products.

Newspapers topped my list as the smelliest non-food item in the dairy. When first unbundled they carried the thick oily scent of ink, which sometimes resembled diesel or tar. Damp, they reminded me of cat's piss. Neither smell was pleasant because both renditions seemed unclean, dirty to the touch – and to the nose. Cleaning products, the ones we used to wash the floor and wipe the counters, and the strong, eye-watering smell of disinfectant, were also contenders for my dairy scents list. The harsh pine smell made me think of the school toilets and sickbay whenever I opened the bottle.

Finally, the few smells that were natural or pleasant: carnations, roses and freesias. We had buckets inside the entrance that contained bunches of flowers. Back then they weren't wrapped in cellophane, and when we lifted them out of the buckets to wrap them in purple or green wax paper they dripped, leaving a trail of round drops across the lino. At the start of spring we always stocked bright yellow daffodils. The flowers didn't smell but I liked the fresh, slightly bitter and earthy scent of their stalks. To me, they were simple, happy flowers, like dandelions or daisies.

Once, around Mother's Day, Mr Bumstead decided to stock orchids, but they were too expensive for our regulars and they didn't sell. As a treat, I was allowed to buy all the wilted flowers for 50 cents a bunch once the petals started to drop. I always took them home, mostly because I felt sorry for them but also because I liked to give them to my parents, who rarely treated themselves to luxuries.

In general no one really valued the flowers or paused to sniff them on their way in or out of the shop. They seemed to be an afterthought, a token symbolising care and attention to compensate for neglect. Women grabbed them on their way to visit sick relatives or friends in hospital while men gripped the bunches firmly, carrying them at arm's length, intent at putting as much distance between themselves and the blooms as possible when they reluctantly bought them late on a Friday evening. There appeared to be a certain shame attached to buying flowers, and taking pleasure from their scent was unimaginable. Smelling flowers was strictly for the sick and girls.

Notes from a lost neighbourhood tainted by narcissism: I don't want any of the corner dairy scents in my perfume. I'm not a fan of food or sweet perfumes; I can tolerate vanilla but only when it's dry rather than milky or caramelised. Strawberry, banana and raspberry don't interest me as notes, nor does the smell of mince and sausage grease. Carnations remind me of cloves, and I find the scent overpowering most of the time.

Daffodil – narcissus – is the only flower I'd consider from the corner dairy. I love the smell of the stalks, the way they conjure up the cool interior of a florist shop. And recently I've spent an awful amount of time focusing on myself, becoming more and more self-absorbed with each passing day. Fortunately, however, I've never fallen in love with my own beauty reflected back at me from the water at the bottom of a plastic flower bucket.

Oakmoss, oak and daffodils. The trees and flowers of England and Wales. But with the memory of the old corner dairy in the back of my mind I wonder if I could construct a lexicon, a chronology, of New Zealand scent.

I wasn't offered the job at The Corner Dairy. Anna texted to say I had some great ideas and showed lots of enthusiasm. She congratulated me on how well prepared I was, claimed it had been a pleasure to meet me, wished me well and offered me a $20 discount code on my next purchase.

I kept thinking about the processes we went through last year as part of the management for change. It was one of the most dehumanising experiences of my life. Week after week we requested updates about the future of our department, our positions, any information that might help us get our bearings during restructuring. And week after week we heard nothing. Then, once in a while, pages of detailed but meaningless nonsense would be circulated around the university and we'd spend hours trying to figure out what was actually being said. The language was impenetrable, even by academic standards; it obscured facts. No one would take responsibility or answer our questions. No one would tell us what was going on. Even the union representative found the situation impossible to navigate. It was all 'wait and see' and 'holding pattern' and we were asked to remain patient. We were assured that our concerns were being listened to. But they weren't. No one listened to us. Our union representatives did their best, of that I'm sure. And I'm certain, too, that the head of department did everything in his power to keep American studies afloat. I can barely imagine the stress he must have been under. In the end only one sentence really mattered: the one telling us that the employer had the right to manage, organise and make final decisions about the operation and policies of the university. We were history.

I remember arriving at work at the end of it all and knowing instinctively that something terrible had happened. There were a number of staff members standing around the office area as I stepped towards my pigeonhole. I flinched when I saw the brown envelope inside, then turned back to face Archer, who was reading a sheet of paper balanced on top of a white envelope. I read my letter and felt sick to my stomach. Not because it came straight out and said I had lost my job but because it was an invitation to meet with various representatives to discuss my 'future forward' or something like that. And that was it. Not once did I get a call from the vice-chancellor, her office or the dean. Just the brown envelope in my pigeonhole and a horrible, sickening dread.

I followed Archer into his office and sat in one of the armchairs he had brought in to make his students feel comfortable during meetings.

'Are you all right?' I asked.

'Yes,' he said.

'Have you seen Jerome?'

'Yes.'

'Is he all right?'

'Yes. He's going across to the English department.'

'What do you mean?'

'He's been absorbed.'

'Teaching American literature?'

'Yes.'

'Oh.' I paused for the longest time, processing the information before responding. 'Good. That's good. Good on him.'

I sat in silence, wondering if I would get sent over to the English department. But I hadn't heard anything. Still, there was a chance, wasn't there?

'Are you all right?' I asked Archer, again.

'Yes. How are you feeling?'

'I don't know,' I said. 'Sick, I suppose. Like I failed an important exam.'

Archer offered to fetch me a drink, and I waited in his office while he went down the hall to the small kitchen then returned with chamomile tea in a cup and saucer. I remember turning the cup around and around but I don't recall drinking it.

'What are you going to do?'

Archer let out a long sigh. 'I guess I'll go home and talk to Renate.'

'Good idea. You're lucky to have someone . . .'

And then I stopped because at that moment it hit me hard that I didn't have a wife, a partner, anyone waiting for me at home. I didn't even have a father or mother; they were both dead.

My home might offer sanctuary, but it wouldn't provide me with a comforting hug or words of reassurance. There was only me. God, it was a feeling of such desolation I almost cried.

Jerome called in again on his way home from university. Maybe the traffic was heavy and he wanted to wait it out at my place or perhaps he wanted a rest before going home to his family. He loved his daughter, Scottie, but I'd heard him complain about the disorderliness and the loss of autonomy that came with parenting. He was so fastidious that he had trouble coping with Scottie's liveliness, loudness and mess. It was only when she behaved like a small adult and sat quietly, her attention fully focused on her iPad or activity book, that Jerome was able to relax and fully enjoy her company.

Sometimes, too, though I had no proof on which to base my observation, I got the impression that Jerome felt undermined by the fact that he earnt less than his wife, Desna. I believed that his ambition, his drive to reach full professorship and head of department, was at least partly motivated by an old-fashioned need to provide for his family, to be acknowledged – and revered – as the head of the house.

I was glad I still made an effort to dress up in the morning. I might not have bothered but one day I caught sight of my reflection in the spare bedroom mirror as I was tidying away a stack of books and was taken aback. As I looked at myself for a full minute it occurred to me that I was on the brink of becoming permanently rumpled. The line between casual and dishevelled had been crossed, and if I weren't careful I'd soon be spending the day wandering about the house in cardigans, trackpants and slippers. Extreme measures were in order.

I pulled out a selection of my work wardrobe, trouser suits and chic pencil skirts combined with fine V-neck cashmere sweaters or blouses. I looked good, and when Jerome turned up in his waistcoat and navy chinos I thought that if we stood together and waved towards an imaginary crowd we might have passed as Emmanuel and Brigitte Macron. Of course, I kept that to myself.

It was nice to see Jerome. Life was becoming far too quiet, devoid of reassuring chatter. I still started each morning well. I got up early and searched the job vacancies and sent off a couple of applications, but by noon I was bored, and by two I was often lonely. I'd become one of those people who went through their days speaking to no one. It was only a matter of time before bumping into a neighbour while putting out the rubbish or chatting to someone on the supermarket checkout was the social highlight of my day. In order to fill the void I might start talking to myself, just for company. That thought unsettled me because I didn't see myself as a 'living alone with no one to talk to' person. In my mind I was still a member of the 'contribute to society' group. I was capable of holding down a good job. I had ideas to share, projects to pursue, a future . . . somewhere. Day by day, however, I became less of myself.

Jerome, on the other hand, was doing well. He had made plans to present at a conference in Melbourne and had applied for funding to visit the Ransom Center in Austin for a few weeks in order to go through the James Salter archives.

'I don't suppose you need a research assistant in Austin?' I asked.

'Excuse me? You want to be my assistant?'

At first I thought Jerome was surprised by my offer but then it dawned on me that no, he wasn't surprised, but flattered. The idea of having an assistant appealed to his vanity. I hadn't realised that he carried his self-importance so close to the surface.

'You know, someone to go through the scraps of paper and order them for you?'

He blushed, a little. 'I think I'll be able to manage, thank you.'

'Well, if it gets too much . . . what with teaching and marking, conferences and overseas travel. Etcetera.'

He caught my eye, and I could see that being flattered had developed into being annoyed. My offer to help had been interpreted as a dig at his previous habit of offloading work onto me. He suspected that, deep down, I thought he was lazy.

'James Salter,' I said, to steer the conversation back to safer ground. 'The famous frotteur of words.'

Jerome relaxed. He was the one who first brought the frotteur reference to my attention. It originated from an interview with Salter in the *Paris Review*, and the only reason I knew about it was because Jerome had his copy signed by Salter himself and had shown me the author's spindly signature, fine pen strokes that looked on the verge of disappearing.

'Have you seen Archer?' I asked.

'Yes. Of course.'

Jerome's response surprised me because he tended to keep his distance from Archer at work. I think Jerome knew he couldn't compete, that, by comparison, he was a lightweight.

'When did you see him?'

'Yesterday. I called in after work.'

'Really?'

'Yeah,' said Jerome. 'Renate's working overseas so I've been going over to see him. Just like I check in with you.'

'Oh.'

Hours and days slipped by. First evenings, then weekends, lost their relevance. I fired off more and more emails to potential employers, careful always to maintain a tone of enthusiasm and optimism. I placed a notice in the university online bulletin, offering tutoring, editing and proofreading services to international students and graduates. I realised that my initial success in scoring an interview at The Corner Shop was far from ordinary and that it had given me a false sense of hope. More and more my applications went unacknowledged. I haunted my inbox, checking and rechecking notifications in case a reply had slipped through. Once or twice I received rejections to my morning emails by noon the same day. Though uniformly polite, they were frequently careless with details. One rejection got my name wrong, turning Siân into Sin. If I had a well-paid job that mistake might have made me laugh, but as it was I couldn't even summon up the energy to flick back a grimacing or disappointed emoji.

I had been sitting at my table for hours, wondering if 'unemployment' or, more specifically, the 'unemployable', had a distinct smell, when my thoughts turned back to Jerome. I recalled what he'd said about checking in on me. I'd always regarded us as colleagues, or friends and equals, but now he clearly viewed me as one of the less fortunate, a kind of pity project. He wasn't so much visiting as carrying out a service.

One summer when I was about seventeen I'd helped my best friend's mother deliver meals on wheels to the elderly in Wainoni and New Brighton. I don't know where my friend was at the time, why she wasn't with us, but I recalled several things about those afternoons. The first was the constant presence of cigarette smoke. My friend's mother was very glamorous and a smoker, and as we drove along she used the cigarette lighter in the Holden to light up. I'd never seen anyone do that before and was enthralled with the way she pushed in the button, allowed the coil to heat and then raised the red-hot tip to the cigarette in her mouth, all with one hand and without moving her eyes from the road ahead. She then replaced the lighter in its slot, again without shifting her gaze from the windscreen. She was so poised that she didn't have to tap the ash but allowed the cigarette to burn until almost all the white paper was gone, perfectly replaced by a smooth stick of ash. Only then did she take the cigarette from her mouth and stub it out in the vehicle's ashtray. How she managed to do that, given the motion of the car and the bumps of the road, I never knew.

The meals were stacked in the back of the car, kept warm under tinfoil. The plates were ceramic, not plastic, and the cutlery was stainless steel. Most often we served meals of mince and veggies, pork and veggies or fish and veggies. Always potatoes. And dessert was something steamed: doughy jam, butterscotch or apple puddings. While I served the meals, my friend's mother would go into the kitchen and collect the plates from the previous day and put on the kettle for a cup of tea. The ritual never varied from house to house.

Another ritual was peeling back the layer of foil from the plate. There was always condensation on the underside, and often a film of moisture had settled over the meat and vegetables, making them look damp and slightly grey. The smell incorporated this dampness, so rather than the individual earthiness of carrots, the sweetness of garden peas or the richness of beef gravy, there was a muddled fug of aromas. Every single meal smelt like leftovers, as if it had already been served the previous day to someone wealthier or luckier than the present diner.

As the meal was uncovered and the smell released, the recipient would lean forward and inhale. They would then raise their clouded or watery eyes and look at me and, with an expression that registered as cheeriness, thank me. Only then would their expression falter. As they looked back at their plate, you could see their mouths quiver slightly, the resigned look on their faces.

I'll never forget that look. A look that said, This is my life now. This is all I can expect. Be grateful and get on with it.

The scent of being discarded: meat and potatoes, sticky steamed stodge. If I add meals on wheels to my memory of working in the local dairy it begins to look like mince, sausage and greasy mutton were central themes, or heart notes, of my adolescence. Perfumes built around vetiver – harvested from the roots of a grass grown in India – often smell of sausages to me. Vetiver is not a note I enjoy, for that reason. I remember that Charles had a bottle of Guerlain's Vétiver and that once, when he wore it, I spent the day thinking someone had brought nutmeg-spiced pork buns into the room. I kept swivelling around in my chair, thinking, where is that smell coming from? Charles didn't suit vetiver. In fact, Charles didn't suit many perfumes that I can think of. If I were to match him to a scent I'd go with something floral, something with hyacinth or lily of the valley, or even lavender. I can imagine Charles in lavender.

I needed to do something with my time, so I blended a perfume for Archer.

Physically, he was a little under six feet and slim. He was neatly dressed, without being stylish. He preferred dark suit trousers and plain cotton shirts. These could be worn with a tie, but he usually left the top button open. He wore rectangular, metal-framed glasses for reading and, like his fountain pen, they were tucked in his breast pocket when not in use. He was balding and had no hair at the front or on the crown of his head. Rather than shave his remaining hair, however, he trimmed it. At staff morning teas he generally stood alone, a glass of tap water in his hand, and to tell the truth, his appearance and manner put me in mind of the straight guy from a seventies American sitcom: a cross between Bob Newhart and Murray from *The Mary Tyler Moore Show*.

If I were to match a perfume solely to Archer's appearance, I would probably veer towards something predictable like tobacco. It was the smell associated with middle-aged men who had a favourite chair and spent their evenings by the fire, knocking dottle from their pipes. Tobacco was manly but unpretentious, comfortable yet lacking in style. But in Archer's case there was an unexpected twist: it turned out he had a crush on Susan Sarandon. He'd watched all her movies, owned many of them on DVD and, a few years ago, hosted a *Thelma & Louise* twenty-fifth anniversary cocktail night for the department at a rented weekend cottage near Matakana. During the screening of the film he plied us with a variety of cocktails mastered during his student bartending days and then, as we became increasingly tipsy and giggly, he started shushing us – which only made matters worse. When we became too rowdy he pressed pause and replayed pivotal scenes over and over again. After three hours of heavy drinking and excruciating stop-start scene analysis, most of us lost the will to live and wandered off to bed before the car went over the cliff.

I didn't want to revisit *Thelma & Louise* with my blend of essential oils. I was worried that if I did I might have to sit through the whole film again, and that was more than I could handle. Instead, I went with a more interesting film, *Atlantic City*. In this Sarandon plays the part of Sally, a waitress in an oyster bar who dreams of becoming a croupier and escaping the grim reality of life in a run-down city. At night, she returns to her dreary apartment and stands at the sink, rubbing half-lemons over her hands, arms and breasts. A neighbour, Lou, played by

Burt Lancaster, watches, unobserved. Later, Burt admits to spying on Sally and describes what he has seen: the ritual of cutting the lemons, placing a bottle of 'gold perfume' on the counter and taking a bar of 'blue soap' from a box.

I played the lemon scene several times, and the more I watched it the more ludicrous it seemed. At first I thought it was beautiful. With its subdued golden lighting it reminded me of a painting, a cinematic version of a Morandi still life. Bellini's *Norma* played on a tape recorder resting on the windowsill and the contrast between the visual – the modest kitchen – and the aural – the magnificent opera – heightened the distance between Sally's internal and external worlds. But, watching the sequence over and over again, I became cranky. If Sally wanted to remove the smell of fish, why did she cover herself in sticky lemon juice when she could use soap? The whole thing struck me as phony.

I created Archer's *Atlantic City* perfume around lemon, using pure lemon oil extracted from the skins of the fruit. I highlighted the lemon with a few drops of ylang ylang oil and then contrasted the sweetness with lavender oil to ground the perfume. Finally, as much for fun as anything, I added a dropper of oil from a tin of smoked oysters. I diluted the result in fractionated coconut oil and called it It's Nothing Weird – taken from when Sally answers Lou's question about why she uses lemons. I hoped Archer would like the perfume as much as Jerome had enjoyed *The Awakening* scent, but really I'd be satisfied if he identified the fish note.

Evenings were the worst. I kept scrolling through university, museum and employment sites, checking for vacancies that may have popped up since I last looked only a few hours earlier. When nothing caught my eye, I'd grow desperate and fire off polite and undemanding follow-up emails, which asked, in a friendly but professional tone, if the recruitment search was ongoing or if the job had been filled. I stressed that I was still interested and available, that I'd be happy to provide further information or meet for an interview. Sometimes, very occasionally, I received an equally polite reply apologising for the lack of communication, thanking me for my interest in a position that was now filled. Although most of my applications and messages were ignored, I continued to wait, counting down the days until I could send a follow-up to my follow-up. I knew the whole thing was a lost cause, a joke, and that no one wanted me. But I still waited. I tried not to lose heart.

Some nights I surrounded myself with paperwork, trying to figure out how to budget for my future. Should I break into my retirement savings? Advertise for a lodger? Rent out a room on Airbnb? Should I sell up and buy a campervan and join the retirement-age nomads who travelled around the country taking seasonal work picking fruit? I didn't know what to do, how to make my life work again. I grew so desperate I considered putting my entire perfume collection up for sale on eBay. Some of the perfumes were vintage, others discontinued formulas, a few were rare. Altogether they would bring in a few thousand dollars. But something always stopped me from listing them. The truth was they made me happy and I didn't want to lose them, at least not through a cold-blooded auction.

When I couldn't concentrate on emails or budgets, I'd walk around my apartment and touch it: the brick walls, the rough beams, the bookshelves, even the polished floor. I'd stand with my back to the window and look in, towards the loft. My desire to remain in my home was as physical as it was emotional, as if saving the apartment were akin to saving my sight, my sense of smell or even a leg. When I thought about having to move I felt bereft, flooded by anxiety. The front of my skull ached from the permanent clamp that grew tighter every day. I found it hard to sleep. I tried drinking water, taking magnesium, avoiding the light, screens and books, but nothing worked. The headache became a fixture, and my body slowly adapted, and then threatened to shut down, reducing my world to the pressing rhythm of find work, get money, keep home.

Sometimes, in an attempt to release my biggest fear and anxiety, I would walk around my neighbourhood, taking note of places I might sleep once I was homeless while, at the same time, attempting to convince myself that it would never come to that. As a cover, I carried a stack of work wanted flyers in my bag. I targeted all the apartments in my neighbourhood, then moved through the well-kept residential streets, dropping flyers in letterboxes – even those clearly marked 'No Junk Mail'. I hesitated in front of a homewear design store I'd been in before, trying to convince myself to risk a cold call, but I couldn't bring myself to go in. My reason was ridiculous. Last time I'd found the interior overpowered by the confusion of smells rising from rose-scented candles, synthetic vanilla reed diffusers, handmade citrus-scented soaps and orchid bath bombs.

To give my outing a semblance of normality I spent a few minutes scanning the books in a pop-up Little Free Library. The shelves were crammed with diet books, celebrity memoirs, scuffed and torn thrillers, and Marie Kondo. Even though I had a stack of unread books by my bed I found two that caught my eye: one about a North Island missionary called Richard Taylor, which I thought Archer might like, and the second a recent anthology of short love poems. This appealed to me because of a handwritten note scrawled across the title page: 'Daryl, I carry your heart with me.' A half-page sketch of a naked man with a droopy penis and a bloody heart cupped in his hands filled the rest of the space and above the sad figure, squashed into a speech bubble above his head, were the words, 'because it is bitter'. I recognised the line at once. It came from Stephen Crane's 'In the Desert', arguably the only poem of his that any student of American literature ever remembered, and sure enough it was listed in the contents. I stared at the image for a good two minutes, trying to put myself in Daryl's shoes, wondering how I would respond if that copy had been thrust into my hands as, what, a Valentine's Day present?

Before returning home I decided to extend my walk and cross into town to check out the perfume counter at The Corner Dairy. I recognised the young assistant as the guy I'd seen during my interview with Anna. He was taller than I remembered, immaculately groomed, his hair neatly parted and brushed back over his ears. His skin seemed less red than before, and I realised that he was really quite handsome in his uniform of a neatly laundered, white dustcoat worn over a black shirt and matching trousers.

He caught my eye and smiled.

'Hi there,' I said as I approached.

He stepped closer to the counter and looked genuinely pleased to see me. Maybe he recognised me from the interview?

'I'm looking for a new perfume and I'm really curious about iris notes. Can you help?'

It wasn't so much a trick question as a test. At a quick glance I could see three iris scents on the shelves, including the most famous of them all, Chanel No. 19, created by Henri Robert for Coco Chanel herself. Chanel was in her late eighties at the time, and the perfume was named after the date of her birth, 19 August. In some ways it was a product of its time, a scent that coincided with the 1970s feminist movement, marking a period when women no longer wanted or needed to smell like a bouquet of flowers. It was, and still is, the perfume women reached for when they were facing a difficult day, when they wanted to appear in charge.

As I waited, anticipating that the assistant would reach down and lift out the bottle of Chanel, every fibre in my body grew tense. If he knew perfume he would have no trouble identifying it. I willed him to hurry up, silently repeating '19, 19, 19' over and over in my mind. I found myself leaning towards the counter, trying to catch his eye and slowly directing my gaze down to the right shelf, as if by some invisible force I could manoeuvre his hand to the bottle.

'I'm not sure.' He scanned the shelves behind him, and his hand hovered in front of the Guerlain display before veering off uncertainly towards some Dior bottles. 'Sorry, I'm still learning.' His face flushed red and I felt sorry for him. 'I could ask one of the others,' he said, glancing down the length of the counter.

'It's all right,' I replied. 'I was curious, that's all. Don't worry about it. Thanks so much, though.' Almost as an afterthought I added, 'It must be great working here, surrounded by so many perfumes. I guess you get to test them all.'

I saw the wave of relief that swept over him. His body relaxed and then, catching sight of another customer, he apologised once more and left. I took a second longer to leave. For some reason I thought he might come back and find the bottle, but he didn't.

I'd lost out to a young man who knew nothing about perfume. Iris. I heard the word form on my lips. Also listed in perfume notes as orris. The assistant had so many perfumes to choose from: CK One, Britney Spears' Fantasy, Bois d'Iris from Van Cleef & Arpels, Prada's Infusion d'Iris, Hiris by Hermès . . . It was such a common note he could have taken a guess and his hand would have landed on something with iris in it. Or he could have gone through the testers and sprayed them until he recognised the distinctive note by its smell. Anything that reminded him of potatoes, carrots, wet soil, green stalks, powdery florals or hairspray would, most likely, be iris-centred. Strangely, I was more bothered that he didn't know what iris smelt like than that he had got the job and I hadn't. It was so disheartening.

Notes for a bitter heart: Should I add iris to my heart notes? There's definitely something magical about iris scents. Because the flower itself doesn't smell, iris perfumes utilise the rhizome. The root is dried for up to three years, allowing the irone molecule, at the heart of the scent, to develop. Once the root has dried it is ground up and distilled to create a butter-like product that smells sweet and earthy, rather like fresh-from-the-garden carrots. The iris butter is then turned into an absolute through extraction using a volatile solvent. This is what will eventually be used in perfume.

Iris? Would it go with oakmoss and oak? Yes, I think it would. The problem is that I'm not sure that iris is a good match for me. Iris is a bit of a shape-shifter. The earthy, carrot aspect is only one of many. Some iris perfumes are powdery, some smell like old-fashioned hairspray and some are austere and cool, the most elegant of scents. Iris isn't comforting, it doesn't fill you with a sense of wellbeing. Rather, it's unflappable and poised, and that can be a hard note to live up to. Iris is a scent for a career woman. I need something more forgiving.

Archer's apartment lay on a busy thoroughfare, overlooking the port and container terminal. It was a part of town I rarely visited, but when I did I was always surprised at how distinct the area was from the rest of the city. For a start, regardless of the weather, it always seemed to be windy. The breeze was fresher than in the inner city or its surrounding valleys, and it carried the unmistakable smell of the sea. Mixed with the marine scent was an equally strong smell of diesel, oily and gritty, though whether from the endless stream of buses and trucks speeding by or from the fuel tanks in the distance, I wasn't sure. Finally, as I passed the large storage silos before turning into the pedestrian alley that led to Archer's, I noticed the smell of cement.

Archer must have been watching me approach as he was standing at the entrance, holding the door open for me when I arrived. He took a step towards me as if he might kiss my cheek, then pulled back and offered his hand. I took it in mine and was startled by how thin and bony it felt. When I stepped back to look at him I saw that he'd lost weight since losing his job. His cheeks were hollowed and his face had a greyish sheen, made more pronounced by the faintest trace of stubble covering his jaw. He looked distracted but then he smiled and I could tell that he was pleased to see me.

'How are you?' he asked. 'Keeping busy?' His voice, I was pleased to note, was as strong as ever.

I'd only visited his home a few times before, after Renate's bypass surgery, when some of us in the department took turns fixing meals or watching her while Archer gave his lectures. The three things that stuck in my mind were Renate's optimism, the fact that neither of them mentioned they were vegetarian but took our food offerings with gratitude, and that the windows were incredibly dirty. It was as if the cement had impregnated the glass, creating an opaque filter that dulled the light from outside.

On this visit the windows were clean, and from a spot near the sliding door that opened onto a small balcony I could see the huge cranes and straddle carriers at work unloading shipping containers.

'We bought the place for the outlook,' said Archer.

I laughed.

'Renate has a bit of a thing for harbours and ports. Something to do with her ancestors being Vikings.'

'Really?'

Archer shrugged and shook his head. 'Maybe not. But the view grows on you. It's got a cinematic quality, it's dramatic, larger than life, a bit *Mad Max*.'

His mention of cinema prompted me to take the scent from my bag. When I passed it to him he did something strange: he shook the bottle vigorously and held it up to the light.

'I was thinking about that *Thelma & Louise* party you had,' I said.

'Don't remind me.'

'And then I went from that idea to Susan Sarandon in *Atlantic City*.'

As I watched, he unscrewed the cap and sniffed. He looked perturbed and sniffed again before passing the bottle back to me to smell. I inhaled and even though the oils were newly blended, and not yet fully developed, it was rather good. I was relieved the fish oil didn't dominate the lemon.

'Thank you,' said Archer. 'No one has ever made me a perfume before.'

'It's nothing weird,' I replied, hoping he might say something about the actual smell of the blend but he didn't. Instead he placed the bottle on the counter and fetched me a glass of water.

'Renate used to make soap using lavender and tea tree oil when I first met her,' he said. 'But since her operation she's become very health conscious, and now she's worried some oils cause hormonal problems. Have you heard about that?'

'I have but I'm not sure I believe it.'

'It's a shame she gave up. She still keeps a collection of oils at our cabin. That's where she was most creative. She planted a native garden because she wanted to explore the plants' medicinal properties.'

I'd never heard Archer mention a cabin before, and I was confused because the *Thelma & Louise* party had been in a rented place.

'That's one of the things I've been meaning to do for a while,' he continued. 'I need to give it a lick of paint and tidy it up, in case we decide to put it on the market.'

'Where is it?'

'Oh, it's kind of remote.' He waved his hand in a distracted way. 'It's not close to anywhere. Do you know Raetihi?'

I nodded.

'Well, if you went west you'd be in the general vicinity. We bought the block when Hester was in high school and Renate started making noises about escaping the rat race and taking up fly-fishing.'

'Oh. I didn't know.'

'It's peaceful.'

'I bet.'

He sighed. 'I've applied for an overseas position, but if that doesn't pan out Renate may want us to relocate to the States to be closer to her family. What are you going to do?'

'I'm still looking for work. I don't want to sell up or move if I can help it.'

'Yeah,' he said. 'Having a home is good.'

'I've been doing the rounds, applying for jobs, putting out flyers. Looking for scraps.'

'Scraps? You're better than that.'

'Maybe. I'm not sure.'

'Well, if you need money you can help me paint the cabin.'

I laughed. 'No, no thanks. I don't do remote.'

We fell silent, our gaze fixed on the cranes unloading the huge ship and the back and forth activity of the straddle carriers receiving the containers. A fly crawled up the window, then took off, flying in a jerky square formation in the middle of the room.

'You can smell the sea from here,' I said.

'That was a drawcard for Renate. She often likes to sleep with the door open.'

'Would you agree that we have a kind of genetic memory

for smells, one that goes further back than direct personal experience?'

'I'm not sure I follow,' said Archer.

'Well, if our sense of aesthetics is embedded in our cultural background, we must also be biased towards certain smells? Renate's fondness for the smell of the sea is inherited from her Viking ancestors, for example. It forms part of her scent DNA.'

'That's possible, but I guess people find some things pleasant smelling, or disgusting, regardless of cultural background.'

'So you think smells are universal, not culturally specific?'

Archer gazed back towards the window, and I could see he was working through my question. 'I think both,' he said finally. 'Some scents, like the smell of rain falling on dry ground, must have universal appeal because they're linked to growth and survival and hark back to the time of the hunter-gatherers. But other scents are culturally specific and our preferences would be inherited or learnt. Buttered popcorn or pumpkin pie seem very American to me, and those smells mightn't translate or be appreciated by other cultures.'

'Do you think there's such a thing as a New Zealand smell?' I asked.

Archer shrugged. 'I don't know. I'm not in position to answer that. You'd have to ask a New Zealander.'

On my way home I decided to make a detour via the rose garden. It wasn't far out of my way and so close to home that it was surprising I hadn't visited more often. In recent weeks I'd found myself wandering past places, shops, galleries, parks, and thought I should go in but I'd kept on walking. Perhaps I hadn't got over the fact that I was no longer a busy person.

The entrance was an imposing black volcanic rock gateway flanked by pōhutukawa trees that dripped with tentacles of pale green moss and lichen. On the far side of the gateway the path disappeared down a slope and out of sight. Unkempt vegetation added to a sense of menace. Before going through the gate I had to remind myself that I'd never witnessed anything out of the ordinary, ever, in the rose garden, and that the last time I visited the only other person I saw was a middle-aged woman walking a Labrador with a bag of poo attached to its lead. The only people there today were a gardener, a young man with dreadlocks bound around his head with brightly coloured cotton strands, working at the beds at the far end, and me.

Most of the bushes were past flowering but here and there occasional bursts of colour captured my attention. Where there were no flowers I noticed the variations in the rose thorns. Some were fine and feathery, needle thin and abundant, as sharp as cactus. Others were larger than my thumbnail, heavy triangles, shaped like rhinoceros horns. The thorns on the oldest bushes were draped in lichen, the gnarled branches all but invisible beneath the thick growth.

Because of the absence of flowers, I spent more time than ever before looking at the name plates at the foot of each bush, repeating the names softly to myself as I passed: 'Madame Plantier', 'Slater's Crimson China', 'Gertrude Jekyll', 'Alfred Colomb', 'Madame Alfred Carrière'. Some of the names were familiar from my granddad Bert's garden, though I couldn't always picture the blooms themselves. Others, like 'Auckland Metro', 'Massey University' or 'Christchurch Remembers', meant little to me in terms of flowers and scent but had associations with places or events I knew. I paused for a moment in front of a thornless climbing rose called 'Nahema'. Because it wasn't in bloom I could only wonder if it bore any resemblance to the perfume I first encountered in the basket under the bathroom sink. If it did it must have a beautiful, rich, deep scent, something that filled the air with its presence and lasted for days.

For forty minutes I circled the garden and criss-crossed the paths before taking a seat under the pergola at the end of the main avenue, near the moss rose. Music from a neighbouring building site reached me, and without meaning to I found myself trying to identify each song. I rarely listen to music as I don't like noise, so I was surprised that even with my limited knowledge I could pick out songs from the 1980s by the likes of Dire Straits, Genesis and Whitney Houston. As I became irritated by the music's impact on my private space, I remembered a conversation I'd once had with a university administrator concerning perfume.

We'd been talking about a student enrolment matter when she paused mid-sentence and sniffed the air. A few moments later she asked if I was wearing perfume and when I replied 'yes' she informed me that the university had instigated a perfume-free policy. I'd never heard of such a thing and asked if she was sure. 'Quite sure,' she replied. I couldn't believe that I'd missed the memo, so asked how long it had been in force. 'For years,' she replied. 'Longer than smokefree.' Seeing my sceptical expression, she continued, 'Lots of people hate perfume.'

'You never wear it?' I asked.

'No.'

'What about soaps and shampoos?'

'That's different,' she said. 'I can rinse them off.'

'Fragrant washing powders?'

'I buy unscented.'

'So you don't like perfumes?'

'No.'

'Fair enough.'

I gathered up my papers and made to leave but she called me back. 'I don't think people should be allowed to force their perfumes onto strangers, do you? It's obnoxious.'

'So you shouldn't wear perfume in public?' I asked.

'No. Not if it impacts negatively on others. Not if it's going to give people a headache or make them sick. That's an abuse of their rights.'

'How would you know if it was perfume causing the headache and not, say, pollution, exhaust fumes or stress?'

'Because.'

I knew of many perfumes that gave me headaches so I couldn't really disagree with her but nevertheless I asked, 'What if it's a matter of taste? In the same way you might not like an offensive word or image on a T-shirt? Or a song played on the radio?'

'That's entirely different. I can stop looking or listening, but I can't stop breathing.'

'True, but you could pinch your nose and walk away.'

The woman gave me a withering look and I apologised.

In fact, the university had no such policy, but the conversation stayed with me and I found myself becoming defensive and then offended. Some, like me, would say perfume is special, a pleasant distraction that adds a smile to the day. In fact, many perfumers defined their creations in terms of art and beauty, compared them to music, painting or even literature. Perfume, surely, could never be the equivalent of secondhand smoke. But then I imagined a time when I might find myself standing outside, huddled in a doorway, furtively spraying my wrists as non-perfume-wearers strode past, sending disapproving looks my way.

I didn't stop wearing perfume, but the conversation made me a little more careful about what I wore. I made an effort to keep to perfumes that weren't overly powerful or skanky. Chypres were out, oakmoss was excluded, as was ambergris, animal musks and funky jasmine. For a while afterwards I went back to colognes and pale roses, especially when I knew I had to attend a meeting. On days when I was unlikely to spend much time outside my office I would sneak a couple of sprays of the Mitsouko that I kept in my top drawer next to my stash of whiteboard pens. Even then I made sure to spray the fragrance onto a handkerchief or scarf, something I could leave in my room.

I began watching the gardener. Pushing his wheelbarrow in front of him, he paused and scooped out a handful of fertiliser dust, sprinkled it under the dripline of each bush and then watered it in from a watering can. The repetitive motion from wheelbarrow to plant and back again was restful, rather like watching folk dancers step in and out of a circle. As the gardener worked his way along the avenue and came closer to where I sat, I got a sniff of dried blood, metallic like iron, and immediately I was back in my grandfather's garden, trailing after him as he tended his roses. For the first time in years I missed him.

I woke up in the night with the smell of mothballs in my nostrils. I hadn't come across the odour in years, yet it was so strong I could almost taste it in the back of my throat. It was fleeting, as if tied to the tail of a dream of which I had no immediate recollection, and I lay awake for several minutes trying to recapture both the smell and its source. But, like a phantom, it was gone.

My room was still and quiet, but through the window I caught glimpses of the moon between the gaps in fast-moving clouds. I closed my eyes and nestled into the silence, but my thoughts were agitated and the imagined smell of camphor rushed back, niggling me until I reluctantly got out of bed and went down to the living space.

Downstairs, the air felt closer, the aroma of wool and lanolin calmed me and held me in its embrace as I sat at the table and began to think. To help me focus, I wrote down the word 'camphor' and, beneath it, ideas relating to smell, images, texture and colour. After a few minutes I stopped and read my list: camphor, mothballs, travelling trunk, folded linen, damp, cool, distance, needlework, sadness, menthol, dark rooms, rose garden, peach tree, pollen, green, wood, dust. I added a second column, this time relating to scent and notes: camphor, wintergreen, rose, orchard, lavender, musk, cedar, violet, mimosa, beeswax, Ambroxan. Once I was satisfied, I searched for and arranged the bottles I'd identified in a row in front of me.

I took two blotters and dipped the first in camphor oil, the second in wintergreen. Waving the blotters in front of my nose while inhaling deeply caused my eyes to prickle as tears formed. To make the test more pleasant, I held the blotters further away then brought one strip of paper slowly closer and closer to my nose, stopping when the scent came into focus. I repeated this with the second strip and made notes of what I experienced. To my nose, the camphor had a strong hint of menthol and was darker and woodier than the wintergreen. Camphor was brown in my mind, whereas the wintergreen was like its name and more mint-like.

I put both blotters to one side for a moment and opened my favourite rose otto. This oil, sourced from Bulgaria, had a beautiful beeswax honey note that was often missing from cheaper versions and added to the complexity of its deep rose scent. I wanted to create the suggestion of crab apple or even apple peel, but as no such essential oil existed I went for a drop of Roman chamomile and another of marigold-scented tagetes, hoping that the combination of the two might suggest something apple-like. Though the result did not instantly bring a freshly picked and quartered apple to mind, there was enough sweetness and sense of ripeness present to satisfy me.

As I worked, an image of a young pregnant woman took shape in my imagination. She appeared to be not long out of her teens, sitting on the edge of a narrow bed in a small dark room. Despite its polished brass top rails and four brass knobs, the cast-iron bedstead was relatively plain, with little in the way of ornamentation. The base under the mattress creaked when the woman shifted her weight. The fresh linen bedcover was cool to her touch; a gift from her mother, wrapped in tissue and folded into a cedar chest with the rest of her trousseau. Though it had been washed since first unpacked, she could still detect the scent of camphor in its folds.

The woman looked at her hands, rested them in her lap. The day before she had collected petals from the late blooms of the single rose bush in her garden. Planted by her husband's predecessor, the bush was small, struggling to establish itself in the tended flower bed. The hedge of wild briar fared much better. The rosehips were bright red and plump and when she gathered them she noticed that the leaves of the bush, when crushed in her fingers, gave off the aroma of apple. The pear trees in the garden orchard were too young to have produced fruit, but the crab apple beyond the edge of the property was doing well, despite seeming so out of place surrounded by a remnant patch of native bush.

The woman, whom I initially represented with a simple, traditional blend of rose, violet and lavender combined with a hint of sweet apple and honey, missed her husband. I imagined he was older than she was, a missionary, sombre-clothed and modest. Now I knew what had provoked the image: not just smell but the missionary book I had taken for Archer from the pop-up library. I searched for a low-key earthy scent and decided on clary sage, a plant that has been used for centuries for its medicinal properties. It felt like a good match for a man of the cloth. In my mind, he was often away, travelling throughout the district, performing his duties with such single-minded devotion and intensity that he lost track of the days and his responsibility towards his young wife left at home.

The woman longed for female company, a close friend to confide in or laugh with. Far away, her twin sister lived not ten miles from the family home, and there were days when the missionary wife wished she could change places, if only to spend time wandering the woodlands at the back of the village gathering small handfuls of bluebells, the scent of which she could still conjure up at night.

Would she ever feel at home in her new country? Would the scents of the land she found herself in, their perfume rising from the dense bush and ferns, the flax and the yellow-flowered trees, ever take the place of the smells of her birthplace, those that reminded her of family and love?

I passed the blotters under my nose and thought about the woman as I arranged the individual notes, grouping them in sets of three. The longer I worked, the more real the missionary wife seemed, and I felt a responsibility to capture her essence. I was also glad to focus on her rather than myself. It took me several hours to find the combination I liked, and another hour before I was satisfied with the concentrations, diluting each fragrant oil in alcohol: sniffing, testing, tweaking. Finally I was happy: wintergreen, rose otto, violet, tagetes, chamomile, lavender, clary sage and cedarwood. The smell was so evocative that I began to hear the rustle of long skirts and a low, soft sigh.

There was a message on my answerphone. I took a deep breath, praying that someone had finally got back to me about a job. Instead, it was Jerome. His nanny was planning to take annual leave and he wanted to know if I was interested in stepping in. Three weeks. Four hours a day, sometimes more, sometimes less. Cash in hand: $22 per hour.

A voice in the background, Desna's, chimed in: 'Tell her beggars can't be choosers.'

There was an awkward silence and then Jerome mumbled, 'I hope you didn't hear that.'

Desna laughed. 'I'm kidding,' she yelled. 'It would be an honour to have a real live professor for a nanny!'

I bristled. My first reaction was, 'How dare she?' My second reaction was, 'I need the money.'

I stayed home all day. I felt safe when I was sitting at my table, surrounded by the scents I loved. I had been toying with a few ideas for my signature scent. At the back of my mind was the perfume I created, The Missionary Wife, and I kept going over and over the question of whether my favourite smells were more influenced by my cultural background or by my familiar, physical surroundings. I spent so little time outdoors that I hardly knew what my natural world smelt like. Beyond the earthiness of ferns, the fluffy pollen of kōwhai or the grassiness of flax, I would be hard-pressed to identify more than a handful of native plants by odour. Kauri trees? Did they have a distinct smell? Their resin might. Had it ever been used in perfume? Would my emotional connection to the scents of New Zealand be different, stronger, if my grandparents had been born in Northland or on the West Coast rather than Britain? I thought they would, that the smells might belong to me. But I would never really know.

I was wearing a calming blend of lavender and vanilla, a favourite combination. It was very basic, one of the first recipes I'd attempted when I started making perfume. It did, though, require discipline to get the balance right. So many of my early experiments had been ruined as much by a lack of direction as a lack of skill. I hadn't identified what I wanted to achieve before I started mixing and blending the oils. The worst were those where I'd started off with a few drops of one oil, added a couple of drops of another, and then kept adding and mixing, trying to make something that 'smelt good'. The end result was always murky, like a paint colour mixed from the dregs of too many tins. One of the things I eventually found helpful was to begin with a word, an object or a mood, something that provided a decent frame for my composition. The word could be as simple as 'calm' but that was enough to direct me towards certain oils and discard others. It helped to make sense of the vast lexicon of smells available. My problem these days was being able to identify a word that described me. I was still incomplete, as Seren would say. I was not yet whole.

'Beggars can't be choosers.' Maybe that was me? What would it smell like, a perfume for beggars who can't be choosers? I guessed something similar to scraping the bottom of the barrel, whether of wine, beer, flour, fish, crackers or apples. Back before our department vanished from the face of the earth, we used to ease our way into level one American poetry with a couple of poems by Robert Frost. One many students liked was 'After Apple-Picking', which on its surface describes the tiring, physical act of climbing ladders and harvesting apples. The students loved the poem because it seemed simple and they could make sense of the images. However, when pressed, few claimed to understand *what* the poem was saying. Some thought it was about picking apples, others thought it had something to do with feeling sleepy and drifting off into an unconscious dream state, while others were certain it was about death. Despite the many different interpretations and lack of consensus, it remained a favourite. As one student said, 'Why does it have to be about anything? Why can't it be about apples and cider? That's a good subject for a poem, isn't it?'

I imagined the bottom of an apple barrel smelt good, whereas the bottom of my barrel was becoming increasingly bitter – but that was to be expected when you'd been discarded, chucked onto the pile of fermenting cider apples. Twenty-two bucks an hour to look after Jerome's daughter? I had a better idea. He could take time off to look after his child, and I could step in and cover his work at the university for $60 per hour. That made more sense to me, and I knew for a fact I would do his job as well as he would. Seriously though, if beggars couldn't be choosers I would rather clean out and paint Archer's cabin than try to keep a three-year-old entertained for four hours a day in a house with no TV.

Just as I was toying with the idea of creating a bottom-of-the-apple-barrel perfume, my email pinged with an invitation to attend a job interview for the position of assistant administrator at the Friends of the Museum. It had been so long since I'd sent off my application that I'd given up hope, and my immediate thought was that they must have chosen someone but the appointment had fallen through. It was doubly important, therefore, for me to make a favourable impression. It was a good position, part time but well paid, and I could see myself in a museum situation. I'd enjoyed my years as a curator and thought I'd love to return to that environment. I spent the rest of the day going through the job description, rehearsing what I would say. I recorded myself on my phone and didn't stop until I was sure I sounded professional and confident. Then I went to my wardrobe to select an outfit, finally settling on a Brigitte Macron-style tailored dress. Finally, I chose my perfume, a beautiful centred incense, Kyoto.

I arrived early and sat calmly listing my strengths to myself as I waited. By the time I was called in, however, all my confidence had left me. I had no recent museum experience, none of my skills were relevant to the position, my dress was too short and my perfume too smoky. I hadn't got the perfume counter position, so what chance did I have now? I knew I wasn't going to get the job but I stayed, clinging to my self-worth as it evaporated into the air.

Seated around the table, poised and alert, was a panel of three: two women around my age and another who was much younger, possibly in her mid-twenties. As they offered me a chair at the head of the table I almost had to stop myself from apologising for taking up their time; it was so obvious that they had no need to hire me – a middle-aged, middle-class white woman. They would be looking for ways to make the Friends more inclusive by reaching out to a younger, culturally diverse community, and they wouldn't be seen to be doing that if they took me on.

In the middle of the table was an instantly recognisable Crown Lynn vase, its simple, elegant profile and shell-like white exterior contrasting with the unrestrained arrangement of kōwhai and fern foliage fanning out from its top. It was a nice touch and I wondered which of the women had brought it in. I had a feeling it wasn't the work of the one leading the panel but, rather, that of the assistant – the woman I assumed took charge of buying milk and biscuits for meetings, or wrote thank-you notes and sent out petrol vouchers to invited speakers. Without thinking I reached out and brushed my hand against the soft leaves, then turned the vase slightly as if that might bring me luck.

'They're beautiful,' I said, and the assistant smiled and replied they were picked from her garden that morning. Before she could elaborate, however, Pam, the woman leading the panel, cleared her throat and the interview proper began.

It was a good interview. Respectful. I was asked questions about my experience, and we talked at length about the role of museum supporters and volunteers and the importance of remaining authentic and relevant in a changing world. I think the use of the word 'relevant' touched us all in some way. With the exception of Jax, the younger woman, we were all of an age where our 'irrelevance' was fast becoming a fact of life.

Pam, the manager of the Friends, had been a senior accountant in a large firm but was now retired. Maureen, the woman who arranged the flowers, was a nurse who worked part time in an aged care facility. She had loved visiting museums as a child and had spent hours wandering the galleries with her own two children, who no longer shared her enthusiasm for the collections. 'They're so busy with study and work, and getting on with their own lives,' she said sadly. 'They don't have time to come here any more.'

Quietness took over the room then, broken only when Jax recounted a story about her own introduction to the museum. She'd gone to London after finishing school and fallen in with the New Zealand expat community, earning money working in bars and restaurants at night while undertaking an apprenticeship to a New Zealand-born jewellery designer by day. After three years she returned home, intending to start her own workshop, but had felt out of sorts, unable to get back into the swing of things. Her problem was that she no longer felt connected. And then one day, with nothing better to do, she found herself at the museum looking at the jewellery on display. She walked through several halls and after an hour or so came across a vitrine featuring some contemporary Auckland jewellers, and there in front of her was a necklace consisting of a row of white shell fragments and two small pieces of driftwood threaded onto strands of linen thread.

'The second I saw it I knew I was home. It reminded me of when I lived out on Te Atatū Peninsula and used to explore the beach and mangroves. The shells on the necklace were like the ones that used to cut into the soles of my feet when I was out on the mudflats. I was amazed that something as simple as a necklace, no more than a string of shells and wood, could conjure up such a strong response and sense of place. It was the push-start I needed.' We sat in silence, and then Pam said what we were all thinking, 'God, I wish I was young again.'

As I was leaving, Maureen followed me out and told me that she'd recognised my name when she was going through the applications because her oldest son, Liam, had been a student of mine. 'I remembered him telling me what a great lecturer you were,' she said. 'You were so informed and enthusiastic. He said you were the most inspiring lecturer he ever had and he wished he'd stuck with American studies instead of going into political science.'

'Thanks.'

'He reckons the university shafted you. Not only you but all of you, the whole department, not to mention humanities in general.'

'Well, probably.'

'Do you know what I heard the other day, from a friend of mine who owns an interior decorating business?'

'No?'

'You'll hate this. The rumour is that the vice-chancellor has put in an order for an office refurbishment: curtains, new furniture, fittings, art – local artists – the works. It's going to cost tens of thousands.'

I didn't say anything.

'Terrible, isn't it. To lay off so many people and then order in new curtains. Mind boggling.' Maureen sighed. 'Anyway,' she added, 'it was good to meet you at last. Thank you for coming in. You were great.'

Not great enough to be offered the job, though.

In the following days I went back over my curriculum vitae, adjusting its template and format in an attempt to make it more eyecatching. To ensure that I'd got it right I watched 'how-to' clips on YouTube and consulted websites dedicated to the subject. When I was finished I felt that I'd succeeded in making my résumé slicker, but it no longer seemed quite as informative or useful in terms of my work record and skills. When I read through the changes I kept wanting to restore the bits I'd cut out.

I wasn't happy with my new truncated CV, but I attached it to my latest round of applications and then sat back, content that I had done a good morning's work. As I relaxed with a cup of coffee – the one made from ground beans I still permitted myself each day – I summoned up the courage to call the human resources person about a data entry position I'd applied for around the same time as the museum job. I was put through straight away and the man who answered informed me that they had drawn up a shortlist of applicants that morning.

'Is my name on it?' I asked.

'I'm afraid I can't tell you.'

I hadn't expected any other response but I had little to lose so tried again. I made my case, stretching the truth slightly by explaining I was trying to juggle dates due to deadlines and travel commitments, and to my relief he softened and said he would look me up. I tried not to raise my hopes, but by the time he came back on the line I had somehow convinced myself that I would get an interview. I had the data entry experience and was confident using Microsoft Excel.

'Si-an?'

'Sharn,' I said.

'I have some bad news, I'm afraid. Unfortunately there was a problem with your electronic application and we couldn't process it.'

My heart lurched. 'What do you mean?'

'Well, we clearly stated that all applications must be in the format specified . . .'

'Yes, I know.'

'. . . and it appears your application was submitted incorrectly.'

'What do you mean, incorrectly?'

'It looks like you failed to attach a current photograph.'

'But that's because I didn't want to be discriminated against because of my age.'

'We don't discriminate and nothing in the Human Rights Act prevents us from asking for a photo.'

'Well, I can send you a passport photo now, then, and you can process the application. I'm presuming that's the only problem?'

'I'm sorry, Siân, I really am. But we can't do that. It would be unfair to the other applicants.'

'What other applicants?'

'The ones who also submitted incomplete applications.'

'You mean all the other middle-aged applicants who left out a photo? Oh, and actually, now I think about it, you should think about the message you're conveying with all those photos of *young white men* on your company brochure.'

There was a long pause and then the man cleared his throat. 'We can't make an exception for you, that would be unfair.'

I grunted.

'And, for future reference, don't assume all senior HR guys are white. That's not cool.'

So help me, I chose that afternoon to go back to The Corner Dairy to check on some new perfume releases I'd read about on one of the perfume blogs. The handsome assistant was behind the counter arranging a display of black and white cube-shaped bottles. He smiled at me and said, 'Welcome to the Perfume Corner,' and although it was unfair to blame him for my ill-judged remarks to the HR officer earlier that day, his friendly manner, and the fact that he had a job, struck a raw nerve and I launched into a nasty attack.

'Do you have any perfumes that smell like laundry musk blended with generic berries?' I asked. 'Something that yells "pink." Anything . . .' I paused and then spat out the word 'pink' once more.

He looked at the bottle in his hand and put it down next to the others on display. 'Pink?' He shook his head.

'Really? Because I think you do. In fact, looking around, I think you'll find that you're drowning in pink. And, for your information, it's not Chanel No. 19.'

I didn't stay to test the new perfumes; I was no longer in the mood. Instead, I stomped off to the city art gallery, where I managed to get even more angry and offended by a small display of Picasso etchings that showed images of what I considered brutalised women. I was still fuming when, less than an hour later, I walked through the university and spotted a crowd of people outside the Student Union building. As I got closer I could see a banner announcing 'Silent Protest – Support the Humanities'. The scene was eerily quiet, despite the crowd milling around. I wasn't going to stop but as I circled around the group I caught sight of an administrator I recognised from the history department and paused to say hello.

'It's very polite, isn't it?' I said.

She nodded and whispered, 'It's silent.'

'Not exactly like the old days.'

I glanced around at the expressionless faces of the protesters and shook my head. I expected the woman to agree but instead she frowned and stepped away, but not before she held her finger to her lips and whispered, 'Shush.'

When I looked at the students nearest me I felt even more out of place. Something about their posture and behaviour put me in mind of passive-aggressive, sulking teenagers. By contrast, the older protesters struck me as spectators rather than participants. I couldn't imagine that the protest would even register with the vice-chancellor, let alone have much impact on the wider public. I heard myself mutter, 'This is nuts,' but when a protester next to me caught my eye and gave me a disapproving look, I apologised. 'Sorry, it's caught me at a bad time . . .' I trailed off, annoyed at myself for being so cynical and bitter, frustrated with them for being so lifeless and precious.

I glanced around, hoping to see someone, somewhere, looking as angry as I felt, but all I saw was Jerome, standing alone with his hands clasped in front of him, a solemn, sanctimonious expression on his face. Seeing him made me feel even more restless. I wanted someone to take the lead and break ranks. I wanted noise. I needed someone to call out, 'Save the humanities,' so I could join in.

A restrained murmur went through the crowd and I turned to see a man holding up a phone, clearly filming a small group holding a 'We support the humanities' banner. I recognised his face. He was a member of the campus security team, out of uniform and dressed casually in ripped jeans and a Rugby World Cup T-shirt. I manoeuvred closer but as I got to his side I stumbled and tripped, falling against him.

'Take it easy,' he said. 'You don't want to start anything.'

'Start anything? Who are you, the Red Squad?'

He pulled a sour face but I ignored him. 'Why are you filming, anyway? It's a peaceful protest.'

'Security,' he said.

'Security? Rubbish.' Once more I heard someone shush me but this time I was too annoyed to pay attention. 'I have it on good authority,' I told the security guard in a stage whisper, 'that you and your mates are going to be replaced by hand-knotted rugs.'

'What the hell . . .?'

'Yeah, haven't you heard? The VC's cutting your budget so

she can buy a pair of leather couches, a few "Keep Calm and Carry On" cushions and some new lightshades. How do you like that!'

'I don't know what you're on about . . .'

'Well, give it time and it will all become crystal clear.'

When I got home I was done for. I'd achieved nothing all day except to mouth off at strangers. I could barely have been more unpleasant if I tried. No wonder I was unemployable.

Notes from a noxious weed: gorse. Despite its prevalence and the fact that it has a lovely creamy, pollen-like, coconut and pale mint scent, gorse is rarely used as a perfume note – perhaps because no one wants to harvest the flowers. In Bach flower remedies gorse is used to counteract pessimism, despair and feelings of hopelessness.

Gorse. It goes to the top of my list of heart notes. Just my luck that I'll never find any gorse essential oil, and if I do track some down I guarantee they won't ship to New Zealand.

I hadn't replied to Jerome. I intended to phone him back about the nanny job but in the end I decided I needed an outing so filled my car, intending to do a quick round of the market garden stalls and call in on him on my way back to town.

Jerome was part of the lifestyle block generation, preferring the quiet of the country and a long commute to the restored, inner-city villas of his colleagues. I'd been to his home a few times, making the occasional detour to drop off books during a weekend drive, attending an end of year barbecue or a birthday party. I used to think that he was still settling in, that he would landscape his property, or plant some trees, but when, on my last visit, I'd asked if he had any hobbies and he replied 'My ride-on mower', I realised that landscaping wasn't part of his plan. Apart from a row of cabbage trees planted along the driveway, and a few tussocks by the house, his entire property consisted of nothing but manicured grass.

It was a beautiful clear day, with blue skies and not a breath of wind. Driving through the suburbs on my way out of the city, I could detect the smell of freshly cut lawns and capture the odd glimpse of people pottering about in their gardens or hanging their washing. The banality of these images put me in a good mood, one that remained with me as I made several stops at the market gardens and herb stalls along the way. When I finally pulled into Jerome's long driveway I discovered cars parked either side. Clearly he was having some kind of do, to which I hadn't been invited. I hesitated but decided that because it was mid-afternoon it was most likely some informal gathering and he wouldn't mind my quickly popping in. To make it less awkward, I'd pretend that I'd bought too much basil and coriander for my own use so had decided to drop some off as I was passing by.

If Jerome was surprised to see me, he didn't show it but graciously accepted the herbs before inviting me in, explaining that Desna had asked some of her friends from work to a barbecue and that he'd included some of his new colleagues from the English department. 'You'll know most of them,' he said as he led me through to the kitchen. 'Brooke's here, with her partner,' he said, referring to the head of English. 'You should go and say hello.'

Arranged on the large kitchen island bench were plates of nibbles and several large pitchers of homemade lemonade. As Jerome filled my glass, he said, 'Saw you at the protest.'

'Yeah.'

'Looked like you were having a go at the security guy.'

'I was a bit tense, angry about something I'd heard.'

'Well, you can take it easy now,' said Jerome.

I followed him outside and we stood on the lawn, staring out past the boundary of his section towards the sea in the distance. I told him about my decision not to take on the nanny's job and he assured me that he understood.

'You don't have much to do with children, I suppose?'

'No. I've seen them around the neighbourhood but that's about it.'

It was meant to be a joke but Jerome was too earnest to catch it so I tried to cover up my awkwardness by asking when he was off to Melbourne.

'Soon. Not long.'

'Desna's not going?'

'No, too much work.'

I followed his glance and saw Desna inside, standing among a group of well-dressed women, laughing over something. She must have sensed Jerome looking at her because she suddenly looked his way, then made a strange grimacing face and shrugged her shoulders in a kind of 'What can I do?' way. Jerome glanced from her to me, and back to her. It was barely noticeable and yet something about their wordless exchange tugged at me. I knew I should leave but perhaps because I hadn't talked to anyone all weekend I stayed put, sipping from my glass.

'I love Melbourne,' I said.

Jerome nodded but his eyes were fixed on a place over my shoulder.

'I found a specialist medical and apothecary antique shop during my last visit and it was like a museum of curiosities. There were lots of strange things like wax models of skin disorders, and glass eyes, but the thing I fell in love with was a large cabinet that must have come from a chemist. All the drawers had small porcelain labels with names like oil of cubeb, pennyroyal and oil of cloves. I would have loved to have bought it . . . but dollars!'

Jerome smiled in a distracted way. 'I have no idea what oil of cubeb or pennyroyal is.'

As he spoke he shuffled slightly to his left, forcing me to turn my back on the house and face him.

'Cubeb smells like pepper, and pennyroyal is like spearmint but less sweet. It has a touch of mothballs. I did buy a couple of sealed bottles of extracts and oils, one beauty was labelled *Oleum Pini pumilionis*.'

Jerome shuffled again. 'I got the funding for the Texas research trip.'

'That's oil of dwarf pine needles and the bottle dates from around 1880. Never been opened.'

'So, I'll be going to the Salter archives as soon as I can organise it.'

'You can make a really tasty pine syrup from the cones. It's European – the tree. So have you bought your tickets?'

'Pardon me?'

'To Austin?'

'I should go and help Desna,' said Jerome.

I turned to see where he was looking and there was Desna, excusing herself from the women she'd been talking to and walking towards a man who'd entered the room. He was wearing a sharp black suit with a white open-necked shirt and had a white pocket square peeping from his top pocket. I saw Desna kiss him on his cheek and then she looked beyond him, towards the entrance foyer. A moment later a well-dressed woman walked in. The vice-chancellor.

It was as if someone had yanked on the laces of a corset fitted tightly around my ribs. There was a sharp pain, followed by a shortness of breath that left me gulping for air. I saw Jerome's face but it was a little blurry, his mouth distorted, and then I realised he was trying to tell me something. Rather, he was telling me something but I hadn't understood. All I heard were the names Warden, Black and Maybank.

'Warden . . .' he repeated.

'What?'

'Anthony Warden.'

'Who?'

'Desna's boss. Anthony Warden.'

I shook my head, but my whole body gave a shudder as I saw the vice-chancellor turn our way. 'What's she doing here?' I pointed to her. 'Is she your friend? You never told me you were friends.'

'Tony Warden,' said Jerome. 'The senior partner of Warden, Black and Maybank. Desna's boss, the VC's husband.'

To my horror I saw the vice-chancellor give a little wave to Jerome, who raised his hand in return. But before I could say anything, Brooke Daniels suddenly joined us, her partner Lisa, a midwife, at her shoulder.

'Hi,' said Brooke. 'How are you? I think you know Lisa, don't you?'

'Lisa?' I added the name to the ones Jerome had handed me. It didn't make sense and then, seeing the young woman scowling with a phone in her hand, I snapped back into the world. 'Lisa! Of course, sorry. I'm distracted. How are you?'

Lisa grunted. 'Busy.'

I tried to smile but once more I found myself looking towards the house, my attention fixed on the vice-chancellor.

'Lisa has a client ready to pop,' said Brooke. 'We might have to dash soon.' A look of irritation passed over her face and I noticed Lisa roll her eyes. 'I told you to take the other car,' she said to Brooke.

'It's all right, I've got tons of marking to do. I thought we'd have a few hours together . . .'

'What do you mean?' asked Lisa.

'Nothing,' said Brooke. 'How are you, anyway, Siân?'

I moved my gaze towards Brooke but could think of nothing to say.

'We have to go,' said Lisa.

'Really? Now?'

'Yes. Now.'

Brooke smiled at me and said, 'Drop in for a chat soon. This week if you've got time. Sorry . . .'

'Now,' repeated Lisa.

The vice-chancellor came out of the house and paused on the deck to look at the view. Then, two feet together like a bright young girl, she jumped down onto the lawn and began walking towards us, stopping briefly to greet Brooke and Lisa as they headed away. A few seconds later she was beside us, smiling at Jerome as she kissed him on the cheek. She half-glanced in my direction and said 'Hi' before turning back to Jerome. 'I always forget what a great place you have here. It's so peaceful. And green. So green compared to the city.'

'Hello,' I said.

She barely glanced at me. 'Tony and I sometimes talk about moving to the country. But we both do such crazy, long hours . . .'

'Siân,' I said.

I saw Jerome drop his gaze, his attention fixed on a patch of dandelions by his feet.

'Siân,' I repeated.

'Oh, sorry. Sorry. Siân.' The VC looked at me and a faint smile flickered on her lips as she held out her hand for me to shake.

'Penny,' she said.

'I know,' I said.

I could feel my heart thumping hard in my chest.

'We've met before,' I said. 'Through work.'

The vice-chancellor's expression faltered and for the first time she looked at me closely. I noticed that Jerome hadn't spoken and I suddenly realised how angry that made me feel.

'Siân,' I said again.

'Of course,' she said. She looked at Jerome and now he spoke: 'From the American studies department.'

A chill went through the air. The faint, puzzled frown left the vice-chancellor's face and her mouth hardened into a smile.

'Of course,' she repeated. 'I'm so sorry, Siân. I was distracted. It's been a hard week.'

'Has it?'

Did she hear the scorn in my voice? She shifted her weight, now facing off against me, but she said nothing.

'It is difficult, isn't it?' I said.

'Yes,' she replied. Without altering the expression on her face she asked, 'How are you, Siân?'

'It's been a hard week,' I said as politely as I could.

To my amazement she replied, 'It's been a hard year. Difficult for all of us.'

I felt my jaw sag and drop open, and a voice inside me protested, 'How dare you. How dare you talk to me like that.'

'How's Tony?' asked Jerome.

'You should go and say hello,' said the vice-chancellor.

'I can't see him,' said Jerome.

'Oh, he's probably popped back to the car for some work files.' Then turning to me: 'Tony and Desna work together. They have a big case . . .'

'Unfair dismissal?' I asked.

'Copyright infringement.'

She didn't even blink when she spoke. She looked straight at me, through me, past me. I was all but invisible.

'You really don't remember me, do you?' I said.

From the corner of my eye I saw Jerome's hand reach out

towards my arm. And I felt his fingers ease gently around my sleeve. But it was the vice-chancellor's expression that engulfed me. Her hard face, the slight twitch of her lips and the look of contempt that she could not conceal as she replied, 'Siân Rees, of course I remember you.' She smiled then, a cold frozen smirk. 'Well, good luck going forward.'

I didn't move.

'Bye Siân,' she said as she turned around and walked back into the house.

Jerome followed her. But not before asking if I was okay.

The open space around me felt very large, and standing on the lawn I felt small. I thought how strange I must look from the air. That someone looking down would see a lone woman, standing rigid, a half-empty glass of lemonade in her hand. Off to the side would be groups of people and kids running around, but here on this patch of lawn was a lone, middle-aged woman, with not so much as a tree nearby to offer shelter. From the air, a person would see the woman put down her glass on the lawn, and even though the grass was neatly mown the glass would tip over, depositing a slice of lemon on the bright green. And then the woman would start to walk. She would walk stiffly, as if the mechanics of moving one foot in front of the other were not yet mastered. She would look ahead and no one would call out to her, or wave, or try to stop her. She would circle the house, back to the long drive where her car was parked. From the air, a person would hear the peep-peep of her key activating the lock of the car, and then, seconds later, see her inside, sitting at the driver's wheel. Sitting. Sitting. Staring.

I went to see Brooke Daniels in the English department. Before I went up to her room I found myself standing in the corridor outside my old office. The smell of the new carpet had faded, but the space did not seem the same as when I worked there. My nameplate was still on the door, which seemed remarkable, but underneath it was a laminated card with the names of several people. I didn't recognise any of them but I guessed they were postgraduates, using my room as their write-up space. Archer's name had gone from his door; there were a couple of screw holes where it used to be. Jerome's nameplate had also gone, but maybe he took it with him when he shifted to the English department.

It never occurred to me when I was offered my American studies job that the whole department would ever cease to exist. Perhaps I missed a message informing me that American history, politics, religion, culture and art were no longer relevant in today's world. Maybe those affected by cuts in music, philosophy, religious studies, linguistics, German, French and Italian were equally bemused. Perhaps we should have seen it coming. But it's hard to predict the end when you believe in what you're doing, when there still seems to be value in knowledge.

When I knocked on Brooke's open door she got up from behind her desk and came around to hug me. I appreciated the gesture but I didn't reciprocate. I wanted to strike the correct tone and maintain a professional distance rather than have her think I was making a casual, social call. Moreover, I wasn't entirely sure I could trust her. I'd grown a little paranoid in recent weeks and begun to dwell on what may have occurred behind the scenes in terms of deciding who kept their jobs and who didn't. I'd always respected Brooke, and had no real reason to doubt her, but we were no longer colleagues or equals and I felt on edge now that I was stripped of my professional identity.

Brooke offered me a seat, then carefully closed the door, assuring me that we wouldn't be interrupted. Back to her desk, she unplugged the phone. It began to feel as if I'd walked into a doctor's consulting room and I almost wondered if she would close the blinds to ensure absolute privacy. She picked up a biro – to record our conversation? – but only clicked it a few times before putting it down. Only then did it occur to me that she was anxious, that my presence made her uncomfortable. When I smiled in an attempt to reassure her she looked relieved and asked how I was doing.

'Not too well,' I said. 'I haven't managed to find work yet.'

She nodded sympathetically and mumbled something about it being tough for people like me, by which I gathered she meant middle-aged unemployed women. 'Have you applied for any overseas jobs?'

I shook my head.

'I'm sure they'd snap you up somewhere. You'd have excellent references.'

'Mmm.'

'I wish I could help,' she said, shifting uncomfortably in her seat.

In normal circumstances I would have nodded and said something like, 'It's okay', but these weren't normal circumstances and I couldn't leave without asking for work, no matter how humiliating it was. I took a deep breath and said, 'I was wondering if you had anything I could do? I'd be happy to help out, even if only for a few hours a week. Do you need cover for anyone on sabbatical? Part-time tutoring?'

As I talked she shook her head gently from side to side, one shake for each negative response.

'Marking?'

She shook her head again.

'Research? Background research?'

It was becoming excruciating for both of us but I pressed on. 'A website? Online presence?'

'Pardon?'

'A blog? I could manage a blog for the department.'

There was a long silence and then Brooke gave a slight shrug and said, 'Sorry. There's nothing.'

She looked so upset I found myself wanting to comfort her.

'It's not your fault,' I said.

'I know,' she replied. 'But I feel like shit not being able to help. The situation is desperate. The place is falling apart. We've lost half of our administration staff, and we're being squeezed in every direction. We're not going to be able to do any research. The VC is freezing all our funding. We're going to be left with teaching, and nothing else. Basically, we're being turned into a polytech. And I'm so, so sorry. I can't imagine how difficult it must be for you. How stressful. I'm so sorry.'

'It's all right,' I heard myself reply. 'I'll find something.'

'You know,' said Brooke, 'it's not meant to be like this. We're actually important. English is important. What you taught . . .' She paused and picked up her biro, focusing on the advertisement printed on its barrel. 'Lisa's struggling with work . . .' She turned the pen so I could see the name of Lisa's agency.

I nodded. 'Midwives . . .'

'Yeah, midwives. They're paid nothing. It's awful.'

She's right, I thought. It was awful. Academics, midwives, nurses, teachers . . . the whole shebang. 'It's all wrong,' I said.

Brooke tried to smile but it only made her look even more worried.

'Are you going to be okay?' I asked. 'Have you and Lisa got support?'

'Lisa . . .' she began but then her voice broke off.

'Have you talked to anyone?' I persisted.

'I'm one of the lucky ones, remember! I've still got a well-paid job.'

We sat facing each other and then we both sighed at exactly

the same time, which made us laugh. I sniffed and reached for a hanky to blow my nose. Brooke rubbed her sleeve across her eyes.

'We started teaching about the same time, didn't we?' she said.

'I think so.'

'You used to come into the Staff Club?'

'Only for the free tampons and aspirin. When I was caught short . . .'

'You know it was Penny who organised those things? She used to bully the local suppliers into donating them. She was tough, even then.'

'She would have just been made a senior lecturer in law?'

'Yes, I guess so. She was always ambitious.'

I took a deep breath. 'Do you think Jerome . . . Do you think he made a deal with her, to keep his job?'

Brooke looked at me and shook her head. 'I hope not,' she said. 'I really hope not.'

It wasn't until I left Brooke's office that I realised how tired I was. I wandered back down the stairs, along the corridor towards my office. Without thinking, I reached for my door key and was surprised that it wasn't in my pocket. I immediately opened my bag and searched inside, and it was only then that I understood my mistake. Heat rose up through my neck and face and I had to steady myself against the wall. A door opened at the end of the hall and a young guy came out, then stopped beside me. 'Can I help you? Are you looking for someone?' he asked as he placed his key in the lock.

'No.'

'Are you all right?'

I nodded and mumbled something about being late for a meeting. That seemed to satisfy him and a moment later he opened the door and disappeared into my old room.

A note of comfort: I am never going back. I'm done with university. I am done. I don't believe there's a scent that can lift me out of this mood of defeat and betrayal. Could Jerome have cut a deal with the vice-chancellor? I don't think so. I'm not sure that would have been possible. But maybe I'm wrong and he did. It would explain why he's still working and I'm not.

I need something to bring me comfort. My father. What did he smell like? Amber comes back to me, the scent of his doctor's bag. A sweet scent. The beer he made. There must be more. I remember things like the smell of milk the time a bottle smashed in the back of his car. We scrubbed the carpet but as the days passed, and the car heated, the smell intensified, turning from sour to fetid, a smell I later associated with athlete's foot. I remember the cocoa he used to make us; unlike my mother, he made it with hot milk rather than water, and he stirred in extra sugar the way we liked it, my sister and I. I remember the smell of medlar jelly, made from a recipe in a large black book of baking and preserves. I helped pick the medlars but I hated them; they reminded me of pears and apples left rotting on the ground, brown and mildewed.

What I remember most, though, is the smell of his homespun jersey. Knitted from dark brown merino wool, it carried the smell of sheep, the beautiful greasiness of fleece. I loved the way the jersey accumulated more and more scents over the years: of garden bonfires, two-stroke petrol, freshly caught fish, wood stain, sawdust, dirt. It came to symbolise his life – not his career, as his doctor's bag did – but his home life, the time he spent with us, his family. Homespun, greasy wool. Another heart note for my perfume. To create that smell I'll try ambergris: it reminds me of stock trucks, sweet like caramel, and milky. It reminds me of this apartment, my home.

All I could smell was smoke, cigarette smoke. Though I was sitting on my favourite chair, beside the window, warm with the sun on my back, I couldn't relax or breathe easily. I kept thinking there must be workmen outside. How else could the place smell so strongly of smoke? But when I stood up and looked out of the window there was no one around, and of course I was up on the top floor. I stepped out into the hallway but that, too, was devoid of life and besides, the whole apartment block was a no-smoking zone. Was the smell coming through a vent? I went and stood beneath the heat pump, then the rangehood, and finally by the ventilation units in the small bathroom and laundry. The smokiness persisted but there was no source.

I tried breathing through my mouth but it didn't help. I moved my chair away from the window and positioned it right next to the solid beam running up from the floor to the ceiling. This was one of my most fragrant beams, a length of timber that, on hot days, smelt of a woolshed. I rested my head against it and inhaled and instead of wool I got smoke. And then the smell transformed, turning to gas. It was acrid and I couldn't shake myself free of it. My hand began to tingle and the tips of my fingers turned numb. I stabbed my fingernails into my skin but I couldn't feel anything. The tingling sensation moved up my arm, and then my head began to throb. A clamp tightened on one side and I began to lose vision in the centre of my eye. I could still see but I had to tilt my head and it was as if I could only see around the object I focused on. Where the object itself should be I could only see a dark hole.

I didn't have any painkillers in the house. It had been so long since my last migraine that I thought I'd outgrown them. If I tried to talk, my words wouldn't make sense. It wasn't that I forgot words but rather that they fell out of range. I knew they existed, but not for me.

I made it to my table where I knew I had lavender, peppermint and rosemary oil, all recommended by aromatherapists to relieve the symptoms of headaches. I would have preferred codeine but I had no choice. The bottles dipped and dived in front of me and when I picked up a vial the letters on the label refused my scrutiny. I could make out the first letter, P, and by tilting my head and closing one eye I could slowly spell out the word petitgrain. The bottle to its left should have been peppermint so I took that and slowly pieced together the letters on its label. My lavender oil was in a larger bottle than the others because I used it more frequently and in greater quantities than many of my other oils. I knew its bottle was near the centre of the row and so it was easier to find.

Although sensation had returned to my fingers and my eyesight was becoming clearer, it felt like someone was pressing their knuckles into my temples and I could still smell smoke. I was anxious that the oils wouldn't get rid of the smoke stench or that they would make me sick. The pain was so intense that I found it difficult to sit upright and it was only because I had the two bottles I wanted so close at hand that I managed to unscrew their caps and take a big sniff. Nothing changed, the smoke refused to budge. The larger lavender bottle was easier to grasp so I raised it to my nose and inhaled once more. Relief spread through me as I finally detected its familiar scent. I closed my eyes and made a conscious effort to slow my breathing. I remembered my father, that one of the last conversations we ever had was about lavender. He'd found a study in a medical journal about its use in reducing anxiety and treating pain and mentioned that he liked the smell of the plant. He said it reminded him of his grandmother and I realised, with shock, that I'd never heard him talk about his grandparents, and that I didn't know their names or anything about them. 'Which grandmother?' I asked.

'The nice one,' he replied. 'The one who brought me home from Ireland. I sent her a fish that I caught. In the post.'

I assumed the pethidine was making him hallucinate, and it wasn't until years later when I met his older brother that I learnt my father had been evacuated during the war, that he'd been shipped off to Ireland where he was billeted with a Catholic family. 'I think he must have gone through hell,' said my uncle. 'He was the only Protestant in the neighbourhood.'

'Do you remember anything about a fish?' I asked. 'He told me he posted a fish to his grandmother.'

My uncle shrugged. He didn't know.

The brothers hadn't kept in touch. They hadn't talked or seen each other since my father left Britain. There were no hard feelings; it was as if keeping their relationship intact had somehow slipped their minds.

'Your dad loved ferns,' said my uncle.

'Don't you mean lavender?' I asked.

'No. Ferns. He had a flower press and he made a little herbarium of the specimens he collected. He took the press to Ireland but I think it must have got lost. Or stolen. He never said.'

I spent two days in bed, barely moving, and on the third day, still feeling the effects of my migraine hangover, I phoned Archer, telling him about my visit to Jerome's and asking if it would be okay if I tagged along on his trip to fix his cabin. To my immense relief he seemed pleased, and said yes.

Before leaving I wrote three more applications. One to the city council for a six-month contract compiling a listing of Victorian landmarks and 'notable' residents, one to the television news reference library for the position of general assistant, and another to the Blind Foundation for the role of fundraiser. I knew I could do all three jobs but I also knew that there would be other, better qualified applicants. I almost didn't bother sending them.

It had been a while since I last went away. As I'd aged, my desire to travel had diminished. When I was younger, holidays were largely a positive experience, something I enjoyed planning as much as doing, but in recent years all my breaks had been hurried affairs, booked in desperation in an attempt to escape work for an extended weekend. Melbourne had been my destination of choice. Getting there required little effort and it was a place I loved; in fact it was one of the few places I could happily live – if it weren't so hot in summer.

Travelling to a hut somewhere near the Whanganui River was not on my must-do list, but I was grateful to get out of town nonetheless. My days were becoming clouded by dread. I found it hard to check my emails, not because I was scared of uncovering yet another rejection letter but because I was scared of having to deal with *any* correspondence, good or bad. I wanted to be left alone, to think or not think, as the mood took me.

Furthermore, I was tired of myself. Job applications forced me to evaluate, and re-evaluate, my skills, my experience, my strengths and weaknesses, a constant competitive ranking that left me convinced I was lacking in every area of my personal and professional life. The more I picked myself apart, or attempted to mould myself to fit employee requirements, the less confident I became. While trying to appear at my most attractive, I became more and more disfigured, unrecognisable to myself. I was a fraud; no one would hire me. I wouldn't even hire me.

There were two messages that had made me panic. Out of the blue, my former real estate agent contacted me. She'd been approached by a cash buyer who was searching for a special inner-city, warehouse-style apartment. My apartment. Was I interested in selling? She would give me a follow-up call on the off chance that I was.

The second message was a reminder that the corporate levy for the apartment was due by the end of the month. The annual fee was $8000, up from the previous year. The levy came on top of insurance, currently $3200. I'd already renewed my policy, but the levy loomed over me, dark and threatening, absorbing all light from my world.

And then, finally, there was Jerome. I'd hoped a few days away would create the distance I needed to think through what had happened at his house. I wasn't even sure what *did* happen at his house. Perhaps it was nothing at all. So why did I feel so sick?

Archer texted to say he was on his way but took an hour to arrive. I spent that time loitering around the entrance hall, persuading myself that he'd arrive in a minute. I caught sight of one of my neighbours, an elderly man, who asked if I was the cleaner. I thought he wanted to know if I was the person who had put the flyer about cleaning work in his letterbox so I said yes, but it turned out he wanted to complain about some black marks on the corridor walls near his apartment. When I explained, he still had a go at me, insisting that I take care of the mess right away. In the end it seemed easier to assure him that I'd fix the problem as soon as I could. This satisfied him for a moment but then, seeing me surrounded by luggage, he grew suspicious and demanded to know who I really was, and what I was doing in *his* apartment block. When I said that I lived on the top floor he accused me of lying. Fed up, I asked what *he* was doing in *my* apartment block. He gave me a look that suggested I was mad and said it was none of my business. The conversation went on for several more minutes and, to my surprise, I realised I was enjoying the interaction. It was so direct and blunt, so ridiculously straightforward after all the mindfulness and careful negotiating of my job interviews. I almost cheered when he called me 'a rude young woman' before stomping off.

When Archer arrived I was smiling, my mood lighter than it had been for days.

'I don't suppose you've heard about the libraries,' asked Archer as he helped me with my bags.

'No. What libraries?'

'The fine arts and engineering libraries. The VC wants to shut them down.'

My spirits crashed. 'I guess she really does hate us, after all.'

We drove in silence, our eyes fixed on the car in front, a late-model station wagon with a curly-haired dog that ran back and forth across the back seat. After ten minutes of constant motion the dog suddenly stopped and placed both front paws on the back of the seat, staring through the rear window. It seemed to be studying us, so I waved at it.

'I really think that the university made a terrible mistake,' I said. 'I mean, on top of everything else, don't you worry that the only people left will be the ones who communicate in bullet points? Haven't you noticed the change already? Students who can't string ideas together because they no longer read books?' The dog began running to and fro again. 'We used to read a lot of books, didn't we?'

'We still do,' said Archer.

'Maybe,' I said. 'The truth is I've only read a couple since leaving work, and one of those was *The Awakening*.'

'That takes me back.'

The dog scrambled between the front seats and took up a position on the passenger side, its head poking through the open window, ears flapping.

'Bet I can guess what you're thinking,' I said.

'Oh yes?'

'Bill Cannastra.'

Archer laughed.

'It's funny how single images take up permanent space in your mind,' I continued. 'They're like the visual equivalent of jingles and sound bites, unenlightening but never forgotten. We had a terrific lecturer back in my first year. He was on a Fulbright exchange, from Brooklyn, and he used to shuffle into the lecture theatre and shamble up to the lectern. He always had a handful of mail and he'd place it in front of him and slowly begin to open each letter, and as he scanned his correspondence he'd start to speak. He seemed to begin mid-sentence, as if thinking aloud, and so it would take a minute to register that the lecture had begun and we'd all end up frantically taking notes, trying to catch up. He never shifted his weight, or moved from behind the lectern, and everything he said sounded like a personal memory he was recalling for our benefit. He was one of those people who was always several steps ahead of the class, so we'd be laughing at a funny anecdote about Marilyn Monroe while he was on to a serious critique of Miller's *After the Fall,* and by the time we caught up he'd already moved on to a reflection on self-destruction and the inevitability of tragedy . . .'

'Sounds terrible. What student wants to get lost like that?'

'No, no. The opposite was true. The way he could connect so many disparate elements in such a conversational manner. We came away from each lecture convinced that he personally knew everyone he was talking about. When he mentioned in passing during a lecture on Ginsberg and Kerouac that their friend, Cannastra, had his head knocked off while leaning out of a subway window, we thought he must have witnessed it.'

'What was the lecturer's name?'

I paused. 'I can see him, his brown suit, the pile of letters, his bony hands and long, tapered fingers. I can recall his glasses, his voice . . .'

'But no name?'

'No, that's the funny thing about it. I can remember the name Cannastra but not the professor who mentioned him.'

'Not so funny when you think about it.'

The car with the dog took an exit ramp and for a while the lane ahead of us was clear, then a bright blue coupe pulled in front of us.

'I wish I could remember his name,' I said. 'I feel a bit guilty about it now.'

'It was a long time ago.'

'But I remember the others: Conway, Stowell, Wearing, Wilcox, Harlan. And the visiting Americans: Brooks, MacManus, Carillo.'

'Did I mention,' said Archer, 'that I've been asked to do a lecture series on American society for the local U3A? I get paid, too. Cash.'

'American society? That sounds like a wide field.'

'They're trying to establish a historical context for Trump,' said Archer.

'At least they're not paying you in book tokens.'

'That's true.'

'It will be fun,' I said. 'Those groups are usually well read and pretty smart.'

The blue car suddenly took off, overtaking a long stream of traffic, and disappeared into the distance.

'I thought I'd start with the Puritans and cover the witch trials, the Great Awakening and the Indian Wars. I'd like to introduce Samson Occom's writing if I can.'

'I don't know him.'

'He was a Mohegan minister during the mid-1700s. Remind me to lend you his *Collected Writings* when we get back home.'

Archer had mentioned when he picked me up that our trip to his cabin was going to take a circuitous route. I assumed he meant he knew some minor gravel back road, once we got closer to the destination. In fact, he wanted to go via Rotorua, to take care of some business. When I asked what kind he merely smiled and said, 'Wait and see.'

'I wonder what house prices are like in Rotorua,' I asked. 'They must be a lot cheaper than where we are?'

'Anything's cheaper than where we are,' Archer replied.

'That's true. Do you think you'll keep your house?'

'Which one?'

'What do you mean?'

'Well, we've got three: our place, Hester's central city apartment and then the cabin.'

'Really?'

'Renate's always been good with money. She takes care of all our investments. What about you? Will you sell?'

'I hope not,' I said.

As the words came out of my mouth I pictured a well-dressed real estate agent walking her cash buyer through the spaces in my loft, pointing out the Oregon timber, the sealed brick walls, the steel frame, the earthquake strengthening, the designer kitchen, the well-appointed bathroom and so on, each part of my home itemised and scrutinised. What would my book collection, my perfume collection, the rows of essential oils say about me? That I was eccentric? Obsessive? Knowledgeable? I imagined the agent describing me as a university professor, as if that bestowed a level of respectability and glamour to the loft. Unlikely that she would mention I was unemployed. Retired, maybe? A university professor looking to downsize? An older woman who needed to trade flights of stairs for easy-access, ground-floor living?

The sun went behind a cloud and a fine mist of drizzle covered the windscreen. By the third sweep, the blades of the wipers caught and squeaked across the glass. In the distance a bunch of cyclists barrelled down the road towards us, taking up the entire width of their side. As they passed I noticed that most of the men were middle-aged, but that in their midst a single, thick-legged woman kept pace. Archer slowed as they raced by. Five hundred metres further on two more cyclists appeared, sprinting to catch the leaders. They were young, barely out of their teenage years and as they flew past, heads down, legs spinning, I caught an image of Charles's face looking up from their saddles and laughed.

'What's funny?'

'Oh, nothing. Just remembering my old boss – something he said a long time ago about bikes.'

In my side-mirror I watched the cyclists disappear, the bright colours of their Lycra tops glowing against the monochromatic scenery.

'Renate has an electric bike,' said Archer. 'It's very handy for getting around town.'

'She must be doing well, then. With her heart, I mean?'

'Yes, fine. Slowing down at work helped. No more eighty-hour weeks.'

'I thought she retired after her surgery?'

'She tried retirement but it didn't suit her, she can't sit still. It's all consultancy now. Lots of travel.'

The drizzle turned to rain and I sat in silence. I preferred living alone to compliance with another person, but thinking about Jerome with Desna, and Archer with his consultant wife, I couldn't help but wonder if I'd made the right decision. I envied the emotional support and financial buffer available to my colleagues. How much easier might my life have been if I, too, had had an intelligent, well-connected 'wife'? It wasn't about the money; I might have liked to be with someone who could advise or reassure me, someone who could provide stability and hope, a doctor for the heart maybe.

'Do you mind if I turn on the radio? I'd like to listen to some music.'

'There's a few CDs in the glove box,' said Archer.

There were five discs: two jazz compilations, an early Bill Evans album, Joni Mitchell's *Blue* and a boxed set of Burl Ives's *The Wayfaring Stranger.* I held up the Ives for Archer to see and he nodded.

'If you like Burl Ives,' he said, 'I have a stack of his albums at the cabin.'

'I like his voice,' I replied. 'And I remember him as Big Daddy in *Cat on a Hot Tin Roof*.'

'Which leads us back to Bill Cannastra,' said Archer.

'Does it?'

'Yes. Because they say the character of Brick was based on him.'

'I didn't know that.'

'That's because you're not as old as me.'

'No, it's because I don't remember everything I've read.'

'That too.'

We travelled through a rural landscape, farmland paddocks and snatches of scrub, large clumps of flax and toetoe lining the drainage ditches, cabbage trees standing tall in paddocks of bright green grass dotted with yellow gorse bushes. A large campervan with a Union Jack affixed to its rear panel was parked ahead of us, barely pulled off to the side of the road. The hazard lights blinked in warning and its occupants stood on the road taking photos of two white horses that were running around and around a paddock. Archer slowed to a crawl as we passed but the tourists barely seemed to notice; they were too busy posing.

We continued in silence broken only when I asked Archer if I would ever find a job.

We'd been travelling for over three hours and it was late afternoon when we finally drew close to Rotorua. I smelt the town before I saw it, and breathed deeply, holding the faint aroma of sulphur inside.

'I love that smell,' I said.

'What smell?'

'The Rotorua smell, of course.'

I watched as Archer inhaled and waited for his response. I saw him take another deep breath and asked, 'Well?'

'The thing is,' he said eventually, 'I don't have a sense of smell.'

'What? What about the perfume I made you?' As the words left my mouth I remembered his unusual response to my gift, that he had never come out and said what he thought of the blend, always deflecting my observations with a question.

'I'm sorry,' said Archer. 'I didn't know how to tell you. You went to so much effort . . .'

'So you can't smell anything? Anything at all?'

'No.'

'Nothing?'

'No. But I sometimes think I can imagine what something smells like based on its taste.'

'So you can taste things?'

'Not as well as I used to but I think I've stored a lot of flavours in my memory after all my years of bartending.'

'A bit like Beethoven with his music?'

He looked uncomfortable. 'I used to smoke sixty a day and I think that caused damage – that and being hit in the face with a baseball bat when I was young. Broken nose.'

'So you have no idea what the perfume I made you actually smells like?'

'Lemons and oysters,' he replied.

'But do you know what lemons and oysters smell like?' I pressed. 'Do you know what a lemon smells like?'

'It smells yellow. And bitter.'

'Oysters?'

'Like a grey harbour, waves lapping against a rocky shore.'

'What about Rotorua?'

'Rotten eggs.'

'No, it's more complex than that, it's mineral.'

Archer dropped me in the gardens by the bath house, promising to collect me in an hour once he'd taken care of his business. He could barely contain the smirk that spread across his face.

Notes from a fossil hunter: It had been many years since I'd last been to Rotorua and in the fading light of early evening I headed towards the edge of the lake, standing on the shore looking out over the dried mudflats that led to the edge of a shallow strip of water. Litter, plastic bottles and pieces of driftwood lay in front of me, rimed in yellow sulphur, a crust of pale yellow also on the mud itself.

By my feet were several pieces of pumice, which I picked up and held to my nose. A small fragment of black, glass-like stone – obsidian – caught my attention and I stooped to take it, scraping a palm full of mud as I did so. Now my hand contained a mound of mud, the obsidian and pumice. These must surely represent some of the earliest scents of the country: volcanic ash and stone, mud, hot springs and geysers – the elemental fire and water at the beginning of any fragrance timeline.

On perfume sites I'd seen advertisements for lava stones, dark beads of scoria. From what I could gather, these porous beads were sprayed with perfume and then worn around the wrist, the scent retained in the bracelet for days at a time. I'd never tried the beads for myself but smelling the pumice in my hand made me consider that the claims were true. Within each pebble was a complex smell of sulphur and earth, sand and limestone, an almost chalky scent. I gathered up more pebbles, rolling them in my palms to warm them before cupping my hands to my nose and inhaling.

For minutes I made a mental scan of all the oils in my collection, wondering how on earth I would recreate the smell of pumice. And then it dawned on me that there was no need to recreate it at all. The smell was already captured within the stone, had presumably been there for many years. Could it date all the way back to the last major eruption? Could I actually smell remnants of that event? Were these stones the scent of prehistoric New Zealand?

I felt something akin to intense hunger arise up inside me and I bent down to collect more stones, filling my pockets with pumice. Smears of mud marked my jeans, and my shoes were completely grey. At one point I turned back to face the gardens and it was as if I were suddenly caught in a time warp – the built-world of humans less than a few hundred metres from where I stood in a primordial wonderland. Had perfumer Ernest Beaux, in the Arctic Circle, experienced the same excitement I felt now, fossil hunting for scent?

From a distance I heard a horn, followed by the sound of my name. Pockets bulging, I slowly plodded back across the mudflats, scrambling up the bank to the gardens in time to see Archer waving at me from the driver's seat of an enormous black car.

'What do you think?' he said as we pulled onto the main highway. It was the third or fourth time he'd asked me and each time I'd said 'amazing' or 'brilliant' although a more honest response would have been 'Why?'

'This beats work and job hunting, doesn't it?'

He ran his hands over the surface of the steering wheel, then brought them back to the ten to two position.

'Oh, I'm so sorry,' I said. 'I'd completely forgotten to ask you about that university job. Did you get an interview?'

'Skyped a few times and I was shortlisted, which was nice of them. But in the end it went in-house, to a specialist in post-modern belief. A nice guy, actually. I've corresponded with him a couple of times and he's very bright.'

'But you should have got it.'

'To tell the truth I'm glad I didn't. I'm a bit old for starting over in a foreign country. And, this way,' he said patting the dashboard, 'I get the car of my dreams.'

Newspaper rustled under my pants as I shifted position. The mud on my trousers had dried and was now scaling off in flakes of grey dust. 'So, it's a 1938 Pontiac,' I said. 'And you've really traded your car in for this?'

'Yes. I've had it in the back of my mind for a while now. It's a nice bit of nostalgia – my father bought one after he came back from Korea.'

'I didn't know you had a thing for cars.'

'I suppose I have,' Archer replied. 'This one's been passed down through the members of one family and it's only done 145,000ks. They've been using it for wedding parties and local tours. That's why it's so great.'

'It smells good.'

'Really? How does it smell?'

'Like an old car.' I inhaled and thought for a minute. 'There's a sweet smell, like almonds mixed with wallpaper paste, and then there's a smell of engine oil and something slightly musty. It actually smells a lot like a mechanics' garage, oil dripped on concrete but with a bit of beeswax. Lots of leather, too. It's warm.'

'Did you notice the patina on the bonnet from where it's been polished all these years. Did you see the way the top layer of paint had worn off?'

I shook my head. 'No.'

'I like the way you talk about the interior,' said Archer. 'Your description reminds me of the way my favourite uncle's car smelt. He had a Pontiac, too. That's another part of the attraction.'

'I sometimes get scents stuck in my head the way other people get song lyrics and tunes in theirs. They're my equivalent of earworms.'

'I had "Big Rock Candy Mountain" playing in my head when I was negotiating with the trader. We were finalising the deal and Burl Ives started going around and around . . .'

'Hah, you don't have a CD player any more.'

The sun had set and Archer switched on the lights. They weren't nearly as bright as I was used to, even on full beam. Following vehicles formed a line behind us, flashing their lights impatiently and then shooting past as soon as we pulled over or reached an overtaking lane. Just when it seemed we were clear of the traffic, the line would form once more and though neither Archer nor I said anything we began to grow edgy, scanning the road ahead for possible shoulders. After one particularly aggressive driver sped by, horn blasting, Archer suggested we might like to look for a motel for the night and carry on with our journey in the morning.

'That's a great idea,' I said rather too quickly. 'I mean, you must be tired and it would be sensible because we could get more groceries in the morning before heading into the wilderness. What do you think?'

'Sounds good to me,' replied Archer.

It had been so many years since I'd been on a road trip that I'd forgotten the strange ritual of searching for a motel. The first drive-by was to get an indication of what was full, and who had vacancies. The next passing was slower as each available motel was scrutinised for appearance. Did the place look inviting, run-down, gloomy? What did the make and model of cars parked in the forecourt indicate about the other guests? Were they tourists, families or itinerant workers? Did it look as if some of the utes might belong to rowdy, late-night drinkers, the type of people who slam doors and yell into the darkness, or were they the functional vehicles of choice for those who favoured quiet mornings spent fishing on the nearby river?

What did Archer's Pontiac say about us? Was it a gangster car or a mid-life crisis car? Never having owned anything but a Toyota Corolla, I felt out of my depth trying to tally the large black sedan in which I sat with my personality, and even harder to match it to Archer's. He was so sensible and self-effacing, so knowledgeable and modest, that the car seemed too much of a statement and far too attention-seeking for him.

In the end we settled on a place that appealed because, from the street, it appeared old-fashioned, somewhat quirky and quiet, and it was surrounded by native bush. It was also cheap and had a two-room unit available.

Although it was dark it wasn't cold and we decided to eat outside at a small table in our private patio area. Cooked on the small kitchen hot plate, our meal was fairly basic: a can of chilli beans, nacho chips and grated cheese served with a tomato and avocado salsa, but because we hadn't eaten since leaving home it tasted delicious, and if we'd had another tin of beans we would have polished it off. I've never been fussed about food or cooking, a fact I believe accounts for my gradual weight gain over the past ten years. I'm certain that if I were more interested in the taste and texture of food, I'd try harder to create interesting meals. But I was happy to eat whatever was easy to fix which, inevitably, meant cheese slapped between two slices of bread rather than a salad or vegetables. The only thing going for me, health-wise, was that I didn't smoke or drink – at least, I didn't drink alone. It took very little persuasion for me to accept a glass of wine when Archer offered it with our meal. I noticed that he held the wine to his nose before sipping it and so I did the same.

'What do you smell?' he asked.

'I've never been very confident about picking out notes in wine.' I swirled the dark red liquid and took a breath. 'It's probably not the best glass for holding the aroma, is it?' I asked. 'It's called a seven, the kind of beer glass that was still common when I was a kid.'

I watched as the wine coated the side and then sniffed. 'Can you smell it at all?'

Archer shook his head.

'So I could say anything?'

'No, because I trust you.'

'Well, to me it smells like black currants, overripe grapes – almost like raisins or maybe even prunes, maybe prunes not raisins. It's rich.' I took another sniff. 'It has depth. You know what it really brings to mind? Christmas cake. It smells like Christmas cake tastes. Rich and spicy, and fruity.'

Archer nodded.

'But,' I added, 'there's something here that smells even better than the wine.'

'My perfume?'

I laughed. 'No. All these ferns.'

Our small garden area was surrounded by a fence made of ponga, and although each trunk had been cut to size, small tufts of new growth had sprouted, slowly turning the fence palings back into trees again. In front of the ponga were more ferns, and the scent that came off them was warm and dusty, earthy and surprisingly sweet.

'Can you remember the last thing you smelt?' I asked.

Archer looked down, rolling the small tumbler between his palms. 'Well, I guess it would be cigarettes, if I'm to be honest. But I do have scent memories that go beyond Camels. Hester, when she was a baby. That was one of the best. If she'd been fed she smelt of warm milk, richer than store-bought milk, more like fresh farm milk. If it was evening and she'd come straight from the bath, she'd smell of baby powder, but I wasn't so keen on that. For some reason the smell stuck in my throat. I preferred how she smelt when I picked her up out of her crib in the morning: her skin was kind of warm and musky, but there'd also be a kind of underlayer of soiled nappy smell that wasn't really stinky so much as grass-like, like something you'd expect from a horse. Have you ever smelt that?'

'I remember my little sister's smell when she was a baby. I didn't like it because it struck me as unhealthy, like a smell belonging to a sick person – which she was at the time. She moved to England about fifteen years ago and married a guy with adult children. He didn't want any more kids so she settled for cats, Burmese, I think. We don't keep in touch. I don't even have friends with kids . . . except Jerome, I suppose. But I didn't get to sniff Scottie when she was a baby.'

'Oh, that's a shame.'

I laughed, but realised Archer was serious.

'I remember the smell of a brand of tea Renate and I used to drink in the seventies when we first met, in New York. It had a very strong smell of cinnamon and orange peel, and cloves too. Genuine hippie tea.'

'I've never been much of a tea drinker. I prefer coffee.'

'Oh, I remember the coffee we had when we honeymooned in Hawaii: it tasted like chocolate hazelnut spread. It was incredibly artificial but we thought it was so sophisticated. But I guess if I had to identify a favourite flower it would be the lilac. It's nicely poetical, too, when you think about it. Whitman and Eliot.'

'Lilacs, yes. They're beautiful. But they don't stick around for long. The flowers.'

'Have you ever tracked the references to lilacs in Whitman and Eliot?'

'Yeah, ages ago, mostly Whitman.'

'What about Faulkner's lilac poem? Do you remember it?'

'Vaguely. But I believe lilacs are everywhere once you start looking. Lilacs, loss and death.'

Archer nodded and I heard him quietly recite the opening stanza from Whitman's 'When Lilacs Last in the Dooryard Bloom'd'. He spoke well and I hoped he'd continue but he caught my eye and stopped.

I said, 'I sometimes come across pieces written by perfume lovers who take great care not to wear their favourite scents in stressful situations. For instance, they won't wear a beloved fragrance to a hospital treatment or to a funeral for fear that it will become forever associated with an unhappy event.'

'And you? Do you avoid perfumes? Do you have a perfume that triggers a "management for change" memory?'

'No, I don't tend to kill off perfumes in that way. And also, my memory's not as good as yours. For example, I'm not sure what I was wearing when we lost our jobs. It was probably something unobtrusive as I'd been warned about perfume allergies. I can't even remember what perfume I was wearing to my father's funeral. It could have been something I made myself. But some people would definitely recall those fragrances. Scent's very powerful. It creates sensory flashbacks.'

As we talked I became aware of the sound of frogs chirping in the undergrowth, and, further away, voices of men and bursts of laughter. To my surprise I realised that most of the day had passed without my thinking about my house or finding work. In fact, I felt calmer and lighter than I'd felt for a long time.

'When I went through Whitman's poems looking for scent references I came across a line that stuck in my mind. It was about body odour, and the smell of his armpits being "finer than prayer".'

'And speaking of sweat,' said Archer, 'I need a shower.'

'Sorry, I didn't mean to suggest anything.'

When Archer excused himself, I stayed outside. I'd let him

finish in the bathroom and get settled in bed before going inside myself. I thought he'd like the additional privacy.

As I waited, I checked my phone for emails and was surprised to see a new message from a woman named Jessica Lee. I didn't know a Jessica and was about to delete the message when the subject, 'Thesis Edit and Proofread', stopped me. Immediately I sat up straighter and read the mail, a brief request from a commerce student seeking help to 'strip back' her thesis. She'd seen my advertisement in the university bulletin and asked if I could contact her, as I sounded perfect for her needs. I guessed she was having trouble ordering her material. It was a fairly common problem among students. Some had trouble communicating in full sentences while others were unsure of how to organise their research into a piece of tidy writing. I could help with that.

I sat back in my chair and the relief at being useful once more hit me with unexpected force. Although it was late, I replied to Jessica's email straight away, explaining that I would be happy to meet her when I got home. In the meantime, if she wanted to send through her thesis I would glance over it. For months everything had gone wrong and the word 'failure' had attached itself to me like a limpet. But now, I dared to hope that that would change. Jessica Lee – I could have hugged her.

With renewed confidence I even fired off an email to my old real estate agent, thanking her for her letter but letting her know that I wasn't interested in selling my home. Then, feeling wide awake and unable to settle down, I decided to go for a quick walk around the bush track behind the motel.

As soon as I got away from the units I realised how dark the night really was. At home the night sky was orange and the street lamps cast their pale light over everything, so even in the dead of night there were shadows and often seagulls flying above buildings. But here the sky was dark and close, overcast with misty drizzle. At the edge of the bush tiny bulbs placed every few metres illuminated the gravel path and sections of greasy boardwalk, and in places where the ferns hung low over the track, beads of water caught the light and glistened. A few minutes into the walk I came across a sign announcing a glow worm grotto, where it seemed as if all the glittering drops from the ferns had been gathered up into one place, sparkling in the night. I checked my phone, hoping that Jessica might have replied, but my inbox was empty. It was late, however. To compensate for my disappointment, I attempted to take a photo of the glow worms. The image was blurry, like lights from sparklers during fireworks, but I didn't mind. I was far more interested in the smell of the damp and mossy scoop in the rock wall, surrounded by ponga and thick growth. If Archer had been there and wanted me to describe the smell, I think I'd have told him to imagine the feel of damp, cool stone tunnels and walls of an ancient catacomb or crypt.

As I wandered back to the unit I wondered if I should cut my trip short and head home in the morning. Jessica might get someone else if I didn't return immediately. Students could be impatient, demanding to be seen at a moment's notice, so different from my day when I spent months at a time trying to avoid any encounter with my supervisor. And when meetings did take place, they were brief and awkward, as if neither of us knew how to broach the subject of my thesis. My research progress was painfully slow because the books I had to interloan from American universities took weeks and months to reach New Zealand by sea. The bibliography in my master's thesis was so short compared with those of my students, yet the amount of time and effort that went into hunting down those meagre sources was far greater.

Jessica could wait, I decided. Before going to bed, I emailed her again and suggested she highlight her main concerns so that we could get straight down to business once I returned. As a precaution I included my cell phone number in case she needed to talk. The last thing I can remember thinking before I fell asleep was, things are going to be okay. I'd made it.

Knowing Archer couldn't smell my perfume allowed me the freedom to spray with abandon. I had with me a container of around fifteen manufacturers' samples, all testers that I'd bought off sellers in the United States. When I first became interested in perfume I would order all the recent releases from the niche perfume houses, justifying the expense by kidding myself that it was money saved because I hadn't bought expensive full bottles. I would have bought even more perfume samples had it not been for the price of shipping, which, when added to the exchange rate, could bump the cost of some 4ml decants up to $50 or $60.

What I hadn't realised was how quickly samples could multiply and take over my life; I had boxes and boxes of them. How to catalogue and arrange the vials was the difficult part. Did I arrange them by house, or was it better to organise them alphabetically by perfumer? I could categorise them by perfume notes or even by season, from spring florals through to winter orientals. It was so hard that in the end I left them unordered, jumbled like the books on my shelves, grabbing one or the other based solely on my mood or what I thought would get me through the day.

During breakfast I told Archer about Jessica's email, and he congratulated me so warmly that my sense of optimism felt vindicated.

'Things are looking up,' he said.

'It's nothing much, really,' I countered, waiting for him to disagree. When he merely smiled over his cup of tea, I added, 'It's a start, though. That's what's important.' Two years ago I would never have dreamed of using the word 'start' in relationship to my well-established career.

'Do you think Jessica likes perfume?' I asked.

'Where did that come from?'

'I don't know. I wish, sometimes, that I had someone to share my hobby with, that's all.'

'Apart from me?'

I laughed. 'Yep. Apart from you. I was thinking of someone with a sense of smell, for a start.'

'Jerome?'

I hesitated before responding. 'I'm not sure what I think of Jerome at the moment.'

'He's okay. Ambitious, a bit of a careerist.'

'You don't think he took advantage of his wife's friendship with the vice-chancellor's husband to keep his job?'

Archer shrugged. 'That seems a bit of a stretch, even for Jerome.'

'But you said he'd steal the dried fruit from the muesli packet!'

'Yeah, there's that.'

While Archer got ready to leave I checked my inbox. Nothing. In case she'd accidentally deleted my response, I fired off another message, warning her that I might be out of range for a short while. Then, because it felt like a new start to my life, the beginnings of an upward curve, I sprayed on my most recent tester, Moon Lake, which I'd liked on first sniff for the way it summoned up all the scents of a summer's day by the water's edge. Archer, I noticed, was wearing the perfume I'd made for him. That seemed pretty weird, considering he couldn't smell it.

It was a beautiful morning with mist lifting to reveal the bush and mountains glistening under a clear blue sky. After a quick stop at the supermarket we were on the road by 10 a.m., the Pontiac chugging away with Archer beaming at the wheel. The day before I'd thought the car too much of a statement, too gangster for him, but I now realised that it was a good fit. There was something old-fashioned and sturdy about it, something that gave it an air of intrepid wholesomeness; it seemed fit for a family on the move, which, in a way, we were.

Archer was the first to break the silence. 'I used to watch *I Love Lucy* when I was a kid, and one of the first episodes I remember was the one where she learns to drive.'

'Oh?'

'She has a Pontiac in the series. A convertible, far more modern than this old faithful.'

'Old Faithful?' I grinned. It was the perfect name.

'She has a driving lesson, crashes the car and then straight after teaches her friend Ethel to drive.'

'You really like women in cars, eh?'

'No. I like redheads in cars.'

'Aah, so that's it. It's redheads: Susan, Lucille . . .'

'Renate.'

'That's okay then.'

As we drove I kept glancing at my phone, hoping for a message from Jessica. Niggling at me was the thought that she might have approached someone else, and even though the scenery around us grew more and more spectacular, I could barely appreciate it. Eventually, the signal became patchy and I gave up, promising myself not to check again until we reached Raetihi.

I'm not sure if it was my focus on the phone, or the combination of an uneven road surface and spongy car springs, but I felt increasingly uncomfortable and asked Archer to pull over at the next rest area for a moment so I could stretch my legs. He obliged, and the minute we got out the car was surrounded by a group of tourists who insisted on taking turns photographing themselves with the Pontiac in the background. I thought Archer would hate the attention but to my surprise he seemed to love it, inviting some of the more curious to climb inside and sit behind the wheel while he took their picture. After a minute or two I walked off a short distance to breathe in the fresh air, and then, despite my promise, checked my phone: a new text message. When I opened it, a photograph appeared, framed within a small box, but because of the glare on my phone I couldn't make it out and had to angle myself away from the sun, placing my thumb and finger on the screen to stretch out and enlarge the picture. The blurred pinkish image wasn't immediately clear and I had to peer more closely, and then, with a jolt, I yelped and jumped backwards, and my phone fell to the ground. I made another sound, a strangled 'eugh' that must have been loud enough to capture Archer's attention because he hurried over to ask what was wrong.

'On my phone,' I said, pointing.

Archer picked up the phone and refreshed the screen. He said nothing, but a moment later the phone beeped again and he read aloud: 'Hi Siân. How do you like my stripped back thesis? LOL. Jessica.'

I snatched the phone off him and deleted the text.

'A penis?' said Archer. 'Was that a photo of a penis?'

Without thinking, I handed the phone back to Archer, then wiped my hands across my trousers as if that might help get rid of what I'd seen.

'Wait,' said Archer. 'That's Jessica? Your commerce student?'

I nodded. 'I think so.' The phone beeped again. 'What is it now?' I asked.

Archer read slowly, 'Send pic of your edits to me? See what you have.'

'Please stop it,' I said. 'Turn it off.'

From the corner of my eye I could see a guy leaning over the bonnet of Archer's car, holding a phone in one hand and making a peace sign with the other. I felt sick. On the ground by my feet was a used tissue, and scattered around the rest area were bits of litter, discarded food and plastic bottles. Everything was so filthy. The fresh air was tainted. The hairs in my armpits began to prickle and bead with sweat. I felt dirty and so, so stupid.

'Can we get out of here?' I asked.

'Sure,' said Archer.

'Can you keep the phone? I don't want it.'

'I can do that for you.'

A burst of air, a long drawn-out whimper, escaped me. 'I really thought I'd found a student. I honestly believed it was a job, that everything would improve. God, I'm so ashamed.'

I couldn't get the image of the penis out of my head. It seemed to be poking out of my phone towards me, as if insisting I take hold of it. The sensation of warm, slightly damp skin against my hand. Prodding, prodding. I kept replaying her mocking words in my mind. Stupidly, I had to keep correcting myself: him not her. There was no Jessica, only some creep with my name, email address and phone number.

'Are you okay?' asked Archer.

'Yes, fine.'

'I'm sorry this has happened to you.'

'It doesn't matter. It's my own fault.'

'No. No, it's not.'

'Thanks.' Tears began to well up in my eyes. 'I thought I'd got a job. I even imagined turning my spare room into an office, a place where I could see students. Oh, my God, what if he gives my number to his friends? I was going to charge $24 an hour. That probably makes me sound like a prostitute, doesn't it?'

'No, not at all. It makes you sound like a tutor.'

'What was I thinking?'

Jessica. Not a well-presented twenty-something. Not a young woman who wore jeans or leggings with sweatshirts, a woman who was often surrounded by friends, who went home to her family during the summer break, a woman who got drunk at parties but not so drunk that she'd feel sick the next day. My Jessica was the type of woman who was a little surprised and secretly proud that she'd made it through to a PhD. Jessica wore perfume and highlighted her hair and waxed her legs and would never send a photo of herself, naked, to a stranger. My Jessica didn't have a penis.

It dawned on me for the first time that the man who'd sent the image had no pubic hair. He'd shaved himself before taking the photo. That's why I hadn't immediately recognised the pink blob. In my confusion I'd thought it was some kind of gelatinous dessert or a creature like an axolotl.

'He had no pubic hair.'

'Really? I didn't notice.'

'What is wrong with this world?'

I felt contaminated. My phone, too. A smell materialised. An awful sweet, musty, sweaty, cheesy smell, tacky in texture. As we drove along the smell turned acrid in my nose and I had to wind down the window to let in some fresh air. Even that didn't get rid of it. It became stronger and stronger and I could practically taste it in my mouth.

'Listen, do you mind pulling over for a moment? I need to get something from my bag.'

'Sure.'

'Sorry.'

I knew that somewhere in my travel case of perfumes was a bottle of 4711, a cologne that accompanied me everywhere. Its aromatic citrus blend reminded me of the coarse paper refresher towelettes you used to get with your in-flight meal on planes. It was the kind of fragrance that could obliterate anything, I hoped. It would have the power to make me feel *clean*.

My bottle wasn't quite half full but it would do. Back in my seat, I sprayed my neck, my collar, my wrists, my forearms and inhaled. Then, while Archer watched, I sprayed the air. The initial burst of cologne caught in my throat, and seemed to fill my lungs, causing me to cough. I sprayed again. Archer sneezed.

'How much do you need?'

'All of it, I think.'

I breathed in and my chest hurt. I began to feel wheezy, and I coughed again and again.

'Can you smell it?' I asked.

Archer shook his head. 'No, but I can taste it in the back of my throat. I think you're going to suffocate us if you're not careful.'

'I'm sorry.'

I wanted to take away the smell of the photo. I wanted to disinfect my surroundings, wipe down every surface and scrub it clean. But even that wouldn't be enough to get rid of the stench. I had to fight an urge to strip down to my underwear and rub my skin in an attempt to rid myself of the 'Jessica' stain.

'Can you pass me my phone?'

Archer reached into his pocket and passed it over. 'What are you going to do?'

I had no idea. I realised in that moment that I lacked the strength to do anything.

'What are you doing?' Archer sounded worried.

'Nothing,' I said. 'Nothing.'

Notes of nothing: The time I was four years old, playing by the creek. I liked the smell of the water, it was swampy, like pond water but also peppery and slightly bitter. It was a good smell. On this day, while poking a stick into the mud, a boy of around thirteen approached me and asked to see my knickers. I said nothing. He told me to go under the bridge with him, and when I hesitated he pulled down his tracksuit pants and hooked out his penis through a tear in his underpants. When I was a teenager, walking home from school, I was approached by a man on a bicycle who repeated, 'I want to fuck you', as he trailed after me all the way home. He was there again the next day, and the next. I took a different route, adding thirty minutes to my journey. At school camp, the instructor with breath that smelt of dog shit, lining us girls up to help buckle our waist harnesses at the top of the abseil rock. On the first day we all stood still, smiling sheepishly, while he fumbled with the buckles and webbing around our crotches. The following day a sense of dread kept us quiet as he pressed his body against ours and ran his hands around our waists, our bottoms. On the third day, half the girls complained of being sick, of having sore throats, migraines and colds to avoid his session. On a plane to Europe, the man in the seat next to mine woke me from sleep when his hand slipped under my blanket and travelled to my inner thigh. In an artist's studio a sixty-something sculptor cornered me and ran his hands over my body while describing how he would have 'had me' in his younger days. The day the dentist stroked my cheek and asked for details of my sexual history while waiting for the anaesthetic to take effect. The evening a man followed me from the train station and along the deserted streets of my neighbourhood, causing me to double back into town and sit in a café until I felt it would be safe to go home. The night the proprietor of the hotel let himself into my room during the early hours of the morning to check I was 'warm enough'. And so it goes on, year after year, all these events and many more where I've let myself down by doing nothing. Not quite nothing, for the one constant in all of these episodes is the smell of my sweat. Not the scent of a healthy body drenched in perspiration caused by strenuous exercise but the sickly stench of onion that arises from armpits tacky with sticky sweat, the result of anxiety and fear.

Poor Archer. He tried everything to cheer me up. 'Did I ever tell you about my first job?' he said, as we ventured off the main road at Horopito to stop outside the vast car wreckers made famous in the movie *Smash Palace*.

'Bartending?'

'No, my very first job.'

I shook my head.

'When I was around sixteen I got a job in a family-owned toupee manufacturing business in New York.'

He glanced across at me and ran his hand over his smooth head. 'I know, funny, right?'

'Was it a good job?'

'I found it creepy, to tell the truth. The hair came from Italy, bags and bags of it, and I had to sort it by type, length and colour. That part wasn't so bad, but once it was attached to lace and made into hairpieces . . . ugh, no thank you.'

The rusting bodies of vehicles extended into the distance. Close to where we sat, Fords were lined up in rows, some stacked one on top of the other. None of the cars were whole. Most had doors or headlights missing, others lacked bonnets or bootlids. From one car to the next, there was such a variety of colour that the car-strewn paddocks took on a painterly, somewhat impressionistic appearance. It was almost beautiful.

'Do you want to have a look around?'

Archer shook his head. 'Not today. Maybe on the way back.'

'Are you sure? They might have some Pontiacs . . .'

Archer wavered, scanned the area between us and the railway line. 'I'm sure they do.'

I expected him to change his mind but he seemed content sitting in the car, taking in the view the way that people who park near airports watch planes land and take off.

'Andy Warhol was a local, though I never saw him.'

'When you made toupees?'

'No. Later, when I was hitting on Renate.'

I waited, knowing he would continue.

'It's a long time ago. Can't believe how long.'

In the distance we could see two men checking out a Holden station wagon, the same model my friend's mother had driven when we delivered meals on wheels. That one had been golden, but the Holden in the scrapyard was a rusted green, faded from the sun.

'Have you heard of the Green Guerillas?' asked Archer.

'No.'

'Well, back in the early seventies a group of activists took over a vacant lot in the Bowery and turned it into a community garden, the first in New York.'

'You've lost me. What's that got to do with Andy Warhol?'

'Nothing. But I used to walk past the restaurant where he dined, Ballato's, on my way to the bar where I worked. After passing his restaurant I'd continue on down Houston Street, and that's when I spotted Renate working in the garden. She wore a yellow headscarf so she was easy to spot. It took me six months to pluck up the courage to talk to her.'

'You were shy?'

'Guess so. She put me in charge of sunflowers.'

The windows inside the Pontiac had started to mist over and the air was cool and a little damp. I stretched and shuffled in my seat, leaning forward to wipe the glass with the cuff of my jumper. The surface smeared and streaked, making it difficult to see. 'I think we should get out and go for a walk.'

We left the car beside the road and began walking along the perimeter fence. Mount Ruapehu, snow capped, stood monumental in the distance. We passed a line of Hillman cars and I stopped in front of an Imp, the car my mother had driven when

I was still at primary school. It had a tendency to roll from side to side with every turn of the wheel. I've never been so sick as I was in that car. Looking at this one reminded me of the taste of vomit rising from the back of my throat and my futile attempts to swallow it back down.

We came to the main entrance and turned in, following narrow shingle and dirt trails between walls of vehicles. Here the cars seemed older and rustier. Glimpsed at the end of one row was grass and a huddle of sheep that slowly and reluctantly made way as we drew nearer. We were standing in the middle of the yard, a small open square of land that was covered in pellets of sheep and rabbit droppings. Ahead of us was a gully filled with dark native bush, beyond that the mountain. Surrounding us, pile after pile of wrecked bodies.

We continued in silence, circling back towards some large corrugated iron sheds. We passed old buses, trucks, a collection of Morris Minors. Many of the cars were adorned with spider webs, spun in the gaps between wing mirrors and bonnets. Like the stacks of chrome bumper bars we'd seen earlier, they caught the light and glinted as we meandered by.

Ahead of us was a shed, and inside we found ourselves surrounded by what, at first glance, appeared to be strange silver eggs. They were headlamps, hundreds and hundreds of them, grouped by model and size on the floor, above our heads and all around us. Few of the hanging lamps had glass, and their disembodied silver sockets followed us around as we moved carefully through the cramped room and on into the next.

'I think I like it better outside,' I said.

'Okay.'

We started back for the main entrance, following a path we hadn't taken before, past the wire remains of car seats, springs and coils spilling out onto the ground in front of us. Some of the springs looked almost new; others were so ancient they were little more than jagged wires poking up out of the long grass.

Archer stopped in front of a large car, the chrome features of its massive art deco radiator grille sweeping elegantly all the way back past a row of vents to its front doors. With the exception of the chromework, the entire car was rusted, small swatches of verdigris dominating the once gleaming black paintwork.

'That's your car,' I said.

'Yes.'

The bonnet was partially raised, revealing a gaping hole where the engine should be. The headlamps were also missing, leaving two featureless sockets staring blindly ahead. The only part of the car that was undamaged was the windscreen. Despite its good condition, patches of lichen, some white, some brown, spread up the glass in dulled rainbow curves.

We climbed in, carefully taking our places side by side. Archer rested his hands on his knees; the steering wheel was gone. I could feel the hard springs beneath me through the tattered seat, patches of straw and grass mixed with metal and leather. Whoever had been here before us had lowered the sun visors. It felt as though the car had been driven to this spot and then left without thought, almost as if the driver and passenger might return, start up the engine and continue their journey.

'Do you get the feeling we belong here?'

Archer laughed.

I turned in my seat, and saw what looked like a nest built in the springs of the back seat.

'Shall we go?'

'Yes,' I said.

Notes for a dear friend: I'm beginning to wonder if friendship or companionship should have a smell. It seems a pity that both love and sex have registered so forcibly in perfume – the first symbolised through roses, the second through layers of skanky musks and heady indoles – and yet friendship has not. A fragrance of friendship might be quieter, less attention-seeking than one symbolising love or sex, but it would have longevity; its base notes would linger, always in the background.

I know, now, that I've found a true friend in Archer. He means more to me than the pipe and slippers man I envisage when I take in his physical appearance. He means more to me than the sly joke of the Susan Sarandon lemon and oyster concoction. In imagining a perfume of friendship the word steadfast comes to mind. I want to honour what he means to me; I want my perfume to be an expression of gratitude. I'm reminded, too, that our friendship is mutual, and so the perfume should represent the bond between us. I will add something that I love to the perfume so when he smells it (which, ironically, he won't) he will be reminded of me.

For Archer I will build a scent around lilacs, ivy, ink and leather. I have a picture in my mind of a man seated in a quiet room, working at a desk. A door opens up onto a small garden; it's spring and the lilac is in bloom. His house is old, covered in ivy. The image references the writers and works he taught, Whitman, Eliot, Faulkner, but only in an abstract sense. I'm not drawing on a line from verse.

Lilac itself doesn't play a major role in men's perfume. It's not traditionally masculine. In fact most people would place it with violets or hyacinth as old-fashioned and fusty, the type of fragrance used to scent linen drawers or bath salts. Using lilac for Archer's scent indicates a softer, gentler side. It also implies a short passage of time: most lilacs bloom for only two weeks or so, not long at all.

I want to contrast the fleeting nature of lilac with something suggestive of a deeper commitment, a relationship that endures after the flowers have faded. A plant with longevity, tenacious in spirit. Ivy. I love the smell of ivy. The first impression you get when you crush the leaves in your fingers is something quite astringent and green, like flower stalks but sharper. Then the smell becomes earthier, partly like freshly dug roots, but then it transforms again, becoming more fungal, almost like a paper bag filled with mushrooms. I like the fact that ivy is common, widespread and frequently overlooked. It's not one of those fussy, special plants that needs to be pampered. It gets on with its life. Importantly, it symbolises friendship, tenacity, eternal love. It's also associated with Bacchus. Archer will know that; he worked in a bar, after all.

Ink and leather: jottings in a notebook. Ink has worked its way into more and more perfumes in recent years. It's a strange note, simple – what you'd expect if you sniffed a bottle of Indian ink. More interesting to me is lampblack, the black pigment used in ink that came from the sooty residue of oil lamps. Lampblack features a nice undercurrent of tar whereas, to me, ink is softer, earthier, like moss. I think lampblack might give body and depth and darkness to Archer's perfume. It is the note of death and decay, the elegiac twist that the scent needs. Leather? Now I think of it I'll leave it out. Lilac, ivy – the scent I love and want to share – and lampblack: a perfume of friendship for Archer. Ivy. The scent is so beautiful I will also add it to my own collection of heart notes as a constant reminder of my bond with Archer.

On a rise above a bush-clad valley, Archer pulled over for a final check of his messages. He climbed onto a boulder, holding his phone high above his head; for a moment he reminded me of the

Statute of Liberty, albeit a balding, wobbly version. He signalled to me and I climbed out to see what he wanted.

'This is the last place you can get reception. Do you want me to check for you, in case someone's got back to you about a job interview or something?'

I shook my head.

Archer touched my shoulder, resting his hand there. 'We can return tomorrow, anyway.'

I used to groan at the number of emails choking my inbox. There were times when I'd wake in the night and see the blue light flashing on my phone and spend an hour or more replying to requests, just so I didn't have to deal with them first thing in the morning. Most of my colleagues complained of the influx. I know that Jerome stopped responding to all of his. He'd forward them on to me with a pitiful, 'So, so sorry but I think you know more about this than me. Would you mind sorting out the details? Sorry to be a drag.' Sometimes I'd snap and return them with a curt, 'Too busy. You do it.' But often I'd feel sorry for the sender, or worry about the reputation of the department if the email went unanswered. I wasted so much time covering his correspondence, reading his grant applications, correcting them, flattering him.

What would I see on my phone now? The chances of it being anything I wanted to see were nil. In fact, I might as well become one of those people who keep their cell phone only 'in case of emergencies'. People like my mother, who succumbed to family pressure but rarely charged the battery. As she'd frequently said, she could always borrow someone else's if she needed to.

Behind me, Archer sighed.

'What is it?' I asked.

'Renate. I've barely seen her since I lost my job. She's always travelling. Guess I never noticed before . . .'

'You were too busy doing your own thing. But she'll be home soon.'

'Yes. I think she's flying in from Australia around midnight, from memory.'

He shrugged and scrambled down from his boulder. 'It's a good view, isn't it? It was even nicer before they started logging.'

The road narrowed and became more and more winding as we descended into the valley and along its floor. A strong smell of burnt rubber from overheated brakes filled the air, combining with the dust that had seeped in through the cracks in the windows and vents. The burning smell got stronger and stronger, and I was about to mention it to Archer when the road flattened out and all of a sudden we were driving through a new landscape of native bush and river flats, lush green paddocks scattered with yellow daffodils. As we drew near to an old homestead, Archer told me that it belonged to his nearest neighbour, Junee, a widow who kept her eye on his property. 'She always airs out the place and turns on the power when she knows I'm coming. We'll have hot water and ice, with any luck.'

We turned through a gateway and bounced along a deeply rutted, overgrown drive that passed through dense bush before finally opening out on a cleared section where a small board and batten timber dwelling with a large verandah took centre stage, surrounded by a smaller shed, picnic table and outdoor fireplace. Gardens occupied a raised bank behind the house, and from where I sat I could make out clumps of daffodils and what looked like lemon trees.

'Here we are,' said Archer. 'Welcome.'

People who are particularly fond of their houses tend to stand outside for longer than usual before unlocking the door and going in. It's a process of taking the measure of a place, reacquainting yourself with its mood or pace. This is what Archer did. He stood still, feeling the fresh air on his face and listening to the birds that called from the trees. He then led the way up to the planted area, pausing to show me the citrus trees planted in the warm shelter of a large water-tank. 'This is my cocktail garden,' he said as he plucked a handful of well-ripened lemons and limes from the tree. 'There's mint by that tap and over there is a cranberry bush and next to it a blackthorn so I can make my own sloe gin.'

Beyond the cocktail garden was a neat arrangement of herbs and native planting, bordered by larger trees. In the ground at the foot of some of the plants were neatly painted name plaques, similar to the type found in botanic gardens. 'This is what Renate refers to as her Mother Aubert garden,' Archer explained. 'I don't know much about it, to be honest, but nearly everything here is medicinal.' We followed a wood-chipped path, pausing to read out the names: horopito, kawakawa, raukawa, rewarewa, tarata.

'How are they used?' I asked.

'I can't tell you. The only one I really know is horopito, which is peppery. But there are a couple of books on the shelves inside that might explain, and I think Renate's recipe book is around somewhere. Go and take a look if you're interested.'

We passed the remains of a vegetable garden that was mostly weeds with rhubarb and fennel to one side, before turning back to the front of the house, inspecting the picnic table made from rough-hewn macrocarpa and the fire-pit, and then finally stepping up onto the verandah where gumboots and boots were neatly lined up beneath an old pew. After unlocking the door, Archer stood back to allow me inside.

As I stepped in I got a whiff of seagrass from the floor, but more noticeable were the beautiful dappled colours of yellow, red and green on its surface from the abstract design on a pane of stained glass hanging on wires from the ceiling. 'Renate had it made for my fiftieth,' said Archer. 'Beautiful, isn't it?'

One wall of the bach was covered from floor to ceiling with books, and against the back wall was a drinks cabinet brimming with bottles and glasses of all shapes and sizes. 'Bathroom through there,' said Archer, pointing to a bright yellow doorway. 'You have the choice of the bed in the loft or the fold-out couch in Renate's study. That's where she keeps her books. Come, I'll show you.'

We entered a small, dark room. The air was cold, and when Archer raised the blind, bottles in various shades of blue and green were revealed, lined up on the windowsill. Built-in beneath the window was a long wooden bench on which stood glass jars filled with various bit and pieces, feathers, tools, and, to one side, a few empty amber-coloured bottles – the type I used for my perfume blends. A glass-fronted cabinet, smaller than Archer's drinks cabinet, displayed more amber bottles, some labelled with the contents, and above that was a shelf crammed with books. 'The reference library,' he said, picking up a book and flicking through its dog-eared pages. Attached to the wall above the couch were two fly-fishing rods made from bamboo.

'It's dark and a bit damp,' said Archer, 'but it'll warm up once we get the fire going.'

'Perfect,' I said.

'Or you're welcome to the loft, if you want. That's where I store my albums.'

I shook my head. 'No, this is fine.'

Only then, after the full tour of the garden and house, did we begin to unpack the car, stacking boxes of food and clean linen in a heap on the table. As we put things away, Archer described the holidays he, Renate and Hester had spent building the cabin. 'We started with all three of us camping out in the small shed. Junee's husband was still alive and he did most of the real construction work on the cabin, but we chipped in as much as we could. It was very satisfying, creating something from scratch, a place built to last. It reminded Renate of her days in the Green Guerillas.'

'So why are you thinking of selling?'

'I don't know if I am, to be honest. But I guess we don't make it down here as often as we used to now that Renate's got so busy with work. I could come down on my own, I guess. Spend my days out on the porch.'

'I don't think so.'

Archer shrugged. 'How are you, anyway? Are you okay?'

'Surviving.'

'Good.'

We devoted the afternoon to cutting firewood and sanding down window frames, Archer up on the stepladder, me working on the sills. We didn't talk much, though every now and again I heard Archer humming to himself, a tune that sounded a lot like '9 to 5', though sung by someone who knew only half of the lyrics. I was beginning to grow tired and bored and was wondering how I could suggest a break without giving up, when Archer called, 'Cocktail hour.' It wasn't quite five.

I hadn't drunk cocktails since Archer's *Thelma & Louise* party, a night that started innocently enough with beer, but soon took off with variations on the classic redhead recipe. Never much of a drinker, I couldn't hold my liquor and was soon out of my depth. One of my last images, before giving up and going to my bunk, was seeing Jerome with his arm draped around Archer's shoulders, telling him how much he admired and respected him, and how professors like him were one in a million. *One in a million!* Jerome must have said it four or five times, before turning to the others and exclaiming, 'Would you look at this guy! One in a million.' Archer, far more sober than the rest of us, laughed off the compliment with a professional, 'Here's to your health!', before shrugging off Jerome's arm and going back to his chair in front of the movie. I didn't wake up until noon.

'So, I was thinking,' said Archer as I followed him to the kitchen, 'that we could start with a nice gin rickey made with my own sloe gin.' I watched as he measured and mixed the ingredients, enjoying the skill with which he worked. He passed the first drink to me and then made himself one, using exactly the same measurements.

'Let's go and sit outside,' he said.

The sun had fallen behind the ridge and the light was beginning to fade but it felt good to be sitting at last, facing each other across the picnic table.

'Points if you can name the novel that features a gin rickey.'

'Something by Hemingway?' I guessed.

Archer shook his head.

'I'm going to go with F Scott Fitzgerald or Truman Capote, then.'

Archer looked pleased.

'I think it's not flamboyant enough for Capote so I'll try Fitzgerald.'

'Yes. But which book?' Archer tapped his glass and waited.

'*Tender Is the Night*?'

Archer shook his head. 'Nope. *The Great Gatsby*. The lunch party when Tom twigs that Daisy loves Gatsby, before they all drive off into town.'

'I was going to say that!' I joked.

'We used to have Gatsby nights at one of the bars where I worked. None of the regulars took part. They'd sit at the counter and roll their eyes, blowing smoke from their cigarettes and downing bourbon, while all around them office workers and East Village types got tipsy and crashed into chairs, calling, "Sorry, old sport!"' He paused and took a sip from his glass. 'So, how do you like your drink?'

'Good. Delicious. There's a bit of fruit?'

'That's the sloe. Plummy but bitter.'

Despite having had only one drink I could feel the alcohol take effect. I hadn't eaten since breakfast; somehow I hadn't got around to it.

'You want another?' asked Archer.

'Maybe?'

We went inside, and as Archer laid the fire I pulled together some snacks: bread and cheese, hummus, smoked salmon, tomatoes and cucumber. I laid out more than I thought we'd need. I was already unsteady on my feet and I wanted to make sure there was food close at hand.

Smoke from the fire sagged and rolled out of the firebox, and I watched as Archer took a deep breath and blew, the embers glowing, then flickering, as the dry wood caught. He continued to puff and within minutes the smoke disappeared as the blaze took hold. He lit the candles on the table, their flames casting yellow circles of light over the polished wood. 'We do have lights, if you want something brighter.'

'No, it's fine.'

We took it in turns to serve ourselves, happy to linger over the meal. Unlike me, Archer picked at his food. I ate most of the bread, relieved that it filled my stomach and cleared my head. Little conversation passed between us but as the meal drew to a close, I asked Archer how long he'd spent as a barman.

'Years, off and on. It was a good job, interesting.'

'Did Renate share your enthusiasm for cocktails?'

He shook his head, but then he reconsidered. 'We used to experiment using the produce she brought home from the garden. The results lacked the depth and complexity of a true cocktail but they were pretty good. You can turn anything into a decent drink once you've mastered the basics of mixing.'

'Perfume?'

He looked puzzled.

'Perfume? Could you translate a perfume into a cocktail.'

'Sure. Easy. What have you got?'

I went into Renate's room and came back with a small vial of Mitsouko, filled from a 1950s vintage bottle I'd bought off eBay when I still had a job and made the occasional extravagant purchase. I'd spent weeks researching old bottles, packaging, batch numbers, doing everything to calm my nerves, but even so I knew I was taking an extraordinary gamble when I bought it. Apart from the obvious problem that it might be fake, I was worried that the juice might have deteriorated. But Mitsouko had been my first strange love and so I did the unimaginable and placed a bid. With the exchange rate and shipping it came to $978, the most I'd ever spent on a perfume – the most I'd ever spend.

I remember how good the bottle felt in my hand when it finally arrived but, despite my excitement, I couldn't bring myself to break open the neck seal and release the perfume. It was too much responsibility. One day, there would be no more vintage Mitsouko; it was finite. The bottle sat on my table for days, and then weeks. In the end, I took the perfume to work and handed it over to Jerome. He was eating his lunch when I went in, and as he took the scent from me he held his sandwich in his mouth so that he could use both hands to release the cap. My eyes scanned from the lettuce escaping the two slices of brown bread to the padded cotton neck protector that he ripped off without a moment's hesitation. Then, pausing to take a bite, he broke the seal on the bottle, all the while chewing the crust of his sandwich. Instead of passing the bottle back to me he wriggled the stopper free and inhaled, still with food in his mouth. He plonked the bottle down. 'Smells kind of fusty, like wet hamsters.'

'Describe the smell for me,' said Archer as he arranged his cocktail shaker and tumblers on the table.

'Well, if I were to express the fragrance in its most basic terms I'd say orange and lemon peel, peach, cinnamon, clove and oakmoss. A perfect fruity chypre.'

'When was it made?'

'Nineteen nineteen.'

'Okay. Wait and I'll see what I can find.'

He went to the bar and began pulling out bottles, holding them up, turning them in his hand, keeping some, putting others back. He disappeared into the kitchen and I could hear cupboards banging. Minutes passed before he returned. He set down his ingredients and said, 'The sidecar. A cocktail that dates back to the First World War. It's very simple: cognac, triple sec and lemon juice.'

By the time he'd described the drink, it was made, and he pushed it across to me. I took a sip and held the mix in my mouth. It wasn't as bitter as I thought it should be for the perfume reference. I passed it back to Archer with a nod.

'Not impressed?'

'No, I like it.'

'That's our starting point. So you understand the basic construction.'

I reached across the table for another taste and, without thinking, drained the glass. 'It needs peach and moss,' I said. 'And something dry, aromatic. It's too sweet.'

I pulled off a piece of bread, hacked off a hunk of cheese and popped it all into my mouth. I noticed that the room was getting increasingly warm; the fire was doing an excellent job. Automatically, I pulled out my phone to check for texts but then remembered 'Jessica' and shuddered. I should have blocked her before now but as long as there was no reception I was safe anyway.

'Peach. I found a tin in the cupboard so let's see what I can do with that. Moss is going to be difficult.' He paused, scratched his head and then I heard him mumble, 'Aquavit? No.'

He began to prepare another version of my cocktail. He put some orange and lemon peel in a silver mixing tin and pressed it with something like a long-handled wooden pestle. Next he added orange wedges and sliced peaches from the tin and pressed again. He caught my eye and held up the pestle for me to see.

‘A muddler,’ he said. ‘I’m not sure how the tinned peaches will go but, as Emerson says, if we aim above the mark we might hit the mark.’

Next he added some bitters, some Cointreau and the cognac, filling the mixing glass almost to the surface with ice. He stirred the drink, then strained it into a highball. He passed a strip of orange peel around the rim of the glass, added a cinnamon quill.

I sniffed. ‘Cinnamon. Orange.’ I then sipped the drink and held it in my mouth before swallowing. I could detect the peach but also the darker aromatic of the bitters.

‘It’s really good.’

‘Is it Mitsouko?’

‘Closer.’ I tried it once more. ‘I like it.’

‘But it’s not right yet?’

‘No. I know . . . give me a go. I know what to do. We need some moss.’

I stood up. The top half of my body felt heavy and I lost my balance and had to steady myself. ‘There’s bound to be some moss outside.’ I took a step and bumped into the table. I reached for one of the candles but Archer got to it first and moved it away. ‘I’ll get a torch.’

It was far darker outside than I thought it would be. I’d forgotten that the night sky here was black. I managed the first step off the deck but missed the next one and stumbled, preventing myself from falling only by doing a little running skip until I regained my balance. I glanced back over my shoulder and saw Archer framed in the light of the door. He seemed to be fussing with his shoes so I set off across the grass towards the shed, anticipating that the older, damper stacks of wood would provide us with all the moss we needed. Behind me Archer called, ‘Careful’ and ‘Wait’, but I didn’t need to. ‘I’m going to muddle some moss!’ I yelled back. That made me laugh. Moss muddler. It sounded like something I should put on my CV. Current employment: moss muddler. Somehow I managed to walk into the picnic table but it didn't hurt. Then Archer was beside me, banging his torch against his thigh, trying to get it going. A dull yellow light flickered and went out. He took me by the arm and guided me across the grass to the shed.

'I don't want that green spongy moss,' I instructed Archer. 'I want the grey hairy stuff, like proper oakmoss.'

I saw Archer crouch down and scrape at something with his fingers, and then he was beside me, a tatter of lichen in his hand. 'Do you think it's poisonous?' he asked.

I shrugged. 'We'll find out.'

I took it from him and sniffed. It was papery and peppery, with a touch of cinnamon.

'What about horopito?' asked Archer.

'What about it?'

'Well, it should have a nice peppery taste. A bit like bay leaf or laurel. We could try it, though it might be too bitter.'

He led the way around the back of the house to the Mother Aubert garden and plucked a couple of leaves. 'Could work,' he said.

'Could work,' I repeated.

'At least it won't kill us.'

'Not if we muddle it up first.'

'Yep. Gently.

'A gentle muddle.'

'That's it.'

Archer steered me back inside and sat me down at the table while he cleaned the mixing glass. 'Remember, you can't go stuffing everything in together and expect it to turn out well. There's an art to it.'

I laughed. He wasn't telling me anything I didn't already know.

I took two leaves of horopito, put them in the bottom of the glass and pressed the muddler hard against them. I must have pressed too hard, or not held the muddler straight enough, because the glass suddenly tilted and skidded out from under my hand, rolling across the table. Archer winced. I started again.

'Don't bruise the leaves. You don't need to apply such force.'

'Don't worry. I know what I'm doing.' In a singsong voice I continued, 'Crush the cinnamon. Add the horopito. Muddle. Two peach quarters. Muddle. Syrup from tin. Muddle. Cognac.'

I was missing the ice. And something else, I couldn't recall what. 'Cointreau,' I went on as I sloshed it out. 'Bitters to taste . . .'

'Not too heavy on the bitters.'

'Bit more bitters! Ice. Stir. Around and around and around, and around. And strain. Into a glass.'

'What about your moss?' asked Archer.

'And,' I said, raising my finger like a conductor counting in an orchestra, 'a garnish of orange rind and a hint of moss and there you have it.'

I slid the glass to Archer and he took a polite sip and coughed. 'Certainly strong.'

'Give it here.' I raised the glass to my mouth, tilted it and then stopped. 'You must sniff it first,' I said. 'Appreciate the bouquet.' I inhaled and something made me sneeze. I sniffed again, more gently, and I don't know, it smelt okay to me. I took a big gulp. Boy, it was bitter but I pretended it was fine. 'Delicious.' I sipped and held the cocktail in my mouth. 'Have you got any absinthe in your cabinet?' I asked. 'I think absinthe is what's missing here. Don't you?'

I could see that Archer was having trouble keeping up with the programme. He looked so puzzled, like a young boy trying to figure out how to tie a shoelace. 'Absinthe,' I repeated. 'The wood of the worm, wormwood.'

'You mean like a Sazerac? Absinthe and cognac.'

'Sazerac? Yep, that'll do it.' I took a long sip of my cocktail.

And spluttered. 'It's not really a Shalimar. It needs more vanilla. Have you got a vanilla pod?'

'What's a Shalimar?'

'The perfume. What did you think? It's what we're making.'

'I thought we were making a Mitsouko.'

I fell silent. I had a feeling he was right. Not that it mattered. They were both terrific perfumes and I could happily drink either.

'Absinthe,' I ordered.

From the corner of my eye I saw Archer wander across to the bar and look inside. His hand reached into the cabinet but then he paused and turned back to face me. 'Are you sure? It's very strong, almost seventy proof.'

'Just for the taste of it.'

He shook his head and came back to the table, carrying a deep green bottle with a label bearing the word 'Sauvage'. That was a good sign. One of the best male perfumes of modern times was Dior's Eau Sauvage. I told Archer so as he pulled his chair closer to the table.

'Do you want to try it first? So you can appreciate how it tastes before you add it to your cocktail?'

'Sure. Why not?'

When he made no move I reached for the bottle and yanked out the cork. I recognised the smell straight away: it was similar to the bottle of Artemisia oil I had at home. I was about to pour the drink into a glass when Archer stopped me. 'No, not like that. We have to louche it.'

'You don't muddle it?'

He shook his head. 'No, I louche it.'

'You're quite louche yourself.'

He looked at me as though he'd heard that joke before, so I shut up and watched as he poured a small quantity of the emerald green liquor into a glass. He passed it to me to smell and I took a deep breath. 'Nice,' I said.

'You wait,' said Archer. 'It'll be even better in a minute.'

He took a spoon with holes and balanced it against the rim of the glass, placing half a lump of sugar on it. Next he put a special straw into a glass of iced water and drew up the liquid, filling the bulb at its end. Then, holding the straw over the spoon, he began slowly to release the water, allowing it to fall drop by drop onto the sugar lump.

The clear green liquid began to cloud ever so slightly in the base of the glass. As Archer continued to drip in water, the level rose but it didn't become cloudy all at once. Rather, a band of clear liquid rested on top of the cloudy base. Finally, only the thinnest film of undiluted, clear liquid remained, hovering above the milky mix. At that point Archer took away the spoon and gave the drink a gentle stir. 'The ritual of la louche, just for you.'

I drained the glass and wiped the residue off my lips with the back of my hand.

'Hmm,' said Archer. 'I think that's enough for one night.'

'Rubbish.'

'You should stop while you're ahead.'

'Says who?'

He smiled. 'Me.'

I saw Archer's hand hover over the absinthe bottle and I snatched it away from him, sheltering it in the hug of my arms.

'That's right. Leave the bottle. I like the taste. It's bitter. Like my heart.'

Poor Archer rolled his eyes at that. 'I think I'll leave you to it.'

'That's right, old sport!' I laughed. I'd always noticed that my humour became sharper and more sophisticated when I drank. Something to do with losing inhibition and opening a direct channel to the creative brian . . . brain.

'Call me if you need anything,' said Archer.

'And I'll be there!'

Archer hesitated but I shooed him away. I had cocktails to

make. Je Reviens! No. 19! And for Jessica, a big glass of Poison. Base note, heart note, top note. Simple.

I felt the light against my lids long before I summoned the strength to open my eyes. I looked around, trying to take in my surroundings. I was surprised to discover I was in a bed, the sofa bed in Renate's room. I was under the covers and, as far as I could tell, I was in my pyjamas. I had no recollection of how I'd got there.

I lay still, listening for the sound of Archer in the next room. Every now and again a wooden board creaked but I couldn't make out the sound of footsteps or movement. I had the distinct feeling I was alone in the house.

Slowly I pieced together the events of the previous night. The introduction to cocktail making, the hunt for moss, the attempt to make Mitsouko, the absinthe, and then what? I had a feeling I'd hunted out some spices from the food cupboard. What had I been making? Poison, wasn't it?

The floor beneath my feet felt uneven but at least it was firm. Little by little events came back to me. I remembered getting undressed. I'd managed that by myself. My shoes were placed neatly on the floor by my suitcase. I hadn't been too drunk to be tidy. That was a good sign. My trousers were hanging over the back of the chair. I needed coffee and then I'd help Archer with the painting. I wasn't nearly as sick as I might have been. I'd got off lightly, all things considered.

The table was clear. All the bottles and glasses from the night before were back on the shelves. The fruit was in a bowl on the bench. The peaches were in the fridge, along with the jar of honey. On the table was a small stem vase containing two daffodils and a sprig of rosemary. I couldn't see Archer outside. He wasn't working on the window frames, and when I went around to the front I realised that his car was gone. I checked my watch. It was almost eleven.

I was halfway through my second cup before I noticed the note propped up on the mantelpiece. 'Checking in with Junee and then will try to phone Renate. Back around lunchtime. Arch. P.S. Keep away from the Bloody Mary. It is not your friend.'

The rafters creaked but, because of my hangover, the sound seemed muffled, as if removed from where I was. It was the sound of absence. To fill that silence I put on one of Archer's classical albums and made breakfast, managing only one or two bites of my toast before pushing it aside. After showering I gathered up some books from Renate's shelves and spread them out before me on the table. I thought I'd read for a moment or two, just until I could tolerate the scratch of sandpaper against timber, and then I'd get on with the sanding.

My attention was drawn to a leather-bound notebook with 'Recipes' embossed in gold on its cover. I opened it and on its first page, in green, purple and yellow felt pen, was the heading 'Rongoā/Mother Aubert'. Picking a page at random, I saw a recipe for an ointment used to treat rashes and bruises prepared from kawakawa. Another page contained a handwritten copy of a letter sent by Mother Aubert in Island Bay to the Sisters of Compassion in Jerusalem requesting seeds. Some of the names were familiar, the same plants I'd seen in Renate's medicinal garden during my tour of the property.

I glanced at my watch: it had gone lunchtime and there was no sign of Archer. I went outside and began walking around the garden, hoping to hear the approach of his car. Every few steps I stopped and listened, straining for the sound of an engine, but the air was still, with not even the rustle caused by the wind through the trees to break the silence. I scanned the driveway but again there was no movement. I was the only living thing and instinctively my hand searched out my phone, even though I knew there was no reception. Feeling cut off from the world, I started for the small rise at the back of the house. Standing on a log, I held my phone high above my head in the hope that one or more bars would light up. None did.

I decided to stroll down to the gate. I walked slowly, listing all the flowers, weeds and bushes I recognised on my way: daffodil, thistle, dandelion, flax, daisy, cabbage tree, rimu, fern and grass. At the gate I tiptoed across the cattle-stop and stood on the side of the road, looking first one way and then the other, listening for approaching traffic. I picked up a small piece of smooth, white rounded quartz that stood out from the rough gravel, dusted it off in my hand and put it in my pocket as if saving it for later. I crossed the road and checked my phone once more. Still nothing.

Unwilling to return indoors, I headed towards the woodshed. What on earth had I been thinking last evening? Now it was daylight I could see small blooms of lichen on the dried timber, green cushions on damp stumps. None of it looked at all like the images of oakmoss I'd seen illustrated in articles. Still, I pulled off a few samples and held them to my nose, enjoying both the dusty, earthy scent of the lichen and the damp, fusty odour of moss.

Back inside I prepared a salad for Archer's lunch. I worked slowly, still expecting him to turn up at any moment but definitely before the table was set. We could have a quick bite to eat and then get on with the painting, putting in a few hours' work before it became too cool or damp for the paint to dry. My sense of disquiet increased but I countered my nerves with a list of sensible explanations for his tardiness: he had decided to go to Raetihi for more supplies, the neighbour had invited him for lunch, his car had got a puncture, he'd been flagged down by cyclists on the Mountains to Sea trail, he'd decided on the spur of the moment to go for a walk by the river, Renate had asked him to call her back in an hour and rather than come all the way home he'd remained within cell phone coverage. He wouldn't be long, I kept telling myself.

I was trapped between two opposing spaces within my brain: one pragmatic, the other fearful. I wanted to escape to bed and sleep, but I went back to the books I'd collected from Renate's shelves and sat down with the intention of committing to memory the names of at least five scented native plants. This punishment, akin to writing lines, was to remind me that at my age I should know better than to drink myself under the table.

The resource I chose was a well-thumbed spiral-bound pictorial book of New Zealand natives, with plants listed alphabetically by their Māori names. I skipped the introductory section and started at 'A', but I couldn't concentrate so flicked forward, lurching from one entry to the next. At 'K' I ground to a halt, staring at an entry headed 'Kāretu' with a photograph of a clump of grass centred on the page.

The word kept blurring at the edges as my eyes struggled to keep the letters in focus. 'Concentrate, idiot.' I began reading aloud from the text in a clear and measured way, as if talking to a lecture theatre of first-year students. The slow, methodical manner made the words easier to absorb, and I managed to grasp some basic facts about kāretu: it was a sweet, vanilla–hay-scented grass; it was similar to the North American sweetgrass used in Native American rituals; Māori fashioned belts from its plaited strands. I scanned down the page to a small pale blue text box and suddenly the skin on the back of my neck prickled and my heart beat faster. There, in front of me, was the title 'Recipe for the grand Māori perfume' with the words 'Taylor notebook', followed by a number at the bottom.

A *grand Māori perfume*? Quickly I traced the listed ingredients with my finger as I read through the recipe. Mokimoki:

an aromatic fern. Tarata: a tree that produces scented resin. Kōpura: a moss or lichen found in the mountains. Taramea. Pātōtara. The names were mostly unknown to me. I couldn't begin to think of how the perfume might smell. Piripiri. I had a feeling this was the same as bidibidi, but I couldn't be sure. There could be more than one piripiri for all I knew. Kāretu – the vanilla-scented sweetgrass depicted in the photo at the top of the page. Hinu poaka. In brackets: pork fat. Pork fat I could almost understand. I imagined it was used for extracting or fixing the scent, just as the early French perfume makers had placed petals from delicate flowers, such as jasmine, onto wooden-framed glass panes spread with lard or other animal fats in order to draw out and capture their smell.

I looked up from the page. Despite spending years of my life focused on scent and perfume culture, I was ashamed to admit that I knew absolutely nothing about Māori perfume. I didn't even know it existed. I stared at the entry, working my way through the ingredients once more. I could 'smell' lots of perfume notes from memory but the only ones useful to me now were fern, moss and vanilla. As I read, I realised the name 'Taylor' was vaguely familiar. I looked for it in the index but there was only one entry, for the page I was on, and there was no bibliography with a list of detailed references. I couldn't even Google him.

There was no point fixating on Taylor. The first thing I had to do was go through the rest of the book and find scent descriptions of all the ingredients. I started with mokimoki. Common name: fragrant fern. There was no information about its smell. All I had were two words: 'aromatic' from the Taylor entry and 'fragrant' from the general entry. To me, aromatic suggested anything slightly bitter and herbal, but I suspected the description in the book was less specific. It could mean simply fern-like. I gave tarata only a brief glance, enough to learn that it was also known as lemonwood and that its leaves, when crushed, had a lemon scent. I was sure it was in Renate's garden so I could smell it for myself. Kōpura wasn't listed in the book, kāretu I'd already covered. Next was taramea. I recognised it immediately from its photograph: the sharp, spiky Spaniard grass that I knew from growing up in Canterbury. I couldn't recall ever having been aware of its scent, which the entry described only as 'sweet'. I felt frustration rise up within me. Why wasn't there more detail? Sweet could cover so many smells, from sugary to syrupy to nectar, honey-like, caramel, jam-like, even berries or fruit. So far, all I'd gleaned about the grand Māori perfume was that it contained elements that were aromatic, fragrant and sweet. It wasn't much to go on.

And where was Archer? I wanted to tell him about my discovery. Discovery. It was such a loaded word, but it described the sense of anticipation and excitement I felt. The next plant I found was pātōtara. Rather, there seemed to be two plants with that name: one a parsley fern and the other a small prickly heath pictured growing out of a patch of stones. The latter was described as having white 'honey-scented' flowers. At last, I thought, a fragrance that meant something to me. Finally, piripiri. I felt a tinge of satisfaction on reading that it was bidibidi but my satisfaction was short-lived because there was a second entry, another piripiri – a filmy fern whose dried leaves were described as smelling like blood.

On the back of Archer's note I made a list of the ingredients, writing their scents next to each plant, and sat back trying to summon the individual fragrances, mentally blending them as I juggled the parts: aromatic fern, lemon leaves, sweet resin, honey-scented flowers, dried blood. I couldn't, though, make them fit into my scent template. I could group some of the ingredients together, such as the lemon and honey, but once I started adding the dried blood I'd get lost.

I wanted to rush home, back to the city, and find a sample of the grand Māori perfume. Maybe the museum had one, a tester of the sweet, aromatic, bloody goodness? I was so impatient to find out what it was like and I felt certain that someone, somewhere must know.

It was more and more difficult to sit still so I headed out to Renate's garden. I found the tarata and plucked a leaf, crushing it in my fingers. Although there was a trace of lemon, I wasn't convinced I'd have been able to identify it without being primed by the description in the book. A few yellow flowers grew in clusters near the ends of the branches, and when I smelt them I detected a soft fragrance that was creamy and sweet, more like pollen than lemon. Finally, I plucked some soft leaf tips and crushed those and immediately the smell of grated lemon rind filled my nose. The scent faded, however, almost before I could fix the fragrance in my mind. I held the crushed leaves up to my nose again, and even though only a minute had passed the smell had all but diminished to a faint veil. I moved slowly through the garden, stopping whenever a name plaque or plant caught my attention. I noticed that the trunk of one large tree was covered with the long-fingered leaves of a climbing fern that I thought resembled the photograph of mokimoki I'd seen. I picked a leaf and bruised it, hoping that the scent would resemble blood, but no. I didn't bother to smell the heart-shaped leaves from the big kawakawa but circled back to the horopito, Archer's peppery plant.

I decided to walk down the driveway again. I remembered how I used to go down to the gate of my childhood home and look for my father coming home, usually about twenty past six. I missed him during the day, waited for him with the concentration and faith of a dog. Now, I watched for Archer with a similar sense of impatience and longing. His continued absence filled me with a dread that I could no longer suppress. I waited thirty, forty minutes, pacing from the gate to the road, where I tracked up and down, willing him into sight, afraid to leave the area in case I missed him. I stayed by the gate like the little girl I'd been, growing lonely as the sun slipped behind the hill. I knew something was wrong. I did what all people who find themselves alone and lost are told to do. I stayed put, waiting for someone to come and help.

Notes from here to there: There was a woman with a toddler on the seat next to me on the bus during the journey from Raetihi to Hamilton. The child was well behaved. He didn't wriggle, or cry, or kick the seats. He spent the entire journey looking at an iPad, building cars from bricks. He was so absorbed in the game that he was completely unaware of me, even when I began to cry. His guardian asked if she could do anything but I shook my head. I told her that my friend had been in an accident, driven off the road, and had been flown to Waikato Hospital. The police explained he was in a critical condition. The woman in the seat next to me said, 'I'll pray for him.' I nodded. She apologised for the smell coming from the boy. 'He needs his nappy changing. I think I might wait until the next stop – it's not far. It's a bit tricky otherwise.' I reassured her that I didn't mind. And that was true, I didn't.

Near Tūrangi I checked my phone and saw the word 'urgent'. The sender and the address were unfamiliar and I thought it must be the hospital, or Renate, or Hester so I opened the message. It contained a photo of an erect penis and the words, 'I'm waiting for you.' The boy in the next seat played his game, his guardian scrolled her phone. The couple across from me looked at their phones. The bus was unusually quiet, but perhaps not. No one texted to let me know Archer's condition. Why would they? I began to imagine I could smell burning brakes. I glanced around to see if anyone else had noticed but the driver appeared settled up in his seat; he didn't move. I could see his face reflected in the rear-view mirror; he looked bored. I could still smell the burning but I didn't speak up.

In recent years there have been a lot of articles about how people in the industrial world are slowly losing their sense of smell. We rely on our sense of sight far more heavily than we used to. Why sniff food when you can read a use-by date? In surveys young people state that they'd rather lose their sense of smell than their phone. And yet when the police officer arrived at Archer's cabin I knew he was a smoker. Not from the yellowish bristles on his moustache but from the smell of his body. Junee, who drove me to the bus stop, smelt of coffee – instant coffee. It was on her breath. The woman from whom I bought the bus ticket smelt of hair product, a sweet fruity-coconut scent. The driver smelt of sweat. Someone behind me was eating a banana. The seats were musty. The bus was burning. I looked out of the window.

I sank into the comfort of my home, exhausted.

The apartment was quiet. The air was still; it soothed me, enfolding me in the warm scent of wool and lanolin. Everything within my home was as I'd left it. It was as if it had been waiting for my return and now I was back it would take care of me and help me to regain some semblance of peace. I never wanted to leave again.

I sat down at my table, drawing in the traces of scent from the oils set out in front of me. The smell was muted, but I could detect some of the notes: the incense-like smell of frankincense, the beautiful rich Bulgarian rose, the smooth amber, the forest floor of oakmoss. I'd missed these smells. It felt so good to feel their presence once more.

I never wanted to step foot outside my home again. I never wanted to return to that hospital corridor, the gleaming linoleum and the smell of disinfectant, half-eaten dinners, sickness and grief. I had got there too late; Archer was dead.

Renate had arrived before me. She sat holding a brown paper bag containing Archer's personal belongings, and took a moment to recognise me as I entered the sitting area outside the morgue. On the bench beside her was a young woman, an almost-identical version of Renate. Although I'd never met her, I guessed straight away it was Hester.

'We're waiting for the funeral director, aren't we?' said Hester. 'We thought he'd be here by now.'

I held Renate in my arms. Her body felt frail and lacking in substance, as if hollow. 'What are we going to do without him? I'm so sorry.'

'I don't know,' she replied. 'Thank you for coming.'

'I got here as soon as I could.'

Despite the gravity of the moment we started talking about transport. Hester asked how I'd got there and when I explained that Junee had dropped me at the bus stop in Raetihi, she commiserated, adding uncertainly, 'We drove down together, didn't we, Mom?'

'How was the cabin?' asked Renate. Her voice sounded automated, as if responding to an on switch. 'I haven't been there for the longest time.'

'Good, beautiful,' I said. 'We only got started on the sanding, though. We were planning to finish the painting but then Archer . . .'

'That's okay,' said Renate.

'Your garden . . .'

Renate nodded and for a moment her eyes flickered, as if fighting to stay awake.

'It's beautiful,' I continued.

'Did Archie show you around?'

I nodded.

'Did he make you a cocktail? He's very good at cocktails. He used to be a bartender at Max's Kansas City? Did he tell you that?'

'That's a bar?' asked Hester.

'Nightclub,' said Renate. 'He was a party boy back then, still going strong at 5 a.m. even when he had lectures to attend.' Renate smiled and squeezed her daughter's hand, but her eyes had filled with tears. 'I often wonder if he wouldn't have been happier staying with that crowd. I think he only got caught up in academia because of me. Out of duty, the belief he should provide. I don't know, but I feel I crushed his spirit in some way, without intending to.'

'No,' I protested. 'He admired you. You're all he ever talked about – you and his work. He loved you so much.' I could feel my eyes prick at the thought of the conversations we'd had but then I realised my gaffe. 'He always talked about you, too, Hester. He was so proud of you.'

'Then why did he buy that crazy car behind my back?' said Renate. 'Why didn't he tell me? He'd been dropping hints for years and all that time I'd said, "You don't need it" or "It will cost a fortune in repairs – you're not a mechanic", and he'd drop the topic for a while but then slowly reintroduce it, hoping I'd come around. He always wanted a Pontiac and I never said yes. I was one of those wives . . .'

I looked at her, uncomprehending.

'You know, the type of wife who says no all the time. In the end the husbands have to sneak off and buy what they want in secret because they're scared of being told off.'

'No, I don't think that's true,' said Hester.

'Then why didn't he let me in? Because I was too mean. I should have said, "Hell yes, let's do it! Life's too short . . ."'

She fell quiet and looked past me towards a space over my shoulder. 'I should have said, "Go for it. You're a saint. You deserve it,"' she whispered.

'You weren't to know,' I said.

The minutes ticked by and there was still no sign of the funeral director. Suddenly, from out of nowhere, Hester asked, 'Do you want to go in and say goodbye?'

The finality of her question brought me to tears. I couldn't imagine anything worse than having to farewell my dear friend. However, Hester must have mistaken my reticence for squeamishness. 'He looks normal. You can't tell he's been hurt.' It was my opportunity to ask what had happened, what had caused the accident, but I couldn't. I wasn't brave enough.

I left Renate and Hester shortly afterwards and went to wait for the northbound bus that would deliver me home. I was glad that so little of the journey retraced the route Archer and I had taken only a few days before. It wasn't until we reached the outskirts of the city that the two journeys merged, but by then I was too tired to notice much.

To my surprise, Jerome visited the morning after my return. I hadn't seen him since his garden party and he seemed grey, his eyes circled with dark rings and his complexion mottled. I invited him in and he came and sat at my table, his hands clasped on the top as if he were a schoolboy sitting to attention. I could think of nothing to say, and after a few moments of awkward silence he stood up and hugged me, the weight of his body heavy against mine. 'I can't believe it,' he said.

It became obvious that he'd already spoken with Renate and had a much clearer idea of what had happened. 'The cyclists who called the ambulance said he was barely conscious when they found him. There was no phone reception so it took about forty minutes to raise the alarm. Can you imagine?'

I waited for him to describe the crash, the tell-tale smell of burning brakes, but instead he became distracted by a pile of papers and books on the end of the table, and started rearranging them into a neat stack. 'He loved you, you know.'

I made a sound, a whimper, and Jerome stopped what he was doing. 'No, not like that. Not in a weird way. I meant that he held you in high regard and thought the world of you. Why else would he refuse to take the job at the university during the restructuring?'

My whole body contracted. 'What do you mean?'

'When he was given the opportunity to transfer to the history department.'

'What are you saying?'

'Just that. He could have moved across but he said he wouldn't do it. He didn't think it would be right to accept unless everyone else in the department got equal treatment.'

'He never mentioned it to me.'

'Because you would have persuaded him to take it.'

I was silent, ashamed of the first thought that entered my head: He was a better man than you.

'Archer's crash,' I said. 'Do they know what caused it?'

'I don't know. I didn't like to press for details, it didn't seem right in the circumstances. I only know that it looked like he lost control and ended up running into the bank. What was he doing with that car, anyway?'

'It was his dream car.'

'I can't believe he's gone.'

Jerome left shortly afterwards. He had a lecture to prepare, and he wanted it to be really good so the students would post positive feedback and boost his chances of being nominated for the top lecturer award. It was only after he left that I realised I hadn't probed him about the vice-chancellor. But, really, what difference did it make? The simple fact of the matter was that I hadn't been considered worth keeping, whereas Jerome and Archer had. I wished with all my heart that Archer had stayed on at the university. He had such a brilliant mind, and now he was gone.

I woke in the middle of the night, and in the fraction of a second from sleep to wakefulness I made the connection between the book I'd picked up from the Little Free Library about the missionary Richard Taylor, intending to give it to Archer, and the recipe for the grand Māori perfume. It had to be the same man, didn't it? Alert, I stared towards the orange glow that filtered through the window as my satisfaction at summoning Taylor quickly faded. Already I missed Archer terribly. In that quiet room I convinced myself that I'd not only been responsible for his death by failing to mention the smell of the car brakes, but that I'd also cheated him out of a job. If it hadn't been for me he would still be at the university, happily researching some obscure topic by day, enjoying the company of his family by night. I could have saved him.

Unable to sleep, I climbed out of bed and went down to my table, hunting out the Taylor volume from my stack of unread books. I discovered that he was Anglican and had settled in Whanganui in the early 1840s. He had spent the next thirty years travelling around the district, making overland journeys that frequently took him upriver towards the volcanic region and Taupō, as well as further afield to Auckland and Wellington. Throughout his travels he made notes, filling volumes with his observations about his missionary work, Māori and natural history. I flicked through the pages in the hope of catching a glimpse of the word 'perfume'. After an hour or so I'd skimmed every chapter but found nothing and so I started up my computer and began searching the keywords 'Taylor' and 'perfume'. My screen filled with links to Taylor Swift's perfume range, fragrances I hadn't tried but which, out of habit, I studied before refining my search for Taylor, the missionary.

As I followed each new link, my mind wandered back and forth to Archer. Small details came to mind. I recalled the way he always acknowledged my input regarding his research, never once taking the credit for material I had unearthed. I recalled the way he used to stand up whenever I entered his office, then come around from behind his desk and offer me the old armchair. I recalled the way he put my name forward to chair sessions at national conferences, his expression of gratitude for my gift of perfume and his unwillingness to admit he couldn't smell it. His beam of joy when he drove up to the lake in his Pontiac. His kindness. His love of lilac and his crazy, all-encompassing knowledge of lilac poems. The more I thought about him, the more perfect he became. I couldn't think of a single time when he'd let me down. Nevertheless, I'd failed him. If I'd been a better person I wouldn't have remained at his cabin, waiting, when it was so clear something had happened to him. I would have gone looking for him and I would have found him. Had I had my wits about me I would have got to him first and kept him alive.

I typed in variations of 'Taylor', 'Māori', 'perfume' and 'plants' but then started adding new searches: 'causes of fatal car accidents', 'faulty brakes', 'sudden death'. I wasn't really concentrating on what I was doing. I was too sleepy to think straight and anyway, since losing my job, I'd grown a little haphazard in my approach to research. I found it difficult to take the time to read documents carefully. When assisting Archer I'd been able to sit still and pore over papers, reading every word and making notes; these days I was more likely to take in information at a glance. I was an expert skim reader, absorbing whole pages and chapters, impatiently scrolling through multiple tabs, scraping together fragments from random sources.

Years before I'd read an article about the smells of an operating theatre. I remembered that fat and flesh burnt by the electric cautery smelt like singed hair. Bone gave off a burnt smell when sawn. But I couldn't remember, at four in the morning, the scent some surgeons applied to their masks to counter the stench of gangrene, rectal abscesses and dead bowels. I opened a new tab and within seconds I had my answer: tincture of benzoin. I followed a link and the screen filled with images of wounds, blisters, cold sores – all covered in a yellow-brownish stain. I knew benzoin was a resin with a sweet vanilla-like smell that was used in connection with amber and gourmand perfumes, but off the top of my head I couldn't remember exactly what it smelt like. Automatically I reached forward to locate a bottle of the oil from my library of scents, but there wasn't one. I searched through all the rows, convinced I'd simply misplaced it, but the more I thought about it the less sure I was that I'd actually used it in any of my blends. My go-to resin of choice had always been frankincense, and I tended to rely on that in combination with amber oil when wanting a warm and sweet base.

I glanced at the window. It was close to dawn and already the sky was beginning to lighten, the dull dark-grey and orange of night replaced with a greenish tinge. It was too late to go back to bed and I was restless after all my hours of reading. My inability to conjure up the scent of benzoin annoyed me. I wanted to smell it immediately, but the only place open was the twenty-four-hour pharmacy, at least an hour's walk from home. I knew it would be more sensible to order the oil online, but less than five minutes later I was following the narrow tree-lined street up the hill, pausing for a moment at the Little Free Library. There was nothing on early missionaries, poetry or natural history but, to my delight, there was a pocket-sized *Observer* book of glass with an image of a blue vase on its cover that I gladly took, despite several of its pages being badly foxed and eaten by silverfish.

At the end of the street I decided to take a short cut through the school playground, passing the sandpit and an old dinghy that was swamped with brackish water under a thick layer of oak leaves. I took another short cut through the back of the church and onto the main road. Ahead of me was a quiet street and beyond that the Domain, dull in the dawn light, though its true colours would soon be revealed.

I struck out across the park, enjoying the uncluttered, open space and the fresh-hay smell of the mown, damp grass that stuck to my shoes. My passage was marked by a trail, two jittery green lines through the silvery dew. Not one of the early commuters and joggers strayed from the hard tarmac and pavements leading towards the main exits.

The sky entered its rainbow phase. The pea-green became lighter and brighter, flushed with pink and rose. I hit the main road, and the scent of grass and earth was suddenly replaced by traffic fumes. A bus pulled out, leaving a cloud of exhaust in its wake. The pavement filled with more people, most younger than me and all either listening to music or looking at their phones. I'd never been able to listen to music when I walked, and the few times I'd listened to podcasts on my way to work I'd found I couldn't concentrate on my surroundings. Once, even though I passed directly beneath a large mimosa in full bloom, I couldn't detect its sweet-powdery scent until I removed my ear buds. The following day I took the same route to work, curious to see if my sense of smell would be disrupted once more if, instead of listening to *This American Life*, I tried one of Debussy's preludes, *Les sons et les parfums tournent dans l'air du soir*. I thought the quiet piano solo might bring out the blossom notes. Once again, though, I found I couldn't get a fix on the fragrance while the music was fighting for attention. I gave it one more go on my way home, but the combination of heat, exhaust fumes and the heavy beat of the bass from the open windows of cars all drowned the mimosa, wilting it in the air.

As I approached the pharmacy a young man came out and began folding away the sandwich board on the pavement. I hurried up. 'Are you closing?'

To my relief he smiled and said, 'No, just swapping it for the daytime sign.'

I followed him inside and stood browsing the shelves until he was ready to serve me. 'Do you have any benzoin?'

'Benzoin?'

Maybe I'd mispronounced it? I tried again, 'Benzoin. In either an oil or tincture. I don't mind which.'

'I don't think so,' he replied. 'Do you mind waiting here while I go and ask the pharmacist? I won't be long.'

He returned after a few minutes to tell me they didn't have the benzoin in stock, but could order it.

'How long will it take?'

'It will be here later this afternoon or tomorrow. Or you might have better luck at one of the mainstream pharmacies.'

'Thanks,' I replied. 'I might try town.'

As the words left my mouth the pharmacist stepped into view from the back of the shop. She was wearing a white coat, and her hair was silver grey with one broad streak of jet black. Metal-framed glasses rested low on the bridge of her nose and her lips were stained bright red. She saw me and took a step forward but hesitated, as if she might as easily turn and go back to her bench. However, a moment later she came through into the shop and stood in front of me.

'We haven't got any tincture of benzoin. But I'm happy to order it.'

Her voice was quiet, as soft as I remembered. But that wasn't what captured my attention. It was her perfume. Issey Miyake. Thora was still wearing it after all these years.

'No,' I said, 'it's okay. I can go somewhere else.'

She looked vaguely relieved. Maybe she was tired because she'd reached the end of her night shift and was looking forward to going home? Nevertheless, she kept her gaze on me, as if searching through her memory. 'It's no trouble,' she said. 'It'll only take a minute and if it's in stock it'll be here this evening. I can give you a call when I come in?'

'You work all night?' I asked.

'Yes.'

She frowned. All I had to say was, 'You don't remember me but I'm Siân.' My name was unusual enough to have rung a bell, and even if it took a moment she would have worked it out. But as I was planning to speak up another possible conversation started playing through my mind: 'I'm Siân.'

'Sorry? Who?'

'We used to know each other, years ago.'

I could imagine her peering at me through the aviator lenses and saying, 'Sorry, I'm not very good with faces.'

We hadn't crossed paths for twenty-five years and although I'd seen the steady softening and slump of my own face and body, she hadn't. I'd never been anything special in the looks department, unlike her.

'So I'll order it for you?' she said. 'What's your name?'

'Rees,' I said.

'Okay, Reese. If you write down your number I'll give you a call tonight.'

I went outside and sat down by the bus stop, facing the main entrance of the pharmacy. I expected her to emerge straight away but it was a good forty minutes before she came out. She began to retrace the route I'd taken, and I trailed after her, maintaining my distance so she wouldn't notice or be alarmed. It was easy to keep Thora in sight. Her slight figure dressed entirely in black resembled a shadow against the grassy expanse of the Domain.

The last time I saw her was shortly after I gave her the perfume in the uranium glass bottle. She'd been with a group of people I didn't know, visiting the art museum where I worked. It was a Sunday and I was taking my turn covering security, walking through the galleries, ensuring that no one got too close to the paintings or touched them.

The main exhibition at that time was a show called *The Art Lab*. Charles had latched onto earthquakes. He'd come across, in an American museum, an image of a 2000-year-old Chinese bronze earthquake detector decorated with dragons and toads, and he wanted me to organise a loan for our gallery. 'Phone the director and tell him we absolutely must have it.' I was used to his style of command but my heart sank nonetheless. When I suggested a written request first, he said, 'You write it and give it to me to sign.'

It was a difficult letter to get right since I hadn't seen a picture of the object and knew nothing about it. I tried to summon Charles's voice, incorporating phrases like 'the tectonic energy that binds our museums across the Pacific', and, much to my relief, he was happy with the result and we faxed it off. By the time we got a reply, turning down our request, he'd moved on to particles and atoms, 'the chemistry that triggers explosions through our cultural imagination'. *The Art Lab* was the heavily curated result.

I was standing on the small mezzanine balcony looking down. Thora had broken away from the group and was by herself, moving quickly past some exhibits, lingering over others. There was one piece in the show I particularly liked, a small assemblage created by a contemporary artist using Victorian microscope slides, and I hoped Thora would notice it and take the time to study the work. Then I'd feel justified in having given her my grandmother's glass bottle. If she ignored it, I'd know I'd made a terrible mistake, one that would trouble me for a long, long time. Just as she was about to look, one of her friends called her over. I saw her hesitate but her friend called, 'Come on!', then crossed the gallery and pulled Thora away from the microscope work. A moment later my walkie-talkie crackled to life and I was summoned to the front desk to sort out some problem with a jammed receipt roll on the cash register. I was still there when Thora passed by, raising her hand in a hello-goodbye wave as she left.

Now, as I watched her crossing the Domain, I thought I should make her a new perfume. I imagined something fleeting, a close-to-the-skin scent that only she could smell when she wore it. Would a traditional water infusion, like rose water or rosemary-scented Hungary water, suit her? Violet water? I'd made it before by steeping violet petals in water for a few days before straining and adding gin. It was a scent that was slightly wistful and melancholic – fragile. But where would I find violets? There were none in the Domain, and I had no memory of having seen them anywhere in the city. Of course, if I really wanted to create a beautiful, sweet and powdery true-to-life violet-based perfume I wouldn't use violets at all. I'd reach for alpha-isomethyl ionone. That would give me the fragrance I desired.

Ahead of me Thora skirted the car park and disappeared over the crest of the hill, on her way home, I supposed, to sleep – or, like me, attempt to sleep.

When I woke with the sun streaming into the loft, my first thought was Archer. I'd dreamt we were in his old office, but he was wearing his full academic gown and congratulating me on my promotion to head of the chemistry department. For a split second upon waking I was so happy, thinking all my troubles were over, and then the truth quickly flowed in, like one of those treacherous Morecambe Bay tides I'd read about in the *Guardian*, the fast flow of water that cut off and then drowned cockle hunters.

I'd wasted another morning, sleeping off my dawn expedition when I should have been going through job vacancies. By my own calculations, I'd applied for over seventy positions. From those I'd had only two interviews: the perfume counter and the museum. I had anticipated at least ten, but, apart from a suggestion that I'd be 'kept on the books', nothing had materialised and I'd all but given up checking my phone or emails. My skin had thickened where rejections were concerned, but I couldn't help feeling dejected when my applications went unacknowledged. I didn't want to give in to failure but it was such a struggle to maintain any sense of optimism. The only good thing was that 'Jessica' had moved on. Perhaps, being young and well educated, he had found a job, something well paid, where he could command the respect he so deserved.

It was time to put my house on the market: I could no longer put it off. No one was going to appear on the horizon and save me, I knew that, but somewhere in the back of my mind I'd hoped for a miracle. That a distant relative, perhaps, had decided to name me in a will and that a letter might arrive telling me I'd inherited a small fortune, enough to pay my mortgage or, at least, provide me with a means to negotiate the bills and the lean years ahead. I had no such relative. I wasn't close enough to my sister to ask for help. In fact, we spoke so rarely I hadn't even told her about losing my job.

It was a Friday. At least it was too late in the day for the agent to visit or bother me with contracts or requests for photographs. I had the weekend to come to terms with my decision. On the count of three I would call the real estate office and ask my agent if she had any work available in her office. I would stress that I was open to anything, anything at all, as long as it paid minimum wage. If the answer was negative, I'd have no other option but to put my home up for sale.

One. As soon as I made the call I'd turn off my phone.

Two. I'd sit still and do everything in my power not to think about the future. I wouldn't imagine what came next: the selling up, the search for a new place to live, the packing, the moving, the unpacking, the endless quiet as one day ran into the next. Instead, I'd picture a vast meadow bursting with wild flowers and clover, a field humming with bees. I'd picture myself spread out on a blanket in the shade of a gnarled old fruit tree. The air around me would be sweet as I breathed it in.

Three. I would go and see Thora, tell her who I was and collect the benzoin oil.

I dialled and it went straight to voicemail. I left a message as instructed. It was done. Phone off.

Four. I would go to The Corner Dairy and cheer myself up by sampling perfumes with a benzoin note. And although it was probably too late, I would apologise to the sales assistant for my bad behaviour last time I visited. It wasn't his fault I was a wreck, and I didn't want to wind up like one of those people who were permanently grumpy, taking out their frustrations on anyone who stood in their way. If I were to survive the next stage of my life, I needed to start making peace with the world; I needed to get back into step with it. Maybe exercise could help.

For a short period during the late seventies my mother became a jogging fanatic. Every day she'd lace up her shoes and run a bridge-to-bridge circuit along the Avon River that took her upstream as far as Avonside and downstream to a footbridge in Dallington. Every now and then I'd tag along, not because I was interested in getting fit but because jogging with my mother was peaceful.

One unusually warm and sunny afternoon in early September, 'too hot for exercise' according to my mother, we went and sat in the shade of a weeping willow that was just coming into leaf, its long dangling branches dotted at regular intervals with the almost fluorescent green of new growth. I don't recall that we talked much. I think we were both watching the slow and steady progress of a bright yellow and pink ball that was floating down the river towards us.

Every now and again the willow would rustle in the light breeze, and there were bees nearby, big fat bumblebees that moved quickly as if in a hurry to get to work. I remember, too, a seagull that landed close by and some ducks that climbed up the bank hoping we might have slices of bread. Sparrows chirped above us in the branches. It was a peaceful scene, straight out of one of my favourite childhood books, *The Wind in the Willows*.

As the ball floated closer, I stood up, half-intending to try and draw it closer with a stick, but there were no suitable twigs or branches and so I contented myself with running my hand over and down some of the slender branches, shredding off the leaves and sniffing them. The smell was nothing special – I might have described it as leaf-like – but my mother, who was watching, mentioned that willow was a significant tree despite being a common one.

Sceptical, I asked her to name three things that made it special.

'Only three,' she said. 'That narrows it down.'

I figured she was bluffing but was willing to give her the benefit of the doubt.

'It's fast growing and the bark contains salicylic acid, which is used in aspirin. The willow pattern is a famous blue and white crockery decoration . . .'

'I know that one,' I interrupted. 'You bought one of those plates.'

'Well, willow is native to China, but those plates are very English. And, finally, here's one you'll like: they're called weeping willows because the drops of rain that fall off their leaves look like teardrops. You didn't know that, did you?'

I shook my head. I'd assumed the name had something to do with the shape of the long dangling branches.

'One more thing,' said my mother. 'I wanted to name you Willow because you were born in spring when the leaves were just appearing.'

I felt a pang of pain when she said that. I'd never really loved my name. I knew it was Welsh and unusual but I was tired of always having to explain its spelling and pronunciation. Willow, on the other hand, would have been both special and simple.

'Why didn't you?'

'Oh,' my mother replied, 'I don't know. I guess we just liked Siân better. It suits you. Willow is a bit, you know . . .'

The ball was downstream of us now, heading towards a bend in the river where litter and lawn clippings caught in the backwater beside the bank.

'What do you think?' asked my mother, breaking the silence that had settled around us.

'What about?'

'Oh, you know. Growing old. Losing your marbles. Drifting off.'

I could honestly say I hadn't given it much thought and it certainly wasn't something that captured my attention as the possibility of being named 'Willow' had.

'When I'm old and going gaga you can push me in the river,' said my mother. 'Pretend I slipped but give me a good shove.'

'What?'

'Mmm,' she sighed. 'It's so lovely here, so peaceful.'

'I wish you *had* called me Willow,' I said.

'Do you? Willow Rees. Maybe.'

Notes from a tree: Willow. Willow Rees. Just as I'd once done with Madeline, I tried the name, practised my signature and called myself Willow when no one was listening. Could I be a Willow? Did I feel like a Willow? If my name had been Willow would it be easier to create a perfume matching my identity? I think so. Maybe.

If I were to make a willow perfume I'd want to include the smell of slow-moving river water. Willow, the perfume, would represent three aspects of the river: the surface, the depths and the bank. The surface would contain remnants of all that is carried downstream. The twigs that fall off trees, the leaves and blossoms that flutter down and float like small vessels, the lawn clippings dumped by local residents when they can't be bothered with composting or removal. The sluggish depths with base notes of mud and gravel, a scent of dank spaces, pond water, the dark shadow of an eel or the flash of a small trout gliding over shingle. The bank: willow, gunnera, flax, sedges, irises and grass. Bitter, leafy green with a hint of vanilla-like coumarin for the grass.

It's been a long time since I floated on a slow-flowing river. A real drifting-aimlessly-on-a-summer's-day experience where it doesn't matter what direction your kayak is facing; you just give yourself to the moment and the will of the water.

Willow Rees. I could never be that person. I was always too busy paddling, scanning the distance for waterfalls.

It was late afternoon, and I decided to go to The Corner Dairy to search out benzoin fragrances before going back to the pharmacy. I knew I was going about it the wrong way, that it would make more sense to try the tincture or oil first, but I was impatient and, to tell the truth, I wanted to see if I got any pleasure from sampling the perfumes.

In the space of time following Archer's death, I'd found it difficult to maintain my previous enthusiasm for my perfume collection. I'd bought and collected hundreds of bottles over the years, and each fragrance told a story, challenged me or provided comfort, just as the books on my shelves did. Not so very long ago I'd have hunted down a tester and spent half a day sniffing my wrist or forearm as I followed the scent's development. I could spend hours arranging my perfumes, ranking and comparing them, layering them or contrasting old formulations with new, but recently I'd been put off by many of the scents I once loved. In the past, I'd found them elegant and well mannered; now they'd become shrill and demanding. Worse, half of them were boring and not worth wearing. I'd developed a strong dislike of anything smelling of almond or marzipan, especially when combined with cherry. Two perfumes I'd worn for years, both created by one of my favourite perfumers, Christopher Sheldrake, nauseated me. Wearing them made me shudder, as if someone had soaked crystallised cherries in almond essence and plastered my skin and clothes with the mixture and then locked me in a small room with the heat turned up.

The Corner Dairy was almost empty when I arrived. Since my last visit they'd constructed a counter resembling the one in the dairy where I once worked. I could see displays of lollies through the glass top of the counter, and on the shelves behind the cash register were neatly arranged empty bottles of Ballins and Leed lemonade, cans of Kandy, Go Cola and Frist, and an entire row of full SpaceMan drink bottles. I could have stepped behind the till and begun to work, picking up from where I left off, but instead I headed towards the perfume counter. There were signs here, too, of a seventies and eighties revival. Perfumes from my teenage years such as Fidji, Anaïs Anaïs, Charlie, Silences and even Fenjal were crowded together, higgledy-piggledy, on top of a painted white dressing table with gold trim. It looked as if someone had raided the shelves of a charity shop: there was also a chipped Lladró figurine, a musical ballerina jewellery box and, poking out of a drawer, a vintage hairdryer case, the old-fashioned kind that included a bonnet resembling a shower cap and a set of Carmen heated rollers.

The assistant was looking over the shop floor, a resting smile on his face that stiffened when he saw me approach. He watched as I scanned the display, shifting his weight from one leg to the other.

'Hello,' I said. 'How are you?'

'Good, thank you.'

'Busy?'

He nodded, and his skin blushed, his cheeks reddening.

I lowered my gaze in an awkward attempt not to stare. 'Long day?' I asked.

'Can I help you with anything?'

'You might not remember,' I said, 'but I came here a while ago and I was really rude and I'm sorry.'

His features relaxed somewhat but his skin became even more red, a butterfly image across his nose and cheeks.

'I lost my job.' As the words came out of my mouth I felt a wave of grief. Though my redundancy had been no secret during my interviews, or in conversations with acquaintances, I'd been too ashamed to reveal it to strangers, in public.

The assistant took a step closer and stopped in front of me. 'Oh, that's so sad. My stepdad lost his job when Hutton's closed in Hamilton a couple of years ago.'

'Terrible.'

'It was hard. Especially for Mum and the younger kids.'

'I'm sorry.'

He nodded. 'Yeah. Well, there's always perfume.'

I laughed. 'That's true.'

'We've got a seventies promotion at the moment with all the old perfumes from back then.' He reached for a bottle of Chanel No. 19 and held it up for me, asking, 'Have you tried this? It's beautiful. Very classic.'

'I have tried it but I don't own it. Something always gets in the way.'

'Yeah, it's so expensive.'

'Could I test it?' I asked.

The assistant held the bottle high above my arm and sprayed. He waited in silence as I raised my skin to my nose and inhaled. I felt my face tighten in concentration and then relax as I exhaled. The assistant kept his eyes on me, but said nothing.

'It's good,' I said, thinking that I ought to feel more moved by it. In the past it had always struck me as such a stunning iris.

He nodded. 'It's one of those perfumes that lifts you up from the inside,' he said. 'And it's stood the test of time, you know. It came out the same year my favourite aunt was born, 1970.'

'Really?'

'Yeah. I should buy her a bottle for her birthday. But I don't think she'd like it. She'd probably think it was a bit old-fashioned.'

Two women approached the counter, drawn to a display of a recent release, a deep violet-coloured perfume in a faceted heart-shaped bottle called Réveil. They took turns spraying the juice onto a paper blotter, wafting the strip in front of them. The younger of the two women pulled a face and dumped the strip on the counter. 'Don't like it,' she said. 'It smells like toothpaste.'

'Re-veil? Ray-veal?' said her lilac-haired friend. 'What is that?'

‘It is kind of original, though,’ said the younger woman. ‘Different from all the other ’fumes we’ve tried today.’

‘I guess. Would you wear it, though?’

The young woman sprayed another paper strip, holding it up to her nose for a second sniff. ‘I’d give it a go if someone gave it to me.’

‘It’s unisex,’ chimed in the assistant. ‘There’s camphor in the opening and then it becomes more creamy and woody.’

‘It’s a nice colour,’ said the second woman, ‘and the brand is famous.’

The assistant left me to talk to the women and I stayed where I was, eavesdropping on their conversation as they began to persuade each other into purchasing the perfume. My eyes took in the large promotional poster above the display. It depicted a naked woman with feline eyes beneath a jungle waterfall. She was standing up to her waist in a pool of dappled purple water and the tagline at the foot of the image read, ‘Reawaken Instinct’.

Both women bought the perfume, even though neither one of them seemed to love it or had allowed time for the top notes to fade and the heart notes to develop. I recognised the process. I’d try a perfume, not like it but then slowly convince myself that my impressions were wrong. I’d argue that I’d misjudged the scent because all the reviews and comments I’d read were positive. I simply hadn’t given the perfume a fair trial; it would grow on me. I’d buy it and wear it for a week and spend hours reading more and more reviews, all the time persuading myself to enjoy it. Then, a year or two later, wearers and reviewers would start admitting they hated it and I’d finally be able to sell it on Trade Me.

‘Reawaken instinct.’ I’m not even sure if that’s possible, given that trusting my instincts in the first place is such a challenge. I think it’s because I grew up in a world dominated by visual cues. From a young age I studied my reflection in the mirror, and was surrounded by family and friends who offered opinions on my appearance. I learnt to see myself and I followed or discarded advice based on my own judgement. But although my instincts offered very clear and precise guidance concerning fashion choices, flattering colours or hairstyles, I was far less confident about the aesthetics of smell. I didn't go through childhood being told, 'This smells interesting on you', or, 'This suits your personality and brings out your character'. The only reference to smell I ever heard on a regular basis as a child was, 'You stink', but that was merely a taunt. Smell was undervalued; no one gave it the thought it deserved. No wonder it became so comically easy to talk myself into or out of any perfume.

The assistant returned. 'It's an interesting perfume.' He pointed at the display with the purple juice. 'But I hate the bottle.'

'Your aunt might like it,' I said. 'Do you have any perfumes with benzoin notes?'

'Benzoin?'

'Yes. I've read that it smells a little bit like vanilla, but with more of a caramel note.'

He shook his head. 'I don't know,' he replied. 'It sounds nice.'

'It's a resin and I think it can also be quite warm, like amber.'

'Do you mean benjoin?'

I nodded, same thing.

'We've got two perfumes with benjoin in their names. I'll get them.'

A second later he returned with two sealed boxes and placed them in front of me on the counter. 'We don't have any testers, I'm afraid.'

I turned the boxes in my hand and looked at the price tags. The first, from a cult American perfumer, was $595 for 100ml, and the second, from a major Italian fashion house, was $295 for the same amount. I knew nothing about either and yet I experienced a familiar burst of excitement, a kind of scented bloodlust, just from looking at the packages. The voice in my head had been turned to full volume and was saying, 'Buy me! This perfume is the one. It will get you out of the fug and back in the game! You need it. After all you've been through recently, you deserve it.'

Luckily, I couldn't afford them. If I'd had a job I might have gone one better than the two women with the purple fragrance and convinced myself to buy both perfumes, unsniffed. At least the old flush of excitement had resurfaced, even if only for a short while.

I left with a manufacturer's sample of Réveil. As I passed through the university campus I sprayed it on my left forearm. The opening burst did smell like toothpaste. As I sniffed my skin, an image of a man standing in front of a cracked bathroom sink entered my mind. I could see him brushing his teeth, rinsing his mouth with a swig of water from the tap and then spitting into the basin. The foaming mixture of paste and food particles swirled in the tepid water, forming a rim that stuck to the stained porcelain. The man, who must be in his early sixties, wiped his mouth with a frayed white towel, then took a cigarette out of his shirt pocket and lit up. That's the perfume I saw when I smelt my arm. In a desperate attempt to rid my mind of the bathroom image I summoned up the glossy sales visual created by the company, and a familiar battle began. Toothpaste man, naked beauty. Stained and cracked sink, jungle and exotic violet juice. Me, the middle-aged woman in high-waisted jeans versus the naked forest nymph with the piercing eyes. Reality and fantasy.

I was almost through the university complex before I realised I'd passed my old building without noticing. As I headed out through the corner of the car park I glimpsed Renate in the distance. She hadn't seen me, and it took a moment for me to decide what to do. My first impulse was to hurry away without stopping but instead I summoned up my strength and walked towards her, wiping my arm with the cuff of my jersey in an attempt to scrub off the overbearing smell that was bonded to my skin.

'Renate!'

She stopped, turned and saw me and, to my relief, smiled. 'What are you doing here?' she asked. 'Are you working again?'

We hugged and I noticed how small she was in my arms. 'I'm on my way to the pharmacy,' I replied. 'What about you?'

'I'm meeting Hester and then I'm taking her down to the cabin for a few days. I should have called you.'

'If anyone should have called it was me.'

'We're taking his ashes,' she continued. 'Some of them, not all. I'm spreading him out – half in New York where we met and half here where we lived. I think he'd like that.'

I nodded. 'It's a beautiful place, your garden . . .'

'Yes, it is. Hester wants to plant a kauri but we don't really know what we're doing beyond that. Archer and I were never very good at ceremonies, we didn't like the fuss.'

Her lips began to tremble and her eyes filled with tears. She pulled herself straighter, willing herself to stand tall.

'I'm so sorry, Renate. I should have phoned you. I wanted to tell you something about the car but I didn't know where to start.'

Renate made a gulping sound and her whole body quivered.

'Do you think there was something wrong with it?' she asked.

I felt heat rise through my body and I found it difficult to look her in the eye. 'Well, it was old, so I guess you can't rule out the possibility that something might have gone wrong.' Almost immediately I backtracked, adding, 'It seemed really well maintained, though. It looked great and ran very smoothly.'

'But they said it was a medical event,' she replied. 'An aneurysm. That's what they told me. But do you think there was a mechanical problem? The car was relatively undamaged in the accident so that doesn't seem right. He just nudged the bank, like he felt something was wrong and had just enough time to pull over. But you think it might have been the car?'

A wave of relief mixed with guilt and sadness went through me. 'I didn't know he'd had an aneurysm,' I said. 'I'm sorry. I didn't realise something had happened to Archer. Jerome said he'd lost control but I didn't know why. I assumed it was something to do with the car, or the road conditions, or maybe that he swerved to miss something . . . I didn't know the details and I didn't like to ask. It's so sad.'

Renate looked confused and I wished I'd kept my mouth shut. I'd raised questions and doubts in her mind and now the only decent thing to do was reassure her. 'I'm certain the doctors are right. They would have done scans and they can see what's happened. If they say it was an aneurysm, it must have been that. That makes sense.'

As I spoke I wondered who I really wanted to reassure. Renate only nodded in response, then said goodbye before hurrying off to meet Hester. I kept on my way, going over what Renate had said, trying to convince myself that Archer's death had nothing to do with his car. I couldn't believe that Archer had crashed because of an aneurysm. He was too full of life and too kind a person for something like that to kill him. His death felt unfair and cruel.

As I went through the Domain, I noticed that groups of people were milling around the tropical glasshouse. Tourists probably, from a cruise ship or a bus tour.

As I reached the main drive leading out of the Domain I began to feel nervous. I recognised the feeling in the pit of my stomach, that resident touch of self-conscious foolishness I'd experienced in the past whenever I bumped into Thora. The mixture of being pleased to see her coupled with the desire to escape as quickly as possible. That was how I felt now, and my first reflex was to reach in my bag for a reassuring spray of perfume, my constant shield and protection in awkward social situations. But there was little point because whatever I sprayed would be tainted with the residue smell of the mouth-spit scent that clung to my skin on my left arm, despite all my rubbing. I should have learnt by now not to spray untested perfumes directly onto my skin. I should have tried it on a blotter first. I should also have learnt that the perfumes I hate the most have an uncanny ability to hang around for hours, whereas the real beauties, those that make me swoon with delight, often evaporate and fade within the hour. This purple muck, I thought as I stepped through the main gates, will probably still be on my skin in the morning. And it will remain on my clothes for even longer. Like a stain.

It was late when I reached the pharmacy, and before going in I did something I only ever did before delivering lectures: I huffed into my cupped hands and smelt my breath. It seemed fine, though I'm not sure I'd be able to tell. And I'm pretty certain it's been disproved as a way of detecting bad breath. The same guy was at the counter and behind him, with her back to the shop, was Thora. I guessed she was filling out a prescription for a woman who sat by a water cooler with a small child curled against her. She smoothed his hair and spoke quietly: 'Not long now, love. We'll get you home soon.' I couldn't tell who was sick but they both looked tired, as if they'd had a long day and there was no immediate promise of relief. Thora came out and handed the woman a folded white bag. After going over the instructions concerning dosage, she reached into her pocket and brought out a lollipop for the child.

Then she turned to me and said hello.

'Hi.'

There was an awkward pause, but then she smiled brightly. 'Benzoin.'

As she reached under the counter, she glanced at me and said, 'I didn't recognise you yesterday. I'm sorry.'

I felt my mouth curl into a smile. 'I wasn't sure, either,' I said. 'But, actually, you haven't changed much. Apart from your hair.' I made a gesture with my hands, the type of stroking pat favoured by hairdressers when discussing a cut or style. 'It's the other way around. Grey and black.'

'Yep.' Thora looked at me, as if taking in my changes. 'Are you still a museum curator?'

'No, not for a long time.'

Thora looked surprised. 'Oh, what do you do?'

I was about to answer when the young assistant beckoned Thora and she excused herself. While she was gone I occupied myself looking at the flavoured lip balms displayed on the counter. Some had easy to recognise names, like vanilla bean or sour cherry, but others were obscure. Stardust. Was it a flavour, and if it was, would it taste of rock and minerals and colour your lips grey?

Thora was soon back, presenting me with two amber-coloured bottles, one containing benzoin and the other friar's balsam.

'I wasn't sure if you wanted the benzoin for your medical cabinet or for making perfume. Do you still make perfume?'

She remembered. I felt a surge of pleasure. 'Yes, I do. It's still a hobby, though, nothing serious.'

Thora lifted the smaller bottle, the benzoin tincture. 'This is probably more useful, but really there's not much difference between them in terms of concentration. It's expensive compared to the friar's balsam.'

'Why is it called friar's balsam? Do you know?'

'No. All I know is that it's been around for hundreds of years. People use it much in the way they'd use iodine, on wounds or blisters. It's a bit messy because it stains the skin dirty yellow. You don't have to take both, or either. I can put them on the shelf.'

'No, I'm curious.' As I spoke I opened the benzoin and inhaled, careful not to breathe in too deeply in case it was very strong. A shot of recognition went through me and I gasped.

'Are you all right?' asked Thora. 'Did you get some up your nose?'

I shook my head, and sniffed again. There it was, summoned from the back of my memory, the smell of my father's doctor's bag. The smell I'd thought was amber was now presented to me in its entirety. 'It's the smell of my father,' I said. 'I didn't know it was benzoin, but this is it.'

I passed the bottle to Thora, who held it up to her nose. As she sniffed she squinted, closing one eye. 'It's quite similar to iodine. I'm not sure I could tell the difference. Why does it remind you of him?'

I explained. 'His bag has a warm, sweet, resin-like scent that reminds me of amber, but now I realise it's benzoin. This is a little bit softer, and it has leather undertones, like handbag leather, and it's a little bit spicy too, as if there's a hint of nutmeg or cinnamon.' I dabbed a little of the tincture on the back of my right hand and sniffed again. 'It will sound silly but I feel like I've solved a puzzle.' I smelt my skin again, noticing that, already, the tincture had mellowed, becoming even more like the smell of the drawer within his bag containing the neatly rolled bandages and cloth tape.

I capped the bottle and held it gently in my palm, warming the glass with my skin. 'It's perfect,' I said. 'It seems to fit.'

'I don't follow,' said Thora.

'I mean it feels like a part of me. Sometimes you get that with perfume, a sense of belonging. It's such a warm, skin scent. Thank you.'

Thora began to say something, then stopped and waited a moment. 'I think that's how your perfume made me feel. You mightn't remember the smell, but whenever I wore it I had the impression that it felt right. It was intuitive. I would have found it difficult to express that same feeling in words. I wore it every day until I almost drained the bottle. And then I kept a little bit back, so I could smell it once in a while. When I sniff it now, I'm reminded of Wellington.'

'I put a lot of boronia in that perfume. And frankincense.'

'Yes, I remember. There's a boronia across the road from the sensory garden behind the Domain. I sometimes pass it on my way home and I can remember the first time I caught the smell of it. It's so distinctive, like cranberries and raspberry jam.'

'It was new to me,' I said. 'Unlike anything I knew.'

'I looked it up a couple of years ago and found out it was named after an Italian botanist and plant collector who died when he leant too far out of a window while reaching for a plant. Did you know that?'

I shook my head.

'I don't remember anything else about him. Just that he was called Francesco Borone.'

As in the old days, it seemed we'd run out of things to say, and we both fell silent, smiling awkwardly at each other, hoping either for a new topic of conversation or for some way of politely exiting the situation.

'I still have all my oils,' I said. 'I could try and make your perfume again, if you like.'

'No, I wouldn't ask you to do that. It's too much trouble.'

'Not at all. It would give me something to do. In fact, I can probably find the original formula in one of my old notebooks.'

Thora looked doubtful. 'I'll pay you.'

'Okay,' I replied. 'If that makes you feel better.'

I walked home, my brain swarming with ideas, not for Thora's perfume but for my own signature scent. As I strolled along I took sniffs of my arm, allowing the benzoin to warm me. Once, I accidentally raised my other arm and caught the scent of the strange toothpaste camphor in my nose. Now that it had dulled it was quite nice. In fact, I wondered if I could make the camphor, wintergreen note work with the benzoin. The latter might counteract the sharpness of the purple scent; it was worth experimenting with.

As I circled behind the museum I made a promise to sit down and begin making the perfume of myself. It was one thing to have scent notes circulating in my mind, and fragments of ideas in my head. Now I needed to organise my thoughts and work.

Notes of my collected selves: This is what my perfume is shaping up to be. I'm a bit disappointed that my character doesn't show through more strongly, that I can't point to it in the way you might gesture towards a statue and say, 'That represents me.' My scent, I realise, has as many negative spaces as positive. It shows what I am not, as much as it tries to embody what I am.

I am not my parents. But now that I have smelt benzoin I know I will include it for the memory it awakens of my father. And yet, if I'd asked him who he was, I'm certain he wouldn't have replied 'a doctor'. That was his occupation, not his identity. So, by focusing on benzoin I am, in a way, misrepresenting him.

My mother is more difficult to reduce to a single note. I cherish the memory of our jogs by the river and will stick with willow, but I'm reminded that 'mother' is a more generic description than 'doctor'. It's the everythingness of it, the way she appeared so often to be a reflection of what we wanted or demanded. I never asked my mother, 'Who are you?' That wasn't a question anyone ever asked mothers and housewives. We always assumed we knew, Carrie and I. In some ways it would have been simpler for me now if my mother had rebelled at some stage in her life and gone off to do her own thing. Then, at least, I could have summed her up in a word.

My own identity, the one that once appeared as clear-cut as my father's, now has softer edges, reminiscent of my mother's. That is one of the reasons, I think, why I haven't been able to make as much progress with my perfume: I lack hard edges.

I'm frustrated, too, that my strongest links to scent continue to be associated with memory rather than the here and now. Truly the only place that speaks to me as strongly as the places of my youth is my home. That and Archer, and he's gone.

What have I really learnt about myself since being kicked out of the university? I've learnt that I was ashamed to have lost my job and yet believed in myself enough that I expected to land something new. I'm alone, not only in the sense that I have no one to talk to, but to the extent that the world has become quiet, and empty. And yet I still believe that something is out there. So do I continue to look inwards, defining myself by what I'm not or what I've lost, or do I reimagine myself as what I could be, my potential self?

First thing the next morning, I found my old notebook with the recipe for Thora's perfume. It took less than thirty minutes to gather together the ingredients and blend her scent. To start, I dipped a clean blotter in each of the oils and passed them slowly in front of my nose in order to reacquaint myself with each note. I decided not to alter the perfume but made it exactly as it had been, filling a 30ml bottle with the result. It was better than I remembered. If I'd been making it for the first time today I probably wouldn't have felt the need to dress it up in the uranium glass bottle. I'd have been happy enough using a dark amber glass bottle, the type that contained most of my blends. I made a second, smaller batch of the perfume for myself. Half of this featured the original formula, but with the left-over juice I substituted my new-found love, benzoin, for the original frankincense. This instilled the perfume with a hint of caramelised-amber sweetness. The benzoin brought out the raspberry jam aspect of the boronia in a way that frankincense had not. I'd created a perfume I would wear myself.

It was close to ten when I made my way towards the museum, intending to spend the day in the reference library. During my sleepless night of Googling 'Taylor' I'd discovered that his journals from the 1830s to the 1870s were held in the museum, and I believed that one of them contained the recipe for the grand Māori perfume. As I was still a few minutes early, I passed some time in the small sensory garden, which contained many common herbs as well as some plants I didn't recognise. Fennel was the most prolific. I picked a few strands of its feathery leaves and crushed them in my fingers, enjoying the aniseed sweetness on my skin. A peppermint-scented geranium caught my attention, and after smelling it I stuffed a palm-full of leaves into the pocket of my trousers to return to later. In fact, I might have paid closer attention to the geranium, a smell I enjoy for its bitter green, stalky note, had I not already spotted the plant next to it: wormwood.

I'd always imagined wormwood would be twiggy and scraggly, like a bush rather than a plant. This specimen, however, was low to the ground with downy grey-green leaves that were closer in appearance to a geranium or daisy than the plant carried in my head. I read the label, *Artemisia absinthium*, which gave the clue to its link to absinthe, the drink Archer had prepared for me during our happy cocktail evening. Mugwort was the name preferred by most of my American suppliers of wormwood oil, even though the mugwort variety of *Artemisia* differs from the stronger absinthe version. Plants with 'wort' in their name had medicinal properties, whereas those ending in 'bane' – ratbane, witchbane or wolfbane – were toxic.

I bent down to the wormwood to sneak a few leaves, pressed them gently into my palm and then inhaled. The smell was very faint. My brain told me it should smell like absinthe, but I wasn't picking up on that note so I assumed the fault lay with my nose. When I tried again I detected the scent of faded canvas, or the sun-baked cotton cloth of the old inflatable lilos we slept on whenever guests came to stay and use our beds. 'It *is* just like a lilo.' I said the words softly, intending them for Archer, though I knew he wouldn't hear. 'I thought it would smell more like absinthe,' I continued. 'I'm a bit disappointed. It's hardly *loucheable*.'

I tried the leaves once more, but it was difficult to gain a clear impression because the smell was so fleeting. I crushed the stems between my fingers until the slightest smear of juice appeared. This time I could clearly detect an aroma of licorice. This was minty, but as I continued to smell a touch of celery leaf surfaced, and then a slight hint of cumin. I inhaled more deeply, the smell caught in the back of my nose and I sneezed.

Again, I squashed some leaves hard in my palm, bruising them, and sniffed. A searing pain went through my nose, as if I'd inadvertently inhaled soap or shampoo. It burnt the back of my throat and made it feel raw, as though I'd just vomited. The burning sensation grew stronger, boring a hole in the back of my nose. I cleared my throat but the rawness grew worse. I could clearly taste the wormwood now. It was like the clear nail product I was given as a child to discourage nail biting. Every time I breathed it felt like a hot flame burning my sinuses, and I kept sneezing. I was still snuffling when I finally reached the museum.

The library was empty when I arrived, and after signing in I made my way to a long table that faced a curved wall with windows looking down onto the atrium below. The table was similar to the one I worked at when I was making my perfumes, but instead of oils and blotters there were containers of sharpened pencils and neatly trimmed squares of recycled paper. At my back were dark stained shelves filled with books about New Zealand history and culture, natural history and the arts.

I sat quietly, my notebook open, while I waited for the librarian to fetch the Taylor material. Had it not been so cold in the room I might have enjoyed the peacefulness. Instead, my thoughts lingered on whether I'd caused permanent damage to my still burning nose and throat, and how misleading the suffix 'wort' was. No wonder it was attached to 'mug'.

After ten minutes, I heard a low jangle of keys and the librarian reappeared, pushing a trolley containing several large volumes. She walked right past me and went back to her computer, where she started typing.

'Are you sure this is the correct reference?' she asked.

'It should be. I saw it in a book containing Taylor's recipe for the grand Māori perfume .'

She looked puzzled. 'There's a bit of a hiccup.'

I went over to her desk, and even though I was convinced I hadn't made a mistake I felt my cheeks begin to redden with embarrassment.

'The problem is we don't have the material you want.'

My heart began to thump in my chest. 'Oh,' I stammered. 'That's odd. I'm pretty certain I got it right. I'm usually quite careful.' I was completely unnerved.

'Let me go and check with my colleague.'

I needed some important papers to shuffle and rearrange in order to take the spotlight off my stupidity, but I had nothing. At a loss, I started picking pencils out of the container on the desk, testing their sharpness against the tip of my finger.

The librarian came back. 'It looks like you might have made a simple oversight concerning the terms "notebooks" and "journals". Easy to do if the reference isn't terribly accurate to begin with. The good news is that the notebook you're after exists. The bad news is that we have the journals, but the item you want is at the city library, in the heritage collection. I've jotted down the reference for you.'

She handed me a piece of paper and took a step back, a small act of discretion for which I was grateful.

'Do you know where to go?' she asked.

I felt myself blush and I could practically hear Jerome spluttering and laughing. Even Archer, who had graciously endured several minor slip-ups while I was carrying out his research, would have raised an eyebrow at such a sloppy start.

'I'm sorry,' I apologised. 'I don't know what to say.'

'Don't worry about it. Perhaps you'd like to look at some of Taylor's journals while you're here. I put a selection on the trolley.'

The neatly transcribed, typewritten volumes she opened in front of me dated from the 1840s onwards, and as I delved into the entries I was taken by the missionary's descriptions of his travels up and down the Whanganui River. The places he described were close to the cleared farms, forestry plantations and bush country I'd travelled through with Archer. Taylor's landscape, though, was primeval and fecund, teeming with life. More than once he described the scenery as 'romantic' and the term struck me as fitting, given the way nature appeared to dwarf him. The power of the natural world was even more accentuated through his references to the mighty river rapids and the occasional rumble and rattle of earthquakes that rocked his camp. I followed him as he walked through dense bush, over bluffs and across volcanic landscapes, but in terms of smell, there wasn't much to go on. There were only a few passages and even those were brief: the earth floor of a church covered in aromatic mānuka branches, another laid with dried fern.

By now other visitors had come into the library, groups of schoolchildren filing in and out, chatting as they picked up books from the shelves or studied the glass-topped display cases. Researchers came and went, talking loudly at the librarian's desk: a man seeking information about a relative killed in Messines, a woman researching 1940s fashion, a university graduate wanting to continue her research into artist Charles Blomfield's letters, a teenager working on a project about influenza. Their requests didn't distract me: I was too engrossed in what I was reading to be drawn back to the present day.

After a few hours I came to the final volume in my selection, an entry that included a cross-country journey made in April 1849 from Taylor's home in Whanganui to Tauranga, and then on to Auckland. A passage jumped out at me. Near Matamata he came across an abandoned mission house, visible from far away because of the number of 'foreign' trees forming a grove nearby. As he drew nearer he began to list the plants he encountered: blooming furze that perfumed the 'wilderness', sweet briar and evening primrose, tufts of strawberry plants, a large woodbine bush, a huge mimosa and wild asparagus. All the windows of the house were broken and the lawn had been dug up by pigs. I reread the passage, marvelling at the detail of the picture he painted. But it was his use of the word 'foreign' to describe the mission house trees, rather than 'exotic' or even 'non-native' that seemed to emphasise a sense of distance between him and his temporary garden surroundings. It was as if, at that moment, he had cast himself in the role of local or even 'native'. Had I been wrong in thinking he didn't feel at home in the bush and forest? Maybe my own lack of familiarity with such an environment had caused me to misinterpret his attachment to the land he journeyed through.

I couldn't rid myself of the thought, either, that after reading more than five volumes of his journals, all rich in observations relating to his natural surroundings, it was a single paragraph describing a missionary garden that spoke most directly to me. My scent imagination had been activated by the descriptions of mimosa, nectar-rich honeysuckle, gorse and briar rose. These were the smells that had a place in my own memory and experience. I could summon up the smell of that garden in a way that I hadn't been able to smell the bush. So, did that make me 'foreign'?

I left the museum feeling deeply troubled and disconcerted. I was born in New Zealand, had lived here all my life and valued notions of the unspoilt landscape, the bush and sea, and yet, when tested, my instincts and preferences sent me sniffing back to Britain. I felt as if my nose had betrayed me, as if in some way it was challenging me with the old taunt, 'Pommy, go home'. The realisation that I was somehow perhaps not *of this land* filled me with a sadness I hadn't expected.

I'd intended to take Thora's perfume to her that evening but I wanted to spend some time alone, studying my notes and planning what to do next. I was pulling out all the oils related to the plants in Taylor's missionary garden, comparing them with the wintergreen and rose blend I'd made earlier for my own imaginary 'missionary wife' perfume, when the phone rang. I was so deep in thought that the sound startled me and it took a second before I could identify its source. I barely got out my greeting before the real estate agent began talking, checking that I was happy for her to visit so that my home could be photographed for the website and print listings. She sounded confident, assuring me that the market was in the seller's favour, that she'd already contacted potential buyers and that my loft would be snapped up in no time – days rather than weeks. 'We'll have you cashed up and out of there in no time,' she said, as if doing me a favour. 'I doubt we'll even go to auction.'

I listened in silence, fighting back the urge to explain that I didn't want to sell. Couldn't she understand that the very idea caused me pain, and that I could barely bring myself to think about moving? Inside I was shouting, 'Leave me alone, it's the only thing I've got left. I don't want to turn over a new leaf or start a new chapter in my life. I want to stay here!' I anticipated the language of her advertising copy, with its clichés about the vendor being 'ready to move on' with 'new adventures on the horizon', and wished I could substitute my own version: 'After years of contentment, the vendor's life has turned to shit. Her loss is your gain, but try not to rub it in. She loved this apartment, it meant everything to her.' That's what I wanted to say, but of course I kept silent.

'I'll bring croissants and coffee and we can have a chat about dressing your place for the open homes,' she said before hanging up.

Would my home really sell in a matter of days? It sounded like a death sentence with benefits. If only I could be listed as a chattel and allowed to stay. 'Don't think about it,' I told myself. 'Go out, get some fresh air and calm down. The situation will seem less bleak when you come back.' I doubted it. I could already visualise the fast-approaching day when I would pack away all my books and perfumes and rest my head against the wooden posts and beams one last time, in a futile attempt to collect and hold the smell of my wool-store loft for future comfort.

I decided to go and see Thora. Again there was a line of people in front of the conservatory but I didn't detour from my path to the pharmacy. I wasn't sure if she'd be pleased or merely bemused to see me again so soon, but attempted to make myself feel less self-conscious by promising to just drop off her perfume. I couldn't face the thought that she might already be talking about me to her partner or family, joking about the strange woman from her past who'd suddenly turned up: a perfume addict not so very different from her customers on the methadone programme.

I looked through the window before going in. The shop was empty and Thora was alone, standing at the counter, staring into space. To my relief, she looked pleased to see me.

'You've made it already,' she said as I handed her the bottle.

She unscrewed the cap and held the bottle up to her nose. 'That's incredible,' she said. 'That smell takes me straight back to my bedroom in Aro Valley. I can see it so clearly, the purple tie-dyed sheet I made into a bed cover, the mobiles I made from driftwood, shell and coloured glass, the posters and pin holes in the walls, the bedside table made from a beer crate covered in tapa. It's amazing.' She dabbed the oil onto her skin. 'It's just the same. Thank you.'

In all the time I'd known Thora I think I only went to her flat once or twice, and the smells that stood out were cat pee and onion. I particularly recall the small white flowers of the onion-weed that grew on the damp bank behind the kitchen, and how the smell was so strong it used to distract me from conversation.

'I like the boronia in it,' I said. 'Whenever I smell it I wonder why I haven't used it again in perfume.' As the words came out I knew exactly why I hadn't used it again. In my mind I associated the smell with Thora, and the truth was I wanted to maintain its special meaning.

'Raspberry.'

I nodded. 'Do you remember the Nina Simone concert?'

'Yeah,' said Thora, 'I do. She was great. Our choir tried "My Baby Just Cares for Me" a while back but it wasn't one of our best. We were a little out of our comfort zone.'

'You're in a choir?'

'Don't laugh. It's made up of local pharmacists. We call ourselves A Spoonful of Sugar. I didn't choose the name. We specialise in arrangements on a medical or drug-based theme: 'White Rabbit', 'Lithium' . . . It's pathetic really but we enjoy it, except only a few of us can hold a tune. We sometimes sing at retirement villages. I know, tragic, right.'

'Not if it's fun.'

'I only joined because my ex insisted. The choir was short of mezzo-sopranos and I fitted the bill.'

'So you can sing?'

'Nah. Not really. I'm okay in the background.'

She looked at the scent in her hand. 'It was so nice of you to make this, thank you.'

It was my cue to leave but as I turned to go, Thora cleared her throat and said, 'I was wondering if you might like to have a coffee, or come over for a drink sometime – if you want. My home's not far and my son's usually out.'

'That would be nice, thanks.'

'The only thing I've got planned during the day this week is the lunchtime protest at the university.' She saw my blank look. 'Against closing down the art history department. But I guess you'll be at work?'

'No,' I bluffed, 'I'll be there, protesting.'

'Perfect,' said Thora. 'But don't take it personally if I'm not very chatty. I'll just be tired.'

The walk back across the park in the late evening light was one of the most peaceful I could recall in months. The sky was streaked in pale rinses of pink and yellow, and to the west towers of cumulus loomed upwards, their rounded shapes flattening into tabletops at their greatest height. The air was warm, and as I walked I could hear the footsteps and jagged breath of joggers catching up to me and overtaking, shambling or running ahead. There were still people outside the glasshouse and this time I wandered over to see what was going on. It was unusually late for the garden to be open, but as I drew nearer I could see a long line that curved around the building. I was nearly at the glasshouse when a youngish man approached and asked me if this was the place to view the corpse flower. Suddenly the queue made sense and I increased my pace, joining the back of the line. How had I not been aware of this? It was such a rare event for this giant to flower, and when it did it would last for only a day or two, all the while emitting a stench of rotting flesh.

The queue moved slowly, but as we edged closer to the entrance the anticipation increased. Now we could see and hear people leaving the garden; some of the children held T-shirts over their noses while others, even more dramatically, fanned their hands in front of their faces and made spluttering noises. I heard one woman complain that she thought she was going to faint from the stench. Another complained that it wasn't as bad as she'd thought it would be, that if she'd known it was just going to smell like a dead rat she wouldn't have bothered coming all this way.

'Did you come far?' I asked the man who'd spoken to me earlier.

'Just from across the harbour.'

'Are you interested in smells?'

'No, not really,' he said. 'But this is special.'

As we took a step forward I realised how infrequently I'd found myself in the company of a group of strangers smelling things. Usually sniffing was a furtive exercise, as shameful as looking at your reflection in a store window or, God forbid, picking your nose. The perfume counter, the rose garden, the sensory garden and the odd flower show . . . that was the limit of my communal smelling experience. I imagined a sniffing club, where people simply sat outdoors, taking in their scented surroundings. It was odd that so many people should line up to sniff something known to be 'bad', given that many of them wouldn't pause in their daily life to smell anything pleasant, unless, of course, it was presented at the table as a tasty meal or a glass of wine.

'What do you think it will smell like?' I asked my companion.

'Everyone says it smells like a dead body,' he said.

'Have you ever smelt a dead body?'

'Yes,' he replied. 'Lots.'

I took a step back to see if he was joking, but his expression remained impassive.

It was our turn to enter. The change in temperature from the fresh outdoors to the warm, humid interior was the first thing to grab my attention, but within seconds I caught a wave of odour, a fetid mixture of flowers rotting in stagnant vase water combined with mouldy carpet. I tried not to look at where the corpse flower stood, preferring to let my nose rather than my eyes guide my sensory response. As I stepped closer, the smell became more pungent, reminding me of the blood-soaked pads that line supermarket meat trays. It seemed well past its use-by date, and then it transformed and became more rotten, as if a rodent or some neighbourhood pet had died in the roof or under the floorboards. The smell wasn't quite as strong as I'd imagined it would be but I could see how it might attract pollinating flies and beetles. Now I looked at the plant, and the strangeness of its purple-red flower and elongated spadix created such a powerful impression that the smell seemed much louder than when I had blocked the image from my mind. Connecting the smell to its source made it easier to make sense of the stink; it was now less abstract, easier to define, just as discovering dog shit on the sole of a shoe provides a context for that particular unwanted odour.

I caught up with the young man and asked him if the smell reminded him of corpses.

'No, it's not as strong,' he said. 'It doesn't turn my stomach inside out. When you see bodies lined up on the side of the road you feel like you're trapped in hell. That's just a stinky flower. It's harmless.'

As he finished speaking a woman behind us made a gagging noise and announced she felt sick. A handkerchief covering her face, she pushed past us and I heard the young man mutter something that could have been 'loser'.

We'd lingered too long in front of the plant and the pressure from behind shoved us forward. Of everyone around us, I think we were the only two not to take photos or selfies. As if you could capture a smell in a photograph.

True to her word, the estate agent was at my door at breakfast time with a middle-aged man, whom she introduced as Ralph, beside her. She kicked off her shoes and strode ahead of me into the living area, which she took in with a glance. I noticed she hadn't brought either croissants or coffee as promised but I didn't feel like eating.

'You've really made it your own,' she said. The photographer began snapping, moving pieces of furniture to accommodate the image he needed. The mug of cold coffee that had been sitting on the bench when I opened the door was placed on the floor as he took a photo looking from the kitchen to the living space. The coats and shoes by the front door were shifted behind the couch to allow a clear image of the beautiful woodwork and cleanliness of the windows. The photographer turned to the area where I worked and hesitated, staring at my table, my notebooks, uncertain how to proceed. I stood back, suddenly unsure of my ground, even though it was still my house and these were my possessions. The agent grimaced, as if she'd encountered an unexpected problem. Turning to me, she said, 'We find the photos work best when there's no clutter.' She corrected herself, 'No distracting objects. The place should appear welcoming and look lived in but not too quirky, if you get my meaning. We want buyers to relate to the space, to feel that anybody could fit in.'

I pretended I hadn't quite understood.

'Would you mind if we cleared away some of these bottles?' she said. Then, as if she'd only just noticed, she added, 'There's quite a strong smell in here. It's almost like something . . .' And her words came to a standstill, unable to articulate the thought. 'Would it be okay to move these?' she repeated. As I watched, she began gathering handfuls of the bottled oils, plonking them down on the kitchen bench. The photographer helped her while I remained rooted to the spot, watching as, in their haste to clear them out of the way, they knocked some bottles over or left them to roll across the bench. 'There, that's better, isn't it,' she said. 'I have a couple of reed infusers for the open home. They create a lovely ambience; they're very refreshing and calming. The frangipani and vanilla scent masks odours beautifully.'

I walked over to the wall as the two of them continued with their work and I stood with my hand against the wooden post, my dear friend. I tried to slow down my breathing, inhaling deeply and counting the seconds between breaths.

'It's a wonderful place,' said the agent, her eyes following the photographer as he went about his work. 'It's so spacious and airy and the younger set go crazy for lofts. We'll focus on the urban professional market, all those young doctors and lawyers wanting a low-maintenance lifestyle property.'

'Won't they be paying off their student loans?' I asked.

'Oh, their parents usually come to the table. Homes like this are great investments, they keep their value.'

I closed my eyes and tried to block out the sound of her voice. I felt the wood against my hand, its familiar scent like a soft fug of wool. I caught my breath as a sob rose in my throat.

'Don't bring your diffuser,' I said. 'If you bring it here I'll throw it out of the window.'

'Sorry?'

'You heard me. If you bring a diffuser, I'll throw it out of the window and then I'll hire another agent to take over the sale. You. Do. Not. Bring. A. Diffuser. Here. Understand?'

'But it creates *ambience*,' she said. 'It's *French*.'

'I don't care. You're not bringing it here.'

The agent and the photographer exchanged glances and went back to their work.

I stroked the rough timber and it seemed to exhale with relief. 'Don't worry,' I whispered. 'I promise I'll do my best to protect you. You'll be okay.' I could feel my legs tremble and without intending to I sank to the ground and sat with my arms curled around my knees, staring ahead, as the agent and photographer looked on in horror and incomprehension.

My thoughts kept circling back to Richard Taylor and the grand Māori perfume. I'd gone back to the museum to read the rest of his journals because I'd grown curious about his background, his travels and, most of all, his personality. I'd warmed to the missionary and my only regret was that Archer wasn't around to talk to. Despite Taylor's attention to nature, none of the journals in the museum suggested he was particularly interested in smell. Since I hadn't found any descriptions of perfume as such in his writing, the recipe lacked the context I sought. And I hadn't even noticed any mention of the plants identified in the grand Māori perfume. Had he ever smelt it and, if so, why didn't he describe the scent?

Having finished the journals I decided to head for the city

library to look at the notebook with Taylor's recipe. There was another reason for going. The real estate agent was true to her word, arriving daily to show people through my apartment, and I needed to get away from the continual intrusion on my space. I felt anxious every time she phoned me, and although she suggested that all I had to do was pop out for coffee for half an hour while she rushed potential buyers through, I ended up fretting about what was being said or planned for my home during my absence.

The ground floor of the library was bustling with activity but as I made my way up to the special collections the noise fell away and I felt myself relax. I presented the reference given to me by the museum librarian to the assistant on the desk, summarising my interest in Taylor's perfume recipe. She listened, then disappeared into a back room. I felt self-conscious standing at the desk so took a seat at a large table. I'd barely sat down before a teenager came running in and hid beneath another table, in the corner. There were just the two of us, me sitting upright, him crouched low on the ground with his hoody pulled over his face. I waited, expecting something to happen, but it was as if we'd both been forgotten. The hands on the clock above the desk ticked, minutes passed, and just as I was about to break the silence and ask the teenager if he needed help, he scrambled out from his hiding place and quickly marched away. A moment later the assistant reappeared, an older man beside her. I guessed, from his reserved, rather intimidating manner, that he was a senior member of staff.

'You're interested in Māori perfume?' he asked.

I nodded, and quickly repeated what I'd told the assistant. The senior librarian listened, then placed in front of me a photocopy of a newspaper article from the 1890s headed 'Ancient Maori Perfumes'. It was an extract from *Nature,* written by missionary and naturalist William Colenso. Here were references to scented ferns, one, *Hymenophyllum sanguinolentum*, described as so powerful that its smell impregnated the papers on which it was dried. More trees and plants were listed, and as I read further I came across a description of the rituals associated with collecting gum from the taramea bush, which Colenso had seen growing high up in the Ruahine Ranges. At the end of the clipping was a short Māori lullaby containing the names of the plants piripiri, mokimoki, tāwhiri and taramea.

'Interesting, isn't it?' said the librarian. 'A bit more recent than your Taylor, though.'

I flicked back through the pages, reading again the descriptions of the scented plants.

'Have you looked through any of the John White material?' he asked.

I shook my head. I didn't like to say that, unlike Colenso, I hadn't heard of him.

'Well, there'll be quite a bit about plants in his Māori pharmacopoeia, if you get around to it. But here's the Taylor notebook.' He placed a bound volume on the desk, adding, 'It's a copy, not the original.' And then, much to my surprise, he pulled up a chair and sat down beside me.

We scrolled through the pages of the manuscript together, pausing every now and again as we tried to decipher Taylor's handwriting that, although neat, was difficult to read. The notes covered a broad range of topics, underlined headings that skipped between botany, birds and fishes, to Māori customs, language and proverbs. As we turned each page I realised I was becoming less and less comfortable with the material in front of me.

'I'm not sure what to do.'

I waited, perhaps hoping that the librarian would offer a suggestion, but he didn't. I sat quietly, thinking, and after some time one cause for my hesitation came to me. I'd spent many years lecturing, writing journal articles, or presenting papers based on research gleaned from women's personal narratives: diaries, notebooks and journals. Much of the material was sensitive and

I'd always been careful to follow ethics procedures, filling out forms and ticking boxes. But it had been a given that my work was vital and, as such, the historical and cultural institution of the university itself had always bestowed authority and provided a buffer between the material and me. Now, I was morally and personally accountable for all my research-based decisions. I had to ask, Did I have any right to research the grand Māori perfume? And it was clear to me that as a Pākehā, with only a smattering of tikanga Māori, I didn't.

'This isn't my story.'

'Probably not,' agreed the librarian, 'but it's your journey.'

The word 'journey', with its hint of personal development, self-discovery and destiny, made me wince. I wished he'd simply said, 'But you were curious and wanted to find out more.'

I felt disappointed. My interest in smell and perfume was genuine, and to lay eyes on what I believed to be the first written evidence of the fragrance was immensely appealing. In that instant a sharp sense of loss came over me, which I found difficult to conceal. But I swiftly realised that it wasn't *only* the fact that I wasn't Māori that was holding me back. There was something more, something deeper, more elemental. My brain searched for what it might, be but at that moment the very act of thinking seemed beyond my capabilities. Feeling my way slowly, I said, 'I think I need to go back to the start.'

'The start?'

I began gently tapping my fingers on the table, and the repetitive action and soft sound sparked thought. 'The plants came first,' I murmured.

The librarian's passive expression gave way to surprise.

'What I need to do,' I continued, feeling more sure of myself, 'is learn a new way of smelling. My aesthetic is all wrong. I don't know *how* to smell native plants because my nose keeps drawing me back to the smells I already know and appreciate.'

The librarian gave me a glance that suggested I'd failed to grasp the nub of the lesson and had gone off on an unexpected tangent.

'Yes,' I said. 'I don't know how to distinguish one plant from the next. I have to teach myself a new way of smelling, so the scents of the individual natives become as easy to locate in my brain as rose, honeysuckle or lavender. I need to start again with the notes.' Though I was still grasping for clarity of thought, the idea of relearning how to smell took hold and dispelled some of my earlier disappointment. 'The plants are my way into the subject. They're the first step towards understanding the traditions and culture surrounding them. That's how I can learn to be of this land.'

'So botany, ethnobotany, tikanga Māori, colonial history . . . That *is* quite a journey,' the librarian said, his face professionally closed once more. 'I hope you're not working to a deadline.'

'I'm not,' I replied.

He patted the volume. 'Do you want to see Taylor's entry for the recipe before you start?'

'No, thanks. It's okay.'

He sighed. 'I won't leave this out for you, then. I'll reshelve it.'

As I walked home I saw that the trip to the library had done me good. It seemed as if a faint trace of order was beginning to return to my life. My future, still uncertain, was not as frightening. I'd started to make decisions, to regain control and a sense of purpose. I was no longer tumbling around feeling lost but had begun to move forward at a gentle speed I could sustain. Yes, I would learn about plants, but it wasn't a race and I had nothing to prove. I didn't have to become an expert. I would take my time, my whole life if necessary, and allow the knowledge to grow, slowly and steadily, naturally. It would enter me, like breath and scent.

I could hear the protest before I could see it. A distorted voice calling through a megaphone and the roar of the crowd's response, 'Shame, shame, shame!' I hurried up the hill, joining a stream of people all headed in the same direction. Some kept to themselves and looked downcast, but others formed lively groups, holding banners between them and chanting as they marched ahead. When I reached the main campus I joined the back of a large mass of people. Voices came from all directions, a chorus gathering momentum in its rallying cry of 'Save the humanities!', 'Arts not cuts!'

A young woman representing the trade union climbed onto the stage and everyone clapped and shouted. Then she launched into an angry and impassioned speech about abuse of power, workers' rights and the necessity for the humanities. As she finished by declaring that an attack on the humanities was an attack on thinking that threatened the very core of learning and education, a cry of support went up and the crowd erupted in cheers. These were quickly replaced by loud booing as the pro-vice-chancellor took the stage. He looked as arrogant as I remembered, and as he spoke about the university's commitment to the arts the booing grew in strength and a chant of 'Shame, shame, shame!' drowned him out. In one brief lull, I heard him sputter, 'The changes we make now will save the arts in the future', but his words were met with 'Liar, liar, liar!' and soon that was all I could hear.

It began to rain, warm, heavy drops falling straight down, saturating us within minutes. Umbrellas appeared, giving the crowd a colourful, festive appearance, and I found myself being pushed closer towards the stage as those around me adjusted their positions, moving to find shelter under awnings and trees. I found a spot beneath a group of gums. Their long strips of bark had been raked and heaped into an untidy mound, and

I reached down and absent-mindedly picked up a handful of gumnuts.

The mood darkened as the vice-chancellor herself reached the stage. Facing straight ahead, her feet slightly apart, she waited a moment, scanning the crowd before speaking. Her voice was clear and calm and the protesters fell quiet. 'Understand,' she said, 'this university loves the arts. We stand by the humanities and all our staff.' Around me people began jostling and again I was shoved forward, so now I was to the side of the platform, close to the steps leading up to the stage. A voice from the crowd challenged her, and the vice-chancellor immediately swung to face the source of the interruption. 'I say it again. These cuts are necessary to save the future of the arts.'

'Bullshit!' said another protester, and people joined in, 'Bullshit' and 'Liar, liar, arts on fire!' rebounding around the quadrangle. I saw the vice-chancellor look around. The dean of the humanities stepped towards her but she motioned him away. Still scanning the faces in front of her, her eyes settled on me and I saw the flicker of recognition.

'Save our staff!' another voice called, and again the chant was taken up. 'Save our staff. Honour learning!'

The vice-chancellor shook her head, and tried to speak again but couldn't make herself heard over the racket. 'One minute!' she ordered. The crowd fell quiet. 'We have the best interests of the university and all our staff at heart . . .'

I felt sick. Everything she said was a lie and even though I wanted nothing to do with her, I knew I had to say something. Even so, I glanced around, hoping that someone else would do the job for me. Sick with nerves, I slowly mounted the steps and a security guard, one of the campus goons, blocked my path. I tried to edge past but he held his ground. 'Let me through,' I said, my voice quiet, barely registering above the crowd. 'It's my turn.' I saw the organiser of the rally glance from me to the vice-chancellor, and in that second she gave a shrug, a gesture so dismissive that it enraged me, and I gave the guard a shove and stepped out onto the stage.

Nothing in all my years of lecturing could have prepared me for the sight of such a large crowd, all strangers. When a lone voice called out, 'Make American studies great again!', I tried to locate the speaker but it was impossible. Someone handed me the megaphone and I stepped forward. 'I am Dr Siân Rees and I was a lecturer in the American studies department . . .' A cheer went up. 'I was employed at this university for almost fifteen years, until the morning I came into work to discover a brown envelope in my pigeonhole. Inside was a letter informing me that my department had been disestablished and that I was redundant. This is what the VC means by management for change – a management that lacks honesty, respect and empathy.'

'Shame, shame, shame!' went the crowd.

'When I lost my job, I discovered that I no longer recognised myself – I lost my identity and sense of self. Moreover, in the face of permanent unemployment I'm about to lose my home, a place I love and cherish. But that's nothing compared with what we, as a society and culture, lose when the arts come under attack. Our collective identity, our cultural memory, the narratives we share must be acknowledged and honoured and we can only achieve that if . . .' At that moment I saw the vice-chancellor roll her eyes and glance at her phone and I lost my composure and train of thought, stammering, 'short-sighted attack . . . egregious business model . . .'

The crowd didn't seem aware of my stumble. 'We support the arts! Save the humanities!' and the sound of spontaneous clapping filled the air.

'American studies, religious studies, art history, history, linguistics, languages, philosophy, classics, archaeology . . . all under threat. So let's be clear, this conversation is not about saving the *humanities*. Rather, it's about saving the university. Because, make no mistake, the university needs us. Without us, it will lose its relevance. It will no longer be a house of learning or command authority and respect. It will be diminished, reduced to a shell. A bland institution offering conveyor belt courses . . .' I couldn't hear myself think. I tried to continue but my growing awareness of the vice-chancellor's restlessness distracted me. I tried to take up where I'd left off, repeating, 'The university needs us', but I was lost, and I stepped away from the microphone.

As I pushed back through the crowd one or two people smiled at me, but most didn't notice me go by. The protest continued, the crowd continued to chant. The energy within the quadrangle rose and fell, and I was just another voice, one of many. But I'd eased my conscience and I felt better. Quite possibly I'd made a fool of myself but at least I hadn't remained silent. And that was enough for me.

Notes for a beating heart: A question mark hangs over my heart notes; I can't complete them yet. At least I now know where to look, where to find the final ingredient for my blend. I've already started my search. As I left the protest the sun came out and within minutes the heat caused the ground to steam. The first thing I noticed was the scent rising from the mound of eucalyptus bark. It was intoxicating, the smell transporting me to a place of piercing light and heat shimmering beneath a cloud of fresh camphor. The steam continued to rise, creating a fine mist that filtered through the trees at the outskirts of the university grounds. It was like being inside a hothouse. Walking past a small planting of native bush I identified a kawakawa, its bright green and caterpillar-nibbled heart-shaped leaves distinctive against the ferns nearby. I plucked a leaf and crushed it, inhaling a scent of peppered baked potatoes. I took some more and sniffed again, aware that I was being watched by a group of students seated on a bench across the small lawn. The scent was muted, but pleasant, far less harsh than the peppery horopito I'd muddled at Archer's. Ignoring the students, I stepped deeper into the bush and went from plant to plant, plucking, crushing and inhaling the leaves. I found a tarata and enjoyed the lemon scent I'd first 'discovered' back in Renate's garden. I took my time sniffing and testing, and as I pushed further into the thicket I realised I felt happy. A weight had lifted, I was having fun.

A list of potential heart notes: wool, dust, oak, mince, daffodils, iris, lemon, oysters, the sea, roses, camphor, gorse, cigarette smoke, pumice, mud, ash, fern, lilac, sweat, ivy, whisky, wormwood, benzoin, paper, willow, corpse flower, kawakawa, horopito, tarata.

TOP NOTES

Notes of relocation: The fold-out table in my caravan isn't big enough to display all my perfume oils. I still have all my scents but they're stored in file boxes, securely stacked in the storage space beneath the back seat that converts into a double bed at night. The oils and tinctures I'm working with for my signature scent are close at hand, lined up neatly on a wooden board placed over the stove and sink top in front of me. I've simplified my original selection. I think the reduction of notes is a response to my new living arrangement but, more than that, I think that I see myself, now, as decluttered, a simpler version of my old self. My base notes are only three: oakmoss, benzoin and ambergris. The benzoin lifts the deep earthiness of the moss, adding light to the base. Ambergris joins the base notes, but I'm using it to represent the wool and lanolin of my beloved home, the place in my heart I will never abandon.

Much as I love the smell, I've dispensed with the notes of oats and gorse as they don't work with the bitterness of my main heart notes: ivy and willow. Combined, oats and gorse would have created a smell reminiscent of a golden coconut biscuit newly baked in the oven. But, even though I'd like to draw on memory associations with my grandfather and his fried porridge, or my own passing fancy with being Gorse Woman, these notes don't represent me and aren't right for this perfume.

The heart notes of my signature scent are deep and dark, like a pool of still water in the bend of a river. Ivy and willow, one plant clinging and the other weeping; barely recognisable as perfume ingredients but I find myself drawn to them all the same. The leaves aren't flashy, they don't announce themselves, but they carry a sense of gravitas, for me at least.

Finally, the place in my perfume's heart I haven't yet filled. The space I've set aside for a new note, a 'discovery'. I still have so much to learn, I need to look and feel and taste and sniff. I need to capture a sense of place, this place, not some land that lies across the ocean. Maybe I will go with tarata. Its lemon note would lift the green of the ivy and willow and possibly provide a bridge to the fresher top notes. Tarata. I can recognise it now by its smell.

So now the top notes. The final addition to my perfume, the bursts of energy, my here and now, and the way ahead.

After my apartment sold, it seemed a good idea to move south, to the island where I was born. My move was a retreat, I knew that, but I couldn't remain in Auckland after losing both my job and my home; it was too painful. There was nothing keeping me there, apart from a sense of loss that I was afraid might take over my life and become a bitter, twisted comfort.

On the day of the protest, after my 'performance' on stage, Thora found me and brought me back to her apartment, and we sat at her table and I told her about some of the things that were important to me: my career, my friendship with Archer, my soon-to-be-taken-from-me home, and my perfumes. I explained that I'd felt deracinated, well and truly lost. I even explained my attempt to recapture myself through a signature scent, as if I might recognise myself through smell. Thora listened and when I stopped talking we sat quietly while I tried to think of something more to add. I rambled on, desperate to fill the space around me. After a while, I grew tired of the sound of my own voice but Thora seemed capable of endless listening. Exhausted, I said, 'Please talk.'

Thora told me about her years at university. After I knew her, she finished her degree in chemistry and then applied for medical school and moved to Dunedin but fell pregnant in her third year and dropped out. Her son's father was also a medical student and they stayed together, off and on, for six years but eventually split, 'and things became dark'. Thora left out the next few years of her story but came back to it again when her son started high school and she returned to university, this time completing a pharmacy degree.

When I said, 'That must have been satisfying', Thora nodded but somehow she didn't look convinced.

'I moved up here when I took the job at the pharmacy. I needed some time out from a relationship and this job was only meant to be for a year, filling a maternity leave position, but I'm still here, eighteen months later.'

'You don't like it?'

She sighed, then replied, 'No. Yeah, it's fine. I don't know. My son is here too. This is his apartment, though you'd hardly know it – he's never here during the day. I'd like to go back to Wellington at some point. I still own a house there, in Newtown. Also, things have settled down with my ex . . .'

'The ex who got you to join the choir?'

'No. It's a bit complicated. There's the choir ex, who's now a friend, and then there's the Wellington ex, who I cheated on with the choir ex. I've finally managed to buy out Wellington ex, so I've got my house back.'

'What would you do if you went home?'

'Research. I should have stuck with chemistry and I'm more comfortable in a lab, it suits my nature – not that there's anything wrong with the over-the-counter pharmacy.'

'But you're okay here?'

She smiled. 'Yeah, fine.' Then she sighed again, caught herself and laughed. 'It's all good. I'm a bit tired, that's all – too many night shifts and stressed customers.'

I stayed for dinner, relishing the novelty of being cooked for. I noticed that Thora was very organised in the kitchen: she measured out all her ingredients using properly marked cups and spoons. Nothing, it seemed, was left to chance. The oven timer was set to roast the chicken, and its flesh was prodded with a thermometer to ensure it was cooked to perfection. Rice was measured and rinsed before being cooked by the absorption method. Aioli was made from scratch, a clove of garlic crushed with a pestle and mortar, the egg yolk and mustard whisked together before Thora began the long, slow process of drizzling in the oil. I could see the look of concentration on her face as she whisked and her satisfaction when the mixture thickened and she added lemon juice and garlic. She caught me looking at her and joked that she'd got lucky, that nine times out of ten the mixture split, but I didn't believe her. The only time she lost her place was when the asparagus went from bright green and crunchy to yellow-green and limp within a matter of seconds. A look of disbelief crossed her face: 'That wasn't meant to happen.' I had to reassure her that I preferred it like that, that it was how my grandmother and mother cooked it when I was a child.

As we ate I told her about Taylor's notebook and the emotions I'd felt when faced with the opportunity to see the recipe for the grand Māori perfume. 'I was really thrown by the experience,' I said. 'The funny thing is that part of me still believes that plants are just plants. They've been around longer than humans so they should be valued for what they are, free from classification.'

'But?'

'But once you know the cultural significance you can't go on pretending they're just plants. And using ingredients from those plants is an act of cultural appropriation.'

'Has that ever stopped you from using ingredients like benzoin or frankincense in the past?' Thora asked. 'Don't most plants have cultural significance, no matter how far removed that culture is from your own? Just because the plants grow on the other side of the world, and their production is out of sight . . .'

'I guess I'm a hypocrite.'

'You could always stop wearing perfume.'

'Yeah,' I agreed. 'I could. Or I could try and learn about both the plants and the culture.'

'Or you could give it five years, by which time the overseas perfume houses will catch on and start making the grand Māori perfume. Then you can go out and buy a bottle from The Corner Dairy.'

'Aw, don't say that.'

'It's only a matter of time.'

I took a breath. 'I'm wondering if I should put some of the money from the sale of my apartment towards learning how to make proper perfumes. I could apply to one of the perfume schools in France.' Merely saying the words aloud frightened me. I had a good idea of how much it would cost to attend a reputable perfume school and I wasn't sure I was brave enough to take the risk. Even if I had talent I might fail and be left with nothing.

'Could you afford it?' she asked.

'I think so.' I felt the knot tighten in my stomach. 'But if it didn't work out I'd be out of pocket.'

'Yeah,' said Thora, 'but then again, it might be the best thing you ever did.'

She yawned and I realised how long I'd stayed, that it was time to go home. I carried our plates to the kitchen and as I turned to leave I saw her standing by the table, her head bowed, deep in thought. It struck me that I might not see her again. Something about our relationship seemed built on distance. We were both too naturally solitary and inward-looking to maintain regular catch-ups and conversations. We needed a bridging friend, someone who would take us under her wing and organise coffee dates. Left to our own devices, we would think of each other on a fairly regular basis but never quite muster the energy to meet. It had always been Archer and Jerome who came to me, in the past. That was how our friendships had been able to develop, through their efforts not mine.

'Before you go,' said Thora, 'I want to show you something.' She led the way down the hall and into a darkened bedroom at the rear of the apartment. She switched on a small bedside lamp and there, filling the entire wall opposite the bed, was something so unexpected I gasped.

'I became interested in uranium glass after you gave me your perfume,' said Thora as I examined the shelves laden with vases, dishes, bottles and small trinkets in various shades of yellow and green. 'I started collecting it when I did my chemistry degree. It was very cheap back then because it wasn't fashionable. Most of the people I knew were collecting Crown Lynn or Pitcairn Island wooden fish, so I had a clear run at glass.'

My grandmother's perfume bottle sat on the middle shelf and when I saw it I felt a pang. I recalled how I had carried it around in my pocket before giving it to Thora all those years before.

'One of the things my Granny Seren told me that never made sense was that her bottle glowed. I think it must have been her imagination – she was a great one for finding magic and meaning in everyday life. She always claimed she had gypsy blood from her ancestors.'

'Did you ever see it glow?'

'No. I can remember watching but nothing happened. Later, when it was mine, I didn't dare test it because I didn't want to be disappointed. I wanted to believe Seren.'

'I hope you don't mind me saying this but I think you might have some serious trust issues.'

'Yeah, probably. Doesn't everyone?'

Thora came over to where I was standing and flicked a switch on the side of the shelving unit. The entire display of uranium glass lit up, each vessel the most incredible, luminous, bright yellow to vivid green I'd ever seen.

'It fluoresces under ultraviolet light.'

I couldn't respond.

'Take a look at your grandmother's bottle.'

I saw how the scalloped design glowed as if lit from within.

'In the old days, before everyone had bright electric lights, people would notice these bottles glow at twilight – that's when red begins to fade and the violet end of the spectrum dominates. Your bottle dates back to the 1890s, so if it belonged to your great-grandmother she might have noticed it.'

'Seren was telling the truth.'

'Yep. It's beautiful, isn't it?' Without turning off the black light she reached forward for my grandmother's bottle and pressed it into my hand, closing my fingers around it with her own. She then turned back to the shelf and quickly rearranged some of the smaller items to close the gap, filling the space once more.

My caravan is parked beside a small dam in the lee of a long row of poplars that provide shelter to the orchard where I'm currently employed. I ended up in Central Otago because it seemed simpler for me to relocate to the caravan I bought off Trade Me than the other way around. I signed up with a local employment agency, a collective made up of growers and orchardists, and began working in a vineyard. I found that I enjoyed the work, finding solace in the quiet retreat. After a few weeks working on the vines I shifted to cherries, and now I'm in an apricot orchard, a family-run business on the outskirts of town.

I thought I might be too old for fruit picking but I'm surprised by the number of workers who are my age or older. We sit together after work, drawing our chairs into a circle, and talk about what has brought us here, and where we'll go once the apricots are finished. Some of my new acquaintances live a nomadic life, travelling in large motor homes and buses from region to region, taking up casual labour wherever they can find it. There are a number of retired builders and tradespeople, but there are teachers, nurses and other professionals too. Many have chosen this lifestyle but some, like me, fell into this new way of working after losing homes or employment owing to earthquakes, restructuring or financial difficulties. Although we come from all walks of life there's a sense of community, an emotional bond that draws us close. We've formed our own small tribe, just as the foreign pickers and students have formed theirs.

The heat here can be intense and most of us start early, moving through the trees before the sun gets too high. The smell that greets me first thing in the morning takes my breath away. It's the scent of overripe apricots, of fruit scattered on the ground where it has fallen or been discarded. Unlike apricots still on the tree, this fallen fruit is rich and sugared, as if made into jam. There's a density to the scent; it can range from honeyed sweetness through to whisky booziness. As the sun climbs higher, the smell of slowly rotting fruit becomes more pronounced and permeates the entire orchard. Insects hum, their ground-level noise a carpet of sound that we climb above every time we move our ladders. The fruit feels warm in our hands but its scent is lighter, fresher. It seems to retain a semblance of its floral beginnings, something like blossom touched with dew.

As the day progresses, my nose becomes less sensitive to the apricots and starts to pick up other smells that linger in the air of the orchard. I notice the scent of grass sweetened with flowering clover. The metallic smell of the ladders, as the aluminium heats up. The smell of sweat and sun lotion, the fragrance of the latter standing out against the quieter, natural smell of the orchard. The leaves and trunks as I brush up against them.

The smell of water drifting from sprinklers during the night hours.

Sometimes, after dinner, I go for a short stroll on the hill behind the orchard, where a single taramea grows up from a patch of dry soil between two rocky outcrops. I sit and look at it; of all the plants I've ever seen it strikes me as the wildest, the most untamable. I've never cut its leaves or smelt its gum.

Up on the hill the smell of wild thyme is so strong that it burns my nose and catches in my throat. It's medicinal and, just like the wormwood in the sensory garden, clears out my nasal passages, at times making my eyes water. There are other wild flowers growing on the hill: viper's bugloss, briar rose with leaves that carry the smell of apple and, everywhere, like black shadows across the land, pine trees. I've made a blend, a response to the orchard hill that I've named Wildings. It's strongly aromatic, the thyme and pine tussle for domination, and I've had to work through many dilutions and variations in order to ensure that neither of these notes overwhelms the rest of the blend.

Through sheer good luck I came upon the heart note of my Wildings scent as I was parking my car in a picnic area at the foot of a popular mountain-biking track. A sign by the picnic table informs visitors that a cottage once stood on the site, but now all that remains is a long-abandoned outhouse and a collapsed wall, stones crumbling into yellow clay and dust. As I stepped out of my car, I caught a smell I still associate with my mother and the cabinet beneath our bathroom sink: jasmine. I looked around but there was nothing close by as far as I could tell. I laced up my shoes, leaning against the crumbled wall for support, and again the smell of jasmine wafted over me.

I set off, and as I reached the derelict outhouse a small white flower caught my eye and I saw that within the walls of the building was a small vine, draped, as if lounging, across rocks that had tumbled into and covered the floor space of the long drop's interior.

At one time, the jasmine must have grown in abundance, its flowers cloaking the entire building, its perfume mixing with that of the toilet itself. When I went back to my caravan that evening I tested jasmine against the pine and thyme and found that its fullness and sweetness worked with the notes in a surprisingly pleasant way. All I had to do to finish my blend was add a slight touch of lemon to cut through the fullness of the jasmine and provide a rush of energy.

On weekends I take my homemade perfumes to the local market where I have a makeshift stall squeezed between a couple that sells deep-fried banana dumplings, and a retired local who paints flower and landscape scenes on river stones. I introduced my Wildings scent a few weeks ago and, to my delight, it has proved popular with both locals and summer visitors. Many of the people who tested it remarked that the smell 'reminded them of something', though not all of them could say what it was. If I wait, however, most of them manage to identify thyme among the notes. Those who can't identify the individual ingredients when they first smell the perfume always nod in recognition once I provide the correct words. 'Of course,' they say. 'It was on the tip of my tongue. I knew I knew the smell but I just couldn't think of what it was. But now you've told me it's so obvious. I get the thyme now. Pine needles. Flowers. Jasmine.'

I love the moment when my customers start sharing their memories of scent with me. One woman, who grew up on a farm on Banks Peninsula, described her childhood, and the mixture of fear and pleasure she used to experience when she had to go outside to the toilet during the night. I listened carefully as she spoke and wrote down what she said after she left.

'The long drop was corrugated iron and almost completely covered in jasmine and honeysuckle. During the day, bees and flies and cicadas created a constant buzz. Inside, the toilet was warm, sometimes very hot from the sun bearing down on the tin. I noticed that the jasmine smelt like the contents of the toilet, and the toilet smelt like jasmine. They were a perfect pair. At night, the scent changed and became cleaner, as if everything had been washed in Sunlight soap. There were hundreds of moths bumping around the outside light. They scared me when they fluttered too close. The long drop itself was like a black well. I thought about all the things that might live in it, down there. When I went out to the toilet at night I could hear the waves lapping below on the beach. The wind used to blow through the macrocarpa hedge. I had a torch, and I balanced it on the frame of the toilet wall. The shadows were scary but beautiful. The toilet roll, spider webs and tendrils of jasmine . . . all crazy, unfamiliar. The outside toilet was peaceful and yet busy with life and smells. Funny what you remember.'

More and more often I've taken to asking people to describe a scent from their childhood, or a favourite scent memory, and it's surprising how easily they are able to pinpoint an exact moment in their life in that way. I make notes once they have gone, a list that grows and grows:

'My grandmother smelt of hairspray and ash.'

'The day my father died I went outside and sat in his car, and it smelt of him. I bawled my eyes out.'

'My mother always sprayed too much perfume. I hated it. It made her smell like an old lady. I think it was called Youth Dew but us kids called it Youth Spew.'

'I got married in Queensland and the gazebo was covered in frangipani. I only have to get a whiff of it and I'm back there, with my wife. Happiest day of my life.'

'I love the smell of swimming pool water when it splashes onto hot concrete. It reminds me of when I was a teenager and spent summers at the local pool with my friends. I like bleach, too, when it dries on your skin.'

'My dog eats poo. I hate it when he licks me afterwards, and I yell at him and my mum says we should get him put down. Dog poo is much worse than sheep poo, but pig shit is worse.'

'My old woollen hunting jersey. One sniff and I'm like, out of here!'

Not long ago a man sidled up and asked if perfume could bring memory to life. I said I thought so, but in most cases it could only be an interpretation of an experience, rather than a literal depiction, so more like a painting than a photograph.

He said, 'I want something that reminds me of the West Coast.'

'The beach or the bush?'

'Where the bush comes right down to the sea. I used to walk through the bush and push through a whole lot of flax. The beach was wild and littered with big pieces of driftwood, huge trunks washed down from the flooded rivers. Foam came off the breakers, and left wobbly marks along the tide. The air was humid and smelt salty, like the sea. It was hazy. I used to go there all the time with my brother. Can you make that?'

I nodded. 'I can give it a go. Why do you want that scent?'

'Because my brother's dead and because it's the smell of New Zealand, where I grew up.'

'The smell of New Zealand?'

'Yeah. That, two-stroke and beer.'

'I spent most of my childhood at my grandparents' house,' I told him, 'by the gasworks. We could make a New Zealand perfume based on beer and gas.'

He thought that was hilarious and then, growing serious, asked how much the New Zealand perfume would cost, adding, 'Can you make it so I can smell it without having to wear it. I don't want, you know, *to wear perfume*.'

I think I did a good job. It's based around the scent of salt air, because I was thinking about his brother and how his spirit might be hovering above the bush, beach and sea. I tried the perfume out on my fruit-picking friends one night as we sat around the campsite. I had three versions, all slightly different, and I set up a blind test, asking them to rank the samples from best to worst. I thought there would be a clear winner – the one I eventually posted off – but the results were completely mixed. I hadn't given any clues to what I made, and everyone came up with their own take on the scent, something within the perfume that spoke to them. Ross, the retired builder, liked the perfume because it smelt like wood shavings.

'Which one is that?' I asked. He held out a blotter and I took it from him and waved it before my nose.

'It's cedar,' I said. 'I was trying for driftwood. You picked it out from all the other notes.'

'My first job was helping my dad down at the mill,' he replied. 'I'd never forget that smell.'

Rosemary, his wife, identified a metallic, fishy smell in one of the testers. An afterthought on my part, falling back on my old trick of oil from a tin of smoked oysters.

'I like the pretty one,' said Miriam. 'The rose one.'

There was no 'rose one', but I'd used geranium oil in the scent she identified, and geraniol, present in both geranium and rose, is rose-like. I'd added geranium to the blend to bring out the impression of flax.

In the end I chose the perfume I liked best, gave it the manly title of West Coaster and sent it off with a piece of the pumice I'd collected from Rotorua when I was there with Archer. I suggested to my customer that he apply a few drops of the oil to the porous stone and carry it in his pocket or on a string around his wrist or neck. I tried it myself on another piece of pumice and enjoyed the way the perfume interacted with the sand-scented volcanic rock.

After making West Coaster I started quizzing visitors to my stall about what, to them, was the smell of New Zealand. Most people responded with either 'the bush' or 'the sea' and I had to probe them to give more detail. 'It's the smell of honey dew on beech trees,' said one woman. 'That's such a great smell, it's so peaceful.'

'The smell is peaceful?'

'I don't know. I guess so. The bush is peaceful, that's what I mean.'

Another person surprised me by responding 'silage'. He had a faraway look in his eyes and when I asked him what made him think of silage he looked embarrassed and said, 'All right, rye grass. Rye grass growing on the Hakataramea hills.'

'Is that where you grew up? On a farm?'

'During the late forties. Best days of my life.'

'What about the wool shed?' I asked. 'I love that smell, greasy wool and a bit of sheep poo.'

He gave me a funny look but nodded in agreement, then said, 'Clover.'

I tried a different way of posing the question: 'If you were going to describe the smell of New Zealand to someone who hadn't been here, what would you say?'

Almost everyone said 'the bush' and 'the beach', although a tourist from New York said, 'fresh air'. I kept asking different people, and quite often men would offer aromas associated with food: roast lamb, fish'n'chips or hāngī or even hokey pokey ice cream and pavlova. If I asked them to name a plant or flower they tended to look uncomfortable, shake their head and say, 'I don't know. The bush?'

'Saturday,' said another, 'when I mow the lawn. Love it.'

There were exceptions, people who were keen to consider the question. 'It's impossible to narrow the scent of New Zealand down to one thing,' said a woman of my own age. 'It's going to be different depending on who you are, where you live.'

'But if you had to,' I said.

'Cabbage trees. The smell of cabbage trees in flower. They're like jasmine or lily, sweet. But lots of natives have beautiful scents. You just have to know what to look for. Have you ever smelt the native Easter orchid? It's fabulous, so strong.'

'Are you a botanist?'

'No. I have a big garden, though. Are you a botanist?'

'No. I don't even have a garden but I'm trying to train my nose to be more receptive to the smells of my surroundings. I think we don't spend enough time thinking about smell. Or smelling things.'

Several nights ago I was sitting at my table, staring into space, when my phone rang. It was Jerome, calling with news. 'Three things,' he began before immediately launching into how he'd been successful in the latest round of Marsden funding. He talked on and on, so gripped with the details of his $900,000 award and new research project that he almost forgot to mention the other two pieces of information: that the cause of Archer's death was confirmed, he'd had an aneurysm while driving, and that Desna was pregnant with twins.

'How did Renate take it?' I interrupted.

'Oh, she's really pleased for me. She says it's about time literature got funded.'

I waited a moment. 'Sorry, I meant about Archer.'

There was an awkward pause, and Jerome came back on the line. 'Of course. I'm really sorry. I wasn't thinking.' I could almost see him, his mortified expression as he tried to backtrack and save the situation. 'She's good. Keeping busy, I think. She misses Archer but having Hester helps. They're very close.'

'That's good. And great news about Desna, congratulations.'

'Thanks, yes. We're very happy. Big changes all around.'

We spent a few more minutes speaking about Renate and Desna, and then Jerome manoeuvred the conversation back to his funding. 'I'm going to buy out all my teaching so I can concentrate on the project. Are you interested?'

My heart missed a beat. 'What?'

'Are you interested in taking over my teaching and being my wingman on the research? It's a three-year project. You could come back and be my assistant. It's well paid. What do you think?'

I could go back.

I've been unable to sleep, thinking about Jerome's offer. Of course I should grab the opportunity to return to academia. Two or three years' employment, slipping back into the university environment, doing the thing I am good at: teaching and research. I could re-establish myself and then, from a position of security, apply to other universities when my contract approaches its end. I'd be stupid not to take up his offer. I'd have financial security and my life could return to normal, just like before.

This past evening, after working all day in the orchard, I was so sore I could barely move. The weather forecast isn't good, hail is predicted, and we've been working extra hard to bring in the fruit. I was so tired I couldn't face preparing dinner but made myself a sandwich, which I took outside and ate while the other pickers complained about the day and discussed their plans for the rest of the season once the apricots are done. The names of their favourite apple orchards were passed around, and those who had past experience promised to put in a good word for those new to the crop. I thought no one had noticed me, but Ross asked if I was interested in the apple harvest. When I hesitated, he said, 'It's hard work but the temperature's cooler so it seems less tiring than apricots, unless the frosts hit, that is. Some of us make cider, which is a bonus, if you're tempted? The apples smell good, too . . .' When I didn't respond immediately, he asked, 'You must be working on a new perfume. What is it?'

I was going to fob him off with the easy answer, a perfume built around the smell of the orchard and the sweet briar on the hillside, but instead I said slowly, 'A signature scent. I'm trying to finish a perfume that summons up my identity. A perfume that explains who I am, that captures my personality and makes me feel whole.'

I inhaled, and the residue of the long day entered my nose: ripe apricots, earth and dust, warm grass, sun lotion, sweat, the poplars, the faintly dank air rising up from the dam, and the fresher water from the sprinklers.

'You don't feel whole?' asked Rosemary. 'How is it possible not to feel whole when you have this?'

SCENTED

Base Notes:
Oakmoss
Benzoin
Ambergris

Heart Notes:
Willow
Ivy
Tarata

Top Notes:
Osmanthus
Apple
Briar rose

Dilute in jojoba oil

ACKNOWLEDGEMENTS

Thanks to everyone who gave up their time and shared their knowledge with me: Janice Lord, Emma Burns, Peter Johnson, Martin Collett, Vincent Micotti, Serena and Harold Jones, Frances Nelson, Gaynor Bradfield, Robin Krug and the NST community, Rhian Gallagher, Alison Ballance, Pip Adam and Sue Wootton.

Thank you to the Glasgow Street Arts Centre Artist in Residence Programme, Whanganui; Mark Rayner, Paul Rayner and Lauren Lysaght for providing a place to write and a warm welcome in October 2018.

Grateful thanks for assistance and funding from the 2016 NZSA Auckland Museum National Research Grant and the 2016 NZSA Janet Frame Memorial Award. Thank you to Jan, Tania and Frankie for making room for me at the Michael King Writers' Centre during August 2017.

Thank you to everyone at Penguin Random House and my publisher Harriet Allan for continued support. Anna Rogers is a sensitive and gifted editor and once again I owe her a debt of thanks for turning my manuscript into a finished novel. Thank you to Louisa Kasza, Rebecca Lal and Maggie Trapp for guiding the manuscript through its final stages. Keely O'Shannessy designed a beautiful cover and Katrina Duncan made it all look good. Thank you.

Thanks to my family: Wendy, Dave and Jan for good company and especially Alex and Harry for their ongoing love and encouragement. Lastly, thanks to Sprocket and Patch, who taught me most about sniffing and never turned down a walk.

It was more beautiful than anything I had ever seen and I didn't have the words to describe it. I felt it though. I let out an incredible whoop of joy and skipped into the air, laughing and laughing; there was so much joy inside me. For the first time in all my memory, I could not contain myself.

As a boy in the early 1940s, young Boden Black finds his life changed forever the day his neighbour Dudley drives him over the hills into the vast snow-covered plains of the Mackenzie country. Unexpectedly his world opens up and he discovers a love of landscape and a fascination with words that will guide him throughout his life, as he forges a career as a butcher and poet, spends a joyous summer building a hut on the slopes of Mount Cook and climbs to the summit in the company of Sir Edmund Hillary.

A moving exploration of one man's journey and the events which shape him, *The Hut Builder* is also an evocative celebration of the mountain world and the wonder of life.

I wonder why Edwin's mother left him – why his mother left and mine stayed? I mean, which is the more damaging – the mother who tells you she loves you and leaves, or the mother who calls you stupid and stays?

This beautifully written novel is about finding love in the most unlikely of places. Set in the southern South Island, it describes the unusual bond formed between sixty-two-year-old photographer Edwin and twenty-two-year-old Matilda, as their relationship grows in ways neither could possibly have predicted.

I liked the look of concentration on his face when we made love. His hands moved gently over my body; it was as if he was turning the pages of some fragile book – the type of book that has tissue pages, like an old-fashioned Bible. He reminded me, too, of a child learning to read. I pictured his fingertips tracing the words on the page, his lips mouthing the sounds, so intense was his focus. 'Edwin,' I teased, 'am I a good book?'

One of the reasons she was attracted to etchings was the deep, rich, black of the oily ink. A good layer of black ink was fathomless, like the sky or the sea at night. It was black as the unconscious mind, full of life but beyond reach.

Quinn is a successful artist creating new works for an upcoming exhibition. She lives on the coast with Marcus, a vet who left his wife for her and lost contact with his young daughter Audrey as a result. Entering their lives is Callum, a deep-sea diver with a love of the ocean. As the countdown to Quinn's exhibition progresses, each must face challenges and make choices that will test their loyalties and have far-reaching consequences for their future.

Reach is about risk-taking and the ways in which creativity, struggle and danger empower individuals and enrich life.

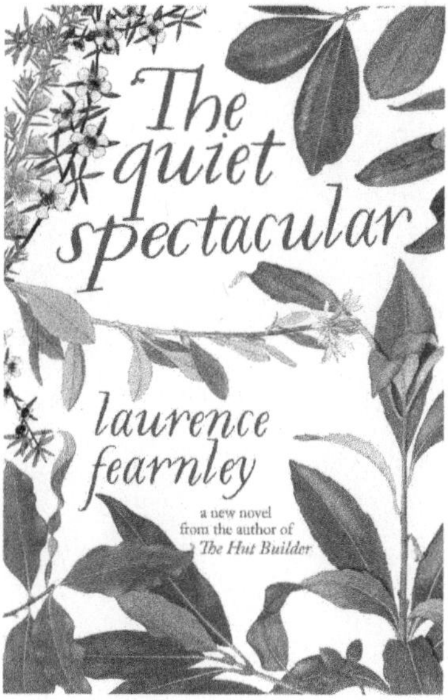

Funny and moving, this novel subverts notions of 'man vs. wild' while showcasing female experience through encounters with family, friends and the natural world.

Loretta is a school librarian, who embarks on compiling *The Dangerous Book for Menopausal Women* while waiting to collect her son from after-school activities. **Chance** is a teenager, who discovers an unusual creative outlet to offset the strain of her controlling mother. **Riva** is the founder of a wetlands sanctuary, who is seeking a way to fulfil her promise to her dying sister to do something 'absolutely spectacular'.

Within a clearing in the woods by a lake stands a den, a secret sanctuary and eventual meeting place for all three women . . .